20p

The Infamous Arrandales

Scandal is their destiny!

Meet the Arrandale family—dissolute,
disreputable and defiant! This infamous
family have scandal in their blood, and
wherever they go their reputation
will *always* precede them!

Don't miss any of the fabulous books
in Sarah Mallory's tantalising new quartet!

The Chaperon's Seduction
Already available

Temptation of a Governess
Available now

and look for two more sinfully scandalous
stories, coming soon!

Author Note

When I was very young I loved fairytales—
especially the story of *The Ugly Duckling*, the
little creature who did not fit in. This is how I saw
Diana Grensham: a young lady who has been told
from a very early age that she is unattractive. She has
therefore hidden herself away from the world, living
as a governess because, as she says, governesses are
of no consequence.

When we meet Alex he is a privileged young man
with looks, health and fortune—a sportsman with an
eye for beauty. The world is at his feet and no one has
ever opposed his will...until he meets Diana. Despite
their differences, Alex is the one man who sees past
Diana's self-effacing shell to the spirited and beautiful
woman inside. He gives her the confidence to believe
in herself.

Alex changes, too. He learns that the hedonistic
world he inhabits is not the one he wants to live in.
He discovers that happiness lies with Diana, but
after all he has done to alienate her how can she trust
him? The ballroom scene at the end of *Temptation
of a Governess* is one of the most touching I have
ever written: so much hangs in the balance, and it is
important that both Diana and Alex get it right. That is
for you, the reader, to judge.

TEMPTATION OF A GOVERNESS

Sarah Mallory

Published in Great Britain 2015
by Mills & Boon, an imprint of Harlequin (UK) Limited,
Eton House, 18-24 Paradise Road, Richmond, Surrey, TW9 1SR

© 2015 Sarah Mallory

ISBN: 978-0-263-24814-2

Harlequin (UK) Limited's policy is to use papers that are natural,
renewable and recyclable products and made from wood grown in
sustainable forests. The logging and manufacturing processes conform
to the legal environmental regulations of the country of origin.

Printed and bound in Spain
by CPI, Barcelona

Sarah Mallory was born in the West Country and now lives on the beautiful Yorkshire moors. She has been writing for more than three decades—mainly historical romances set in the Georgian and Regency period. She has won several awards for her writing, most recently the Romantic Novelists' Association RoNA Rose Award in 2012 (for *The Dangerous Lord Darrington*) and 2013 (for *Beneath the Major's Scars*).

Books by Sarah Mallory

Mills & Boon Historical Romance
and Mills & Boon Historical *Undone!* eBooks

The Infamous Arrandales

The Chaperon's Seduction
Temptation of a Governess

Brides of Waterloo

A Lady for Lord Randall

The Notorious Coale Brothers

Beneath the Major's Scars
Behind the Rake's Wicked Wager
The Tantalising Miss Coale (Undone!)

Linked by Character

Lady Beneath the Veil
At the Highwayman's Pleasure

Stand-Alone Novels

The Dangerous Lord Darrington
Bought for Revenge
The Scarlet Gown
Never Trust a Rebel

M&B *Castonbury Park* Regency mini-series

The Illegitimate Montague

Visit the Author Profile page
at millsandboon.co.uk for more titles.

To Kathryn, my lovely editor,
and all the team at Richmond,
without whom these books would never happen.

Chapter One

The April sun shone down brightly on the low-slung racing curricle as it bowled through the lanes and Alex Arrandale felt the winter gloom lifting from his spirits. A gloom that had settled and remained with him since he had heard of the shipwreck that had taken the life of his brother James and made him, Alex, the eighth Earl of Davenport. He had neither expected nor wanted the succession. James was only two years his senior and, at thirty, everyone had thought there was plenty of time for him and his countess to produce an heir. That was why the couple had set out on their sea journey, sailing south to warmer climes that the doctors advised might help improve Margaret's health and allow her to conceive and carry a boy child full-term. The couple already had a healthy little girl, but a series of miscarriages had left the countess very worn down.

They had never reached the Mediterranean,

a storm off Gibraltar in October had run their ship aground and all lives had been lost. The news had reached Alex several weeks later and the depth of his grief had been profound. Even now, six months on, he still wore a black cravat as a sign of his loss. In all other aspects of his life his friends found him unchanged. He had spent the winter as he always did, at a succession of house parties where hunting, gambling and flirting were the order of the day. Only his closest friend saw anything amiss in his frantic pleasure-seeking.

'Everyone thinks it is because you do not care,' Mr Gervase Wollerton told him, in a moment of uncharacteristic perception. 'I think you care too much.'

Perhaps that was so, thought Alex as he slowed and turned his high-bred team of match greys through the gates leading to Chantreys, but he had been earl for a while now and it was time he made a few changes.

The drive curved between trees that were not yet in full leaf and sunlight dappled the track. Alex slowed, conscious that there might be holes and ruts after the winter. He was just emerging from the woods when he spotted a figure sitting on a fallen tree, not far from the side of the road. It was a young woman with a sketchbook. She had cast aside her bonnet and her red hair glinted with gold in the sunlight. He knew her immediately. He had not seen her for years but the red hair was unmistakable. It was Diana Grensham, sister of the drowned countess and governess to her only child and the other Arrandale waif who had been taken into the late earl's household. She was so engrossed in her work that she did not even notice his arrival. Alex drew his team to a halt and regarded her for a long moment, taking in the dainty figure clad in a serviceable gown of green and yellow and with her wild red hair gleaming about her head like a halo.

'Good afternoon, Miss Grensham.'

She looked up, regarding him with a clear, steady gaze. Her eyes, he noted, were unusual, nut brown but flecked with green and while she was no beauty her countenance was lively and her full mouth had an upward tilt, as if a smile was never far away.

'Afternoon?' Her voice was soft, musical and held a hint of laughter. 'Heavens, is it so late already?'

'You are not surprised to see me?'

She closed her sketchbook and rose to her feet.

'I knew you would come at some point, my lord,' she told him. 'It would have been better if you had given us notice, but I am sure Mrs Wallace will be able to find some refreshment suitable for you. If you would care to drive round to the stables I will go and tell her.'

She took a few halting, uneven steps and he called out to her.

'Let me take you to the house. Stark, get down and hand the lady into the curricle.'

She stopped and turned, saying with a challenge in her voice, 'Because I am a cripple?'

'No,' he replied mildly. 'Because I want to talk to you.'

She handed her sketch book and pencils to the groom and climbed easily into the seat unaided, affording Alex a glimpse of embroidered white stockings beneath her skirts. He could not recall ever being told why she limped, but there was clearly no deformity in those shapely ankles, or in the dainty feet encased in the neat but serviceable boots.

When she would have taken her sketching things back Alex stopped her.

'Stark can carry them to the house. It is a fine day, let us drive around the park before we go in. I want to talk to you about the children.' Without waiting for her assent he set the greys in motion. 'I hope you do not mind?'

'Do I have any choice?'

'I thought it might be easier to talk out here than in the house.'

'You are probably right,' she told him. 'You are

a favourite with the girls and they will want you to themselves as soon as they know you are arrived.' She added thoughtfully, 'Although Meggie might demand to know why you have not been to see them before this.'

'I have been very busy.'

'Too busy to comfort your niece?' When he did not reply she continued. 'She and Florence were left to our joint care, my lord.'

'You do not need to remind me.' He flicked his whip over the greys' heads. What could he say? He knew it was contemptible, but looking back and considering his brother's death, he knew that he had been unable to face anyone's grief save his own. He was a renowned sportsman, a hard rider, deadly with sword and pistol and a pugilist of no mean order, yet he had shied away from visiting James's young daughter and witnessing her distress. He had told himself that her aunt was the best person to comfort little Meggie. Diana had been governess for four years to both James's daughter and little Florence Arrandale, a cousin whose own mother had died in childbirth and whose father had left the country under suspicious circumstances. James had taken the child in as a companion for Meggie and the two girls had been brought up almost as sisters. It was assumed that Florence's father was no longer alive and James had provided for her in his will, including consigning her to his brother's care. At eight years old, both girls would be missing James and his wife, the only parents they had ever known. Alex featured in their lives as a favourite uncle, visiting occasionally to bring treats and play with them for an hour or two before returning to his own hedonistic life. He might be their guardian now, but what did he know about bringing up children, or comforting them? It was no defence and deep inside he knew it, but it was easy to push aside such tiny pinpricks to his conscience.

'At least you corresponded with me,' Diana went on. 'I should be grateful you did not leave that to your man of business.'

'James's wife was your sister, your sorrow was equal to my own and I wanted to send my condolences.'

A black-bordered letter with a few trite sentences. How cold and hard that must have appeared to her.

Her hand came up, as if to ward off a blow. 'Yes, thank you.'

It occurred to Alex that she shared his dislike of overt emotion, so he did not pursue the matter, merely asked after the girls.

'They seem happy enough, but they miss their mama and papa. I know Florence is only a cousin, but her grief is equal to Meggie's, I assure you.'

He said with real regret, 'I am very sorry that I did not come to visit them sooner.'

'Well, you are here now, and they will be very glad to see you. What is it you wanted to discuss with me?'

'I was thinking that the girls might like to go to school.'

She paused, then said slowly, 'You are aware that the girls' education is my responsibility? Your brother was very clear about that.'

'Of course, but that does not mean I cannot take an interest.'

'No, indeed. But I do not think school would be right for them. Especially not at present, so soon after their loss.'

'Very well, but they might prefer another house, where there are less painful memories.'

'They are very happy here, my lord. It has always been their home.'

He felt the first stirrings of irritation. He would have to admit why he wanted them to move out.

'But it is now *my* house, Miss Grensham, and I wish to use it.'

'Well, there is nothing stopping you,' she replied. 'In fact, the girls would be delighted to see more of you.'

'That is not the point. I wish to bring friends here, and it would not be…appropriate for there to be children in the house.'

'What do you mean?'

He gave an impatient sigh. 'Do I need to spell it out to you? I am a bachelor.'

He kept his eyes on the road ahead but he was very aware of her enquiring scrutiny and found it disconcerting.

She said slowly, 'Am I to understand that you and your guests might act in an, an unseemly way?'

'It is a possibility.' His mind ranged quickly over his friends. 'More than a possibility.'

'It is certainly to your credit that you wish to protect the children from such scenes,' she told him, 'but I think in that case it would be better for you to hold your parties elsewhere. The Davenport estates comprise several excellent properties.'

'I am well aware of that,' he ground out. 'But I want Chantreys.'

He kept his eyes on the road but felt her clear, enquiring gaze upon his face.

'And why is it so important to have this house?'

Because it is where he and James had spent most of their childhood. Where they had been happiest. Alex knew that if he said as much she would turn the argument against him and appeal to his better nature to allow the girls to stay. And he had long ago buried his better nature well out of reach. He set his jaw.

'Miss Grensham, perhaps you are not aware of the pressures that are brought to bear on the head of any family to marry and provide an heir. Old family friends, relatives I have never even heard of all think they have the perfect right to interfere in my life.' His lip curled. 'It is assumed that I shall find a wife before the year is out. My intention is to show the world that I will not be coerced into marriage. I want to hold the biggest, most scandalous party of my career here at Chantreys. It is close enough to town for me to invite the *ton* to see just how disreputable an Arrandale I am and to put paid once and for all to their infernal matchmaking!'

There, he thought grimly. That should do it. But when he glanced at the dainty figure beside him she was displaying no sign of shock and outrage. Instead she had the nerve to laugh at him.

'That is the most ridiculous thing I have ever heard and I shall certainly not remove the girls from Chantreys merely to allow you to indulge such selfishness.'

He brought the curricle to a stand and swung round to face her. He held his anger in check as he said with dangerous calm, 'Miss Grensham, have you forgotten that I am now the earl? These properties are mine, to do with as I will.'

She met his eyes steadily, in no wise troubled by his impatient tone.

'I think *you* have forgotten, my lord, that you promised the girls might remain at Chantreys.' Her smile did nothing to improve his temper. 'You wrote to me, do you remember?'

'Yes, I remember.'

He forced out the words, recalling the letter he had received from Diana Grensham shortly after the news of the shipwreck, asking his intentions regarding his brother's wards. He remembered his own grief-racked reply, assuring her that Chantreys would be the girls' home for as long as she thought it necessary. The terms of the will had been quite specific. He and Diana Grensham were joint guardians of Meggie and Florence, but James had added a rider that Diana was to have sole charge of their education, being the person most fit and proper for that responsibility.

'I have kept your letter very safe, sir.'

'The devil you have!'

His hands tightened on the reins and the horses sidled nervously.

'Perhaps we should move on,' she said in a kindly voice that made him grind his teeth. 'There is a chill in the air and I should not like your team to come to any harm.'

Diana folded her hands in her lap as the earl set off again. She resisted the temptation to cling to the sides of the curricle, so noted a Corinthian as

Alex Arrandale was unlikely to overturn her. Not physically, that was, but she could not deny that sitting beside him was causing no little disturbance to her spirits. Her conscience was already pricking her for the way she had questioned his reason for offering to take her up. It had been a civil invitation and she had responded childishly, doing the very thing she hated most, drawing attention to her infirmity. Her only excuse was that his arrival had caught her unawares. Suddenly she was confronted by a man she had only previously seen from a distance, a sportsman renowned for his strength and prowess. To look around and see him sitting in his low-slung curricle, easily holding in check those spirited greys, had thrown her own shortcomings into strong relief. She had no doubt that when he saw her take those first, hobbling steps towards the house that he had looked upon her with pity, if not disdain.

Not that he had said as much and she berated herself for being over-sensitive. It was a relief to turn her thoughts to the future of Meggie and Florence. She felt on much safer ground there but even so, to oppose the new earl at their very first meeting was not an auspicious beginning to their acquaintance. It could not be helped, the well-being of her charges was paramount. The new Lord Davenport had shown himself to be selfish and insensitive, but that was the case with most rich and powerful noblemen so it did not surprise her. What she had not expected was the attraction she felt towards the new earl. It was so strong it was almost physical and it shocked her. Whenever he had visited his brother in the past she had made sure she remained in the school-room, sending the children downstairs with their nurse to join the family. James and Margaret had been more than happy to include Diana in any family party, but they knew how much she hated her deformity and respected her wish for privacy when guests were present.

The late earl and his wife had been doting parents and, apart from short visits to other Daven-port properties, the children had spent their lives at Chantreys. Diana had become their governess four years' ago. She had been just eighteen and declared that she did not want to be presented, hating the thought of being paraded around Court and all the required parties, to be gawped at and pitied because she could not walk gracefully. Her parents had been relieved, not only to be spared the cost of a court presentation but also the em-barrassment of having to show off their 'poor little cripple'.

She had met Alex at James and Margaret's wedding, of course, but a vigorous young man just entering Oxford had given no more than a cursory glance to the eleven-year-old sister of his brother's bride. Since then Diana had kept out of his way, but she had followed his career and knew his reputation as a fashionable sporting gentleman devoted to the pursuit of pleasure. He was a perfect example of the notorious Arrandale family and nothing like his staid and respectable older brother. Now, sitting beside him in the curricle, she was very aware of the size and power of the man. His shoulders were so broad it was impossible not to bump against him as the vehicle swayed on the uneven carriageway, and he was not even wearing a many-caped greatcoat to add to their width, merely a close-fitting coat that was moulded to his athletic body with barely a crease. His hands, encased in soft kid gloves, guided the team with the ease of a master and the buckskins and top boots he wore could not mask the strength in those long legs.

It was not that he was handsome, she mused, considering the matter. His features were too austere and rugged, the nose slightly crooked, possibly from a blow, and there were tiny scars across his left eyebrow and his chin that were doubtless from some duel. His dark-brown hair was untidy, ruffled by the wind rather than by the hand of a master, and beneath his black brows his eyes, when they rested on her, were hard as slate.

No, thought Diana, as he brought the team to a plunging halt at the main door, he could not be called a handsome man, yet she found him disturbing. Possibly because he was now the earl, and technically her employer, even if her late brother-in-law's will gave her joint guardianship of Meggie and Florence. There was no doubt he could make life difficult for her, if he so wished. She would have to tread carefully.

'Can you get down?' he asked her. 'I cannot leave the horses.'

'Of course.' She jumped out. 'Take them to the stables and I will fetch Meggie and Florence to the drawing room.'

She thought he might argue and want to continue their discussion indoors but to her relief he drove off without a word and she limped up the steps into the house.

Word of the new earl's arrival had preceded her, thanks to his lordship's groom and she found Mrs Wallace bustling through the hall. She stopped as Diana came in and beamed at her.

'Ah, Miss Grensham, I have taken the liberty of putting cake and lemonade in the drawing room, and Fingle is even now gone to draw off some ale, since we know that Mr Alex—Lord Davenport, I should say!—is quite partial to a tankard of home-brewed.'

'Thank you, Mrs Wallace. I will go up to the children.'

'They are with Nurse now,' said the house-keeper, chuckling. 'They was all for dashing out to meet his lordship, so excited were they to hear he was come, but I sent them back upstairs to have their hands and faces washed.'

Smiling, Diana made her way to the top floor, where she found her two charges submitting reluctantly to Nurse's ministrations.

'Diana, Diana, Uncle Alex is come!' cried Meggie, running to meet her.

'I know, and once you and Florence are ready I shall take you to the drawing room.' Diana smiled down at Meggie, thinking how much she looked like her mother, with her fair hair and deep-brown eyes. Would Alex see it and take comfort, as she did? A tug on her gown brought her attention to her other little charge. Florence was as dark as Meggie was fair but no less lively, her grey eyes positively twinkling now.

'Can we still call him Uncle Alex, even if he is now the earl?'

'Of course we can,' declared Meggie. 'He is still *my* uncle, and you have always called him Uncle Alex. Nothing has changed, has it, Diana?'

Diana merely smiled, but as she accompanied her charges to the drawing room she was very much afraid that everything was about to change.

The new Lord Davenport was already in the drawing room when they went in, standing with one arm resting on the mantelshelf and gazing moodily into the empty hearth. At the sound of the children's voices the sombre look fled, he smiled and dropped down on to the sofa, inviting the children to join him. They raced across the room, greeting him with a hug and a kiss upon the cheek. Diana walked forward more slowly, surprised at the change in Alex from autocrat to friendly, approachable uncle. The girls settled themselves on either side of him, chattering non-stop, and she heard Meggie asking him why he had stayed away for so long.

'I have had a great deal of business to attend,' he told her. 'But it was remiss of me not to come and see you, and I beg your pardon.'

'Diana said you would be busy,' said Florence. 'She said you would also be very sad, because Papa Davenport was your brother.'

'Did you weep?' Meggie asked him. 'Florence and I wept when we were told that Mama and Papa had drowned. And Diana did, too.'

'No, I did not weep,' he said gravely. 'But I was very sad.'

'Diana hugged us and that made us feel better,' said Meggie. 'It is a pity you were not here, Uncle Alex, because she could have hugged you, too.'

Diana smothered a laugh with a fit of coughing and turned away, knowing her cheeks would be pink with embarrassment. She might consider the new earl selfish and insensitive, but she was grateful to him for adroitly changing the subject.

'I think it is time we had some of this delicious cake that Mrs Wallace has made,' he declared. 'Perhaps one of you young ladies would cut a slice for me?'

Recovering, Diana moved towards the table to help the girls serve the refreshments. She was relieved that the gentleman showed no signs of wishing to quarrel in front of the girls and she was content to remain silent while he talked to them about how they spent their days and what they had learned in the schoolroom. The children were bright and as eager to learn as Diana was to teach them and she was very happy, once they had finished their refreshments, for Meggie and Florence to take the earl up to the schoolroom and show him their work. Diana remained below. It would do him no harm to enjoy the company of his wards for a while, so she took her tambour frame into the morning room to await their return.

Lord Davenport came in alone some time later and she could not resist a teasing question.

'Have they exhausted you?'

'By no means, but Nurse reminded them that Judd would be waiting in the stable to give them their riding lesson and even I could not compete with that treat.'

'No, they love their ponies and I can trust Judd to look after them.'

'You can indeed. He threw me up on my first pony and is devoted to the family.'

His good mood encouraged her to touch on their earlier discussions.

'You see how happy they are here, my lord.'

Immediately the shutters came down.

'They might be as happy elsewhere.'

'In time, perhaps, but not yet.' She felt at a disadvantage with him standing over her so she put aside her sewing and rose. 'They are content during the day, but they are still not sleeping well. They have suffered bad dreams and even nightmares since they learned of the shipwreck. Chantreys is their home; they know it and love it. It would be cruel to uproot them now.'

'I am informed there are very good schools, where they might mix with children of their own age and rank.'

'They have that here,' she replied. 'They have friends amongst several of the local families and the servants here all go out of their way to look after them. They do not want for company.'

'But perhaps a broader education might be beneficial. A school would provide masters in all subjects.'

'Perhaps, but the very best masters are to be found in London and living here we have access to them. There is also much to be learned from the entertainments to be found in town. Their education will not be found lacking, I assure you.'

Alex felt the frown descending. It was a novel experience to have anyone oppose his will.

'Do you maintain that you can teach the girls everything they require?' he demanded.

'I do. I will not be moved, my lord. Meggie and Florence will remain here.'

There was a calm assurance in her tone that caught him on the raw. Did she think to defy him?

He said softly, 'What would you wager upon my having you and the children out of the house by the end of the summer?'

That determined little chin lifted defiantly.

'I never wager upon certainties, my lord, you will not do it—unless you mean to evict us bodily?'

She met his eyes steadily and he realised she had called his bluff. He would not do anything to hurt the girls, but neither would he capitulate that easily.

'No, I intend that you shall go willingly.'

'What you *intend*, Lord Davenport, and what will happen are two very different things.'

His temper flared at her calm defiance.

'This was always a good marriage for your sister,' he threw at her. 'My brother took her despite her lack of fortune. I suppose he kept you on out of charity.'

It was a low blow, unworthy of a gentleman, and Alex regretted the words as soon as they were uttered, but surprisingly she was not crushed by his comment, instead she drew herself up and her eyes flashed with anger.

'He kept me on because I am an excellent governess!'

Admiration stirred. She was only a slip of a girl, why, she barely came up to his shoulder but she was not afraid to meet his steely glance with one equally determined. There was also a glint of mischief in her eyes when she continued.

'Margaret was always the beauty, but I had the brains.'

He laughed at that.

'Very well, Miss Grensham, we will agree— for the moment!—that you are a suitable governess for Meggie and Florence, but this is *not* a suitable house for them, you must see that. There is only the one staircase, and the building is so small that every time the children left the schoolroom my guests would be bumping into them. It will not do, the girls must leave. You may have the pick of my other properties.'

'I do not want any of your other properties.'

Alex bent a long, considering look upon Diana. Most people found his stare unnerving, but she merely replied with quiet determination, 'If you insist, then I shall oppose you, sir.'

Anger stirred again. Did she dare to set up her will against his?

'You would be ill advised to cross swords with me, Miss Grensham.'

'I have no wish to cross swords with you, Lord Davenport, but I will not move the children, and since I have your letter, you cannot make me.' She added, with deliberate provocation, 'Unless you wish to fight me through the courts?'

When Alex drove away from Chantreys the spring day was ending and the clear sky left an unpleasant chill. He had failed in his quest and was in no very amiable temper. As the younger son of an earl, with a sharp mind and excellent physique, he was accustomed to succeeding in everything he attempted. His godfather, an East India merchant, had left him a considerable fortune, which had given Alex the independence to pursue his own interests once he had left Oxford. He had thus arrived in town endowed with excellent connections, good birth and considerable wealth, all the attributes he required to do very much as he pleased. He was not used to failure and it irked him.

He could easily purchase another property close to London and leave Diana and the children to live at Chantreys. He knew that this would be the most reasonable course of action, but when he thought of Diana Grensham he did not *feel* reasonable. Her opposition had woken something in him, some dormant spirit that wanted to engage her in battle. He never enjoyed losing and he certainly had no intention of being beaten by a slip of a girl with hair the colour of autumn leaves.

Chapter Two

Alex was still mulling over his defeat as he drove into town and his mood was not improved by the knowledge that he had promised to attend Almack's that night. The Dowager Marchioness of Hune had written to tell him she was helping to launch a young friend into the *ton* and asked for his support. Lady Hune was his great-aunt and one of the few Arrandale relatives who was not pressing him to marry. Also, he was fond of her in a careless sort of way and he had agreed to look in. Well, he would not go back on his word, even if it meant entering the notorious Marriage Mart.

After a solitary dinner he walked the short distance to King Street, where his mission was soon accomplished. Miss Ellen Tatham was a lively beauty so it was no hardship to stand up with her and once he had done his duty he made his escape and rewarded himself with a visit to a discreet little house off Piccadilly, where he could be sure of more congenial company.

The house was owned by Lady Frances Betsford, a widow and the youngest daughter of an impoverished peer. Despite being an accredited beauty, she had been unable to do better than a mere baronet for a husband. However he had died within twelve months of the ceremony and left his widow with a comfortable competence. She had lived in some style in town for the past five years, moving in all but the highest circles, tolerated by the ladies and sought out by their husbands. Her name had been linked with several prominent society figures in the past and most recently it had been coupled with the new Earl of Davenport.

Alex had known Frances for years. There had been a brief liaison, when he had first arrived in town, and she was keen now to get him back in her bed. Alex was well aware that her renewed interest in him stemmed from his accession to the peerage. That did not overly concern him, he knew his world and viewed it with a cynical eye. Lady Frances wanted to be a countess and she was not ineligible. Her birth was good, she was beautiful, intelligent and no *ingénue* who would bore him within weeks. That was a definite advantage, he thought as he walked into her crowded drawing room. He watched her as she leaned over Sir Sydney Dunford's shoulder to advise him on his discard and realised just how little he cared if she shared her favours with other gentlemen. That, too, he thought, was in her favour. Theirs would be a civilised arrangement with no messy emotions to get in the way.

A tall, elegant figure clad in Bath coating and stockinette pantaloons broke away from the crowd and greeted Alex with a languid wave.

'Well, Alex, have you fixed the summer party for Chantreys?'

'I'm afraid not, Gervase.'

'Pity,' replied Mr Wollerton, shaking his head. 'Lady Frances will be disappointed.'

'That can't be helped—' Alex broke off as the lady in question approached, hands held out and a smile on her carmined lips.

'My lord, I had quite given you up.'

He saluted her fingers.

'I told you I should be late, Frances.'

She gave a soft laugh and slipped her hand through his arm.

'So you did. Come along and join us. What will you play, Loo? Ombre? Commerce? Or shall we play at piquet, just you and I?'

He looked down into her beautiful smiling face. After Diana Grensham's obstinate refusal to agree to his plans, the warm invitation in those cerulean eyes was balm to his battered spirits. What could be better than an hour or two spent in such agreeable company? It would help put the unsatisfactory visit to Chantreys from his mind.

'Piquet,' he decided.

Her smile grew. She moved closer and murmured for his ears only, 'And afterwards?'

Her full breasts were almost brushing his waistcoat and he could smell her sweet, heady perfume enveloping him. She was voluptuous, desirable and knew how to please a man. The invitation was very tempting, but there was a restlessness in his spirits tonight and he was reluctant to commit himself. He gave an inward shrug. It was very likely that in an hour or so he might feel differently.

He smiled. 'Let us begin with piquet and see what happens.'

Alex's restless mood did not abate and even Lady Frances's charms could not detain him. Soon after midnight he made his way back to his rented house in Half Moon Street. Piccadilly was busy, as always. Carriages rumbled past him and the flagway was bustling, mostly with gentlemen going to or from some evening entertainment. One or two females were on the streets, gaudily dressed and clearly offering their services to any man with a few coins in his pocket and time to spare. One of the women approached Alex but he waved her away. As she turned and flounced off the flaring light from a flambeau picked out the red glow in her hair. It was garishly unnatural, nothing like Diana Grensham's glorious autumn tints, that thick auburn hair and her eyes the colour of fresh hazelnuts. A man might gaze upon her for ever without growing tired of the view.

A *frisson* of alarm ran through Alex and he gave himself a shake. By heaven, what was wrong with him tonight? Diana Grensham was not his type at all, she was stubborn, opinionated and what had James been thinking of, to give her sole charge of the children's education?

The answer of course was that she was not an Arrandale, a family renowned for loose living. James had been the exception, a steady, sober young man who took his responsibilities seriously.

'Confound it, so, too, do I!' declared Alex furiously as he turned into Half Moon Street. No sooner had he uttered the words aloud than Diana's reprimand came to mind and he stopped, a wry smile tugging at his mouth. How could he say that when he planned to set the *ton* by the ears with an extravagant ball to which he would invite all the very worst rakes and reprobates of society?

Yes, it would be selfish but the spirit of devilry appealed to him and it would show all those

top-lofty dowds that he would not be bullied into
settling down. He would take a wife when he was
ready and not before. He reached his door and
trod up the steps, the smile fading as quickly as
it had come. That did not solve the problem of
the girls, though. He could not hold such a party
at Chantreys while they were in residence.

'It would do the children no harm to live elsewhere,' he muttered, handing his hat and gloves
to a sleepy servant and taking the stairs two at a
time. 'In fact, it would be good for them and she
should be made to see that.'

His man jumped up in surprise as Alex burst
into the bedchamber.

'My lord, I wasn't expecting you so early—'

'Never mind that, Lincoln. Do I have any engagements on the morrow?'

'Why, no, my lord, nothing apart from your
tailor.'

'Well, he can wait.' Alex shrugged off his coat
and handed it over. 'As soon as it is light send a
message to the stables. I want my curricle at the
door by nine tomorrow morning.'

Alex once again felt his spirits lifting as he
drove his team towards Chantreys. The house had
always been the favourite of his childhood and
now, as he regarded the east front, bathed in the
bright spring sunshine, he was struck anew by its

beauty. Completed soon after the Restoration, the walls were of dressed chalk enhanced with decorative Bath stone at the corners and around the windows. It was small but perfectly proportioned, topped with a steep-pitched roof surmounted by a balustraded platform above which rose the elegant tall chimneys. It was a work of art in its own right and would make an excellent setting for the paintings and sculptures he had acquired over the past few years. It was also perfect for the kind of intimate parties he intended to hold here for his close friends.

It was nearing midday by the time Alex pulled up at the door. He left his groom to take the equipage to the stables and walked to the open door, where the butler was waiting to greet him.

'Miss Grensham and the children are on the west lawn.' Fingle took Alex's hat and gloves and carefully placed them upon a side table. 'Would you like me to announce you, my lord?'

'No, no, I will find them.'

Alex strode across the entrance hall and made his way through the drawing room from where the long windows gave direct access to the gardens. There was no sign of anyone on the terrace or parterre, but the sound of childish voices and laughter led him through a gate in the high hedge between the formal gardens and the extensive lawns that led down to a large ornamental lake with the park and woods beyond.

A lively game of battledore and shuttlecock was in progress with Meggie and Florence ranged against Diana. They were all so engrossed in their game that at first they did not see him and he was able to watch them at their sport. The little girls dashed back and forth, laughing and shouting with delight as they patted the shuttlecock back to Diana, who rarely missed a shot. Alex kept his eyes fixed on Diana and it took him a moment to realise what was different about her. As she ran and turned, covering the ground, there was no sign of that ugly dragging step he had noted the previous day. Meggie sent the shuttlecock sailing high into the air and Diana leapt up to reach it.

'Bravo, Miss Grensham!' he called out appreciatively. 'A fine return.'

'Uncle Alex!'

The girls raced towards him. Diana, he noted, lowered her racquet and watched him, her manner reserved. Unsurprising, he thought, considering their encounter yesterday, but there was nothing to be gained by recalling that, so he greeted her cheerfully.

'Taking advantage of the good weather, Miss Grensham?'

She relaxed slightly and warily returned his smile.

'It is a reward to Meggie and Florence for their hard work in the schoolroom this morning.'

'Must we go in now?' asked Florence, clearly reluctant.

Alex shook his head.

'You need stand on no ceremony with me. I have interrupted your game.'

'We are not doing very well,' Meggie confided. 'Diana is so much better than us.'

'Well, let us see if we can even things up a little,' said Alex, spying a fourth racquet lying on a nearby rug. 'What do you say, Miss Grensham, you and Florence against Meggie and myself?'

The girls squealed with delight but Diana shook her head at him. 'You did not come here today to play games with us, my lord.'

A few unruly red locks had escaped from their pins and he wanted to reach out and tuck a stray curl behind her ear. He would very much like to play games with her, if they were alone... The thought seared him, sending the hot blood pulsing through his body and he had to struggle to concentrate. They had been talking of battledore, not flirtation.

'The honour of the Arrandales is at stake,' he declared, fighting down his baser instincts.

He stripped off his coat, revealing an exquisitely embroidered waistcoat, more suited to

Bond Street than a country garden, but he did
not care for that. 'Fetch me a racquet, Meggie!'

A fast and furious thirty minutes ensued.
Diana, Alex noted, was at first a little shy of
having a gentleman present. She was favouring
her left leg and limping badly but Alex ignored
it, giving no quarter in his returns. To his satisfaction her competitive spirit soon won through
and as she lost herself in the game, running and
straining to reach every shot he sent her way he
saw no signs of the ungainly limp that affected
her walk. The game only ended when Fingle appeared with a tray of refreshments for them all
and a gentle reminder that Cook was even now
preparing nuncheon for the schoolroom party.

'Then tell Cook to set another place for me,'
declared Alex. 'That is, if Miss Grensham has
no objections?'

The girls immediately voiced their approval of
the idea and Diana spread her hands.

'It will be nursery fare,' she warned him.

'Then Fingle shall look out a decent claret to
sustain me,' declared Alex, nodding at the butler.

Fingle bowed and went off to inform Cook of
the change. Alex took the tankard of ale from the
tray and sat down upon the blanket while Diana
poured lemonade for Meggie and Florence. He
watched the rise and fall of her breast beneath
the low-cut neckline of her gown and again felt

that stir of attraction. He dragged his eyes away. This was no part of his plan.

'Is this how you spend every day?' he asked her.

'Whenever the weather permits. Fresh air and exercise are very beneficial to growing bodies.'

And those already full grown.

Diana was unable to stop her eyes travelling over the earl's muscular form as he lounged on the rug, his long legs, encased in their pantaloons and Hessians, stretched out before her. She knew he was considered a Corinthian, a man of fashion but also a sportsman, and it was not difficult to believe it when one observed those powerful thighs, or the broad shoulders, deep chest and flat stomach, accentuated by his close-fitting waistcoat.

Having served the girls, she picked up her own glass of lemonade and made her way to the only free space upon the rug, acutely aware of the awkward, dragging step caused by her shortened left leg. It was not very pronounced and had never prevented her from excelling at the more energetic games she had played as a child with her sister and cousins, but she could never forget it when she was in company. She could never walk with that smooth gliding elegance that was required of young ladies. Her mother had developed a habit of averting her eyes whenever Diana limped into a room.

When her sister had suggested that Diana should become governess to little Lady Margaret and Miss Florence, Diana had accepted readily. All talk of a court presentation and a London Season ended and Diana saw the relief in her mother's face when she knew she would be spared the embarrassment of introducing her crippled daughter to society.

'You look very serious, Miss Grensham.' The earl's voice jerked her out of her reverie. 'Have I said anything amiss?'

'No, not at all.' She pushed away the unwelcome memories. 'You asked how we spend our days here. We are always up by seven-thirty and after breakfast we work at our lessons. Then, in the afternoon, there are more lessons or if the weather is fine we might walk, or play games out of doors. Our days are very full, the girls are learning to play the harpsichord, plus all the accomplishments necessary for young ladies, such as sewing, singing and dancing, but at eight years old I think there is time enough for that.'

'I am not questioning your skill as a governess, Miss Grensham.'

Diana noted that Meggie and Florence had grown tired of sitting down and were playing battledore again, there was no one to overhear them.

'No?' she challenged him. 'Yesterday you suggested I might have been given the post because I was a poor relation.'

And a cripple.

Diana did not voice the words but they were there, all the same.

'I beg your pardon for that.' He sat up. 'Why *did* you take the post?'

'I have always been interested in book learning,' she replied, avoiding his eyes. 'As Meggie's aunt, I was able to be so much more than a mere governess.' She explained, to fill the silence. 'You know how James and Margaret liked to travel, and then there were the house parties to attend and visits they were obliged to make. The children could spend most of their time here, in familiar surroundings, and when their parents were away I was always here with them.' She plucked at her skirts. 'In the event, it was fortunate. When the news came, that Margaret and James were drowned, I could comfort the girls.'

Alex recognised the pain shadowing her eyes. He was not the only one to have lost a sibling when that ship was smashed against the rocks off the Spanish coast.

'And who comforted *you*, Diana?'

He was not sure if she shuddered or if it was merely a shake of the head, but she did not answer him.

'We had best go in now.' She scrambled to her feet and shook out her skirts. 'Meggie, Florence, bring the racquets, if you please, we must put them away safely. Fingle will send someone to bring in the rug and the tray, my lord, so do, pray, go on ahead with the girls, I will follow in a moment.'

Alex said nothing, but as he accompanied the children into the house he suspected that she did not wish him to see her walking with that dragging step.

The schoolroom was on the top floor, as it had been during his own childhood, but it was barely recognisable. It was no longer dark and austere. The walls were painted white and covered with prints and drawings, many of them clearly the work of childish hands. The girls carried the racquets to the corner cupboard and he strode ahead to open it for them. As he did so his eyes fell upon an object in one corner and with a laugh he pulled out a small cricket bat.

'I remember this,' he declared. 'Old Wilshire, the estate carpenter, made it.' He grinned down at Meggie. 'Your father and I used it when we were here.'

'We still use it, Uncle Alex,' said Florence, coming up. 'Diana taught us how to play.'

'Well, well,' he said, grinning. 'Then you must show me just how good you are.'

'Perhaps another day,' put in Diana, following them into the room. 'This afternoon we have work to do.'

'Then I shall join you, if I may!'

If anyone had told Alex that he would enjoy spending the day with two eight-year-old girls, eating bread and butter in the schoolroom, listening to them reading their books and joining them for games of dominoes and spillikins he would have laughed at the idea, but when Nurse came in to take Meggie and Florence off for their dinner he was surprised to see that it was nearly five o'clock. The day had the charm of novelty, of course, and it was undoubtedly helped by Diana's presence. She was a lively companion and clearly very proud of her charges. Alex took his leave of the girls, almost as sorry as they were that there had been no time to try out the old cricket bat and promising that they should do so on his next visit.

'Thank you,' said Diana as she accompanied him down the stairs. 'It was very kind of you to give up your day for Meggie and Florence.'

'Kind?' he repeated, surprised. 'I am not renowned for being *kind*, Miss Grensham! No, I enjoyed myself, else I should not have stayed so long. They are delightful children, although I should not want charge of them every day, as you do. Do you ever have time to yourself?'

'Why, yes. Nurse takes care of the children now, leaving me free until about eight, when I go up to wish them goodnight.' She paused as they reached the entrance hall. 'Would you care to step into the drawing room, my lord, while you wait for your carriage?'

'Oh, I am not going yet.'

'But you will wish to be back in town in time for dinner.'

'I thought I might dine here. If you have no objection?'

He watched her dark lashes sweep down, shielding her thoughts as she said politely, 'It is your house, my lord.'

His lips twitched.

'Be honest, you are wishing me in Hades.'

She flushed at that, but shook her head.

'I apprehend that you wish to discuss the children's future.'

'Pray do not show hackle, Miss Grensham. We have had a pleasant day and I thought it would be useful for us to become better acquainted. As you reminded me, we are both guardians of Meggie and Florence.'

'Yes, of course. Then if you will excuse me, I will go and find Fingle and tell him to lay another place...'

She hurried away upon the words and Alex went into the drawing room. So far so good. Diana had thawed a little and he had no doubt now that he could achieve his object in coming to Chantreys: they could have a reasoned and logical discussion about moving the girls to one or other of his properties. Upon reflection he did not think Davenport House would be suitable, it was in the far north and the climate was rather harsh, but there was the estate in Lincolnshire, or the manor house north of Oxford. They both had large grounds where Miss Grensham could exercise her charges to her heart's content.

Chantreys was too perfect to be wasted upon children. Its light rooms would show off his growing art collection to advantage. It was the smallest of the properties he had inherited and it had plenty of snug little bedrooms well suited to late-night assignations, yet it was also close enough to London to invite parties down for an evening.

A shade of unease possessed him. Was he being selfish, to move the children out of Chantreys? He could hardly continue his bachelor lifestyle here with the children in residence. His father would not have worried about such things, but then his parents had rarely considered their children, leaving them to be brought up by a small army of nannies, nurses and tutors in

some distant wing of whatever house they were
occupying at the time. Chantreys was different,
there was no convenient wing in which to shut
the children away, but even so the earl and his
countess had contrived to avoid too much contact, spending most of their time in London and
driving down to Chantreys only occasionally to
visit their offspring. Alex had quickly learned not
to reach out for Mama, lest he make her gown
grubby, or to speak unless Papa addressed him.
He had learned to keep his emotions in check,
to keep everyone at bay except James. And now
even James was gone.

Alex paced the floor, disturbed by his memories. The drawing room suddenly felt close and
confined and he walked to the French windows
and threw them open. He stood there, breathing in the fresh air. To one side he could see the
empty lawns, stretching beyond the formal gardens. He had enjoyed playing outside today. It
reminded him of those far-off days when he and
James had been left to amuse themselves, playing cricket on that very same grass. Only there
had been no warm and loving governess like
Diana Grensham to look after them, to join in
with their games so energetically that her hair
escaped from its pins and bounced around her
shoulders like a fiery cloud. His eyes narrowed,
as if he might better recall the image she had pre-

sented, her hair curling wildly about her head, breast heaving from the exertion, eyes bright and sparkling. It was clear the children adored her and she was devoted to them. Well, let her argue her case again over dinner. Perhaps this time he would listen.

The door opened and he turned, expecting to see Diana there, but instead it was Fingle.

'Miss Grensham sent me to tell you that dinner would be served in an hour, my lord, and to see if you required anything in the meantime.'

'Yes, I require her company.'

The butler was an old and trusted retainer and at these words he bent a fatherly smile upon his master in a way that made Alex feel about ten years old.

'Miss Grensham has gone to her room to change for dinner, my lord. I am sure she will be downstairs again just as soon as she is ready.'

Alex kept his lips firmly closed, fighting against the impulse to demand that she hurry up. That would sound petulant in the extreme. He had set out that morning with the intention of holding a reasoned discussion with Diana. To order her to attend him would immediately put up her back. She was not a servant to be commanded. He curbed his impatience to see her again and asked Fingle to bring him some brandy.

* * *

Diana made her way to the drawing room shortly before the dinner hour. As she walked in the earl gave her a frowning look.

'Are you still in mourning?'

She glanced down at her lavender silk.

'No, my lord. This is my best evening gown.'

She could have added that it was the *only* evening gown. She had never needed more. When she had first joined the late earl's household she had always been invited to join the family for dinner, whenever they were in residence at Chantreys, but one never knew how many guests would be present, and Diana preferred not to be subjected to the stares and pitying looks of strangers. After a while the invitations had stopped.

'It looks very much like mourning,' he told her.

'One might say the same of your cravat, my lord.'

For a long moment they regarded one another, before the earl looked away and walked to the sideboard.

'Sit down, Miss Grensham. Can I get you a glass of claret, perhaps. Or Madeira?'

'A little wine, thank you.' She moved to a chair opposite the one he had been occupying, glad that he was pouring the claret and not watching her limp across the room. 'What is it you wish to discuss with me, sir?'

'You are very direct.' He handed her a glass and returned to his chair. 'I have already told you, I thought we should become better acquainted. You were always absent whenever I visited the house in the past.'

'Then the earl and countess would be present. I was not required.'

He stared at her over the rim of his glass.

'Were you avoiding me?'

She was surprised that his question did not offend. She replied, equally blunt, 'I was avoiding everyone.'

'Because you limp,' he said. 'What happened?'

'A broken thigh bone, when I was very young.' She paused to taste her wine. 'The doctor set it badly, and although others were brought in they could not undo his incompetence. I was left with my left leg shorter than the right. It does not prevent me from doing anything I wish, but it looks ungainly and makes people uncomfortable. They do not wish to see deformity in the drawing room.'

'Have you ever considered that if you were to be in society more, people would become accustomed to your...' he paused '...your deformity?'

'Perhaps, but I go on very well as I am. The children no longer regard it.'

He held her eyes.

'But you must take them out and about. Does that not make people uncomfortable?'

'Oh, no,' she said quietly. 'I attract no attention at all in the street. Governesses are of no consequence, you see.'

Fingle came in to announce dinner and Lord Davenport rose.

'Shall we go in?'

He was holding out his arm to her. Diana hesitated, tempted to tell him such courtesy was unnecessary, but he would know that. Silently she slipped her fingers on to his sleeve. It was impossible not to feel the hard muscle beneath the soft wool of his coat. He exuded strength and power, and she felt a tiny tremor of excitement at his proximity.

'Oh.'

Diana stopped as they entered the dining room. Two places were set at the table, facing each other across the width rather than at either end.

'I told Fingle to set it thus,' remarked her companion. 'I thought it would be an advantage not to be peering the length of the table and shouting at one another.'

He guided Diana to her seat and held her chair. She sank down, suddenly nervous. She had never dined alone with a man before. *We are here on business*, she told herself sternly. But when the earl took his seat opposite and smiled at her it felt strangely intimate, even though the daylight was still streaming into the room.

The earl's unexpected presence at dinner had certainly put Cook on her mettle and Diana decided there could be no complaint on the number and variety of dishes that appeared on the table. If the earl was not satisfied with the ragout of lamb and tender young carrots and turnips then there was a cheese pie or a fricassee of eggs and a dessert made with some of Cook's preciously hoarded quince jelly.

For many months Diana's meals had been taken alone or with the children and at first she was a little nervous to be in company, but the earl was determined to please and be pleased. He was an excellent host, ensuring that she had her choice of every dish on the table and keeping her wine glass filled. He was at pains to draw her out and she was surprised how easy it was to converse with him. By the time the meal was over she was quite relaxed in his company.

'I had best leave you to your brandy,' she said, when the clock chimed the hour.

'No, please. Stay and talk to me.'

She chuckled. 'We have talked throughout dinner.'

'But not about the children.'

She was disappointed. They had been getting

on famously, and now they would argue again. She knew it. He signalled to Fingle to refill her wine glass and she did not object. She would not, of course, drink brandy, or port, or even Madeira after dinner. That would be foolish and could lead to her becoming inebriated, but a little more wine might stiffen her resolve when dealing with the earl.

Alex signalled to the servants to leave the room. He had enjoyed dinner, surprisingly so. He had decided at the outset that he would spare no efforts to charm Diana, but in fact it had been no effort at all. Her education had been thorough and she was an avid reader. Although she lived confined he learned that she corresponded with several long-standing friends and no one had ever cancelled the late earl's subscription to the London newspapers, so she was well informed and eager to learn. Their discussions ranged from politics to art and philosophy, and if he introduced a subject of which she knew little, her questions and comments were intelligent and interesting. He made sure the wine flowed freely, and as he encouraged her to talk and express her opinions she began to relax, to blossom. Whenever some particular subject caught her interest she would become animated, waving her hands, challenging his views and not afraid to put her own. The one topic they had not touched upon was the children and their removal to another property, but it would soon be time for him to leave, and since that was the reason for his being here, he must make the attempt.

As Fingle shepherded the footmen from the room Alex refilled his glass and sat back, regarding the petite figure sitting opposite him. She would never be a beauty. No coiffeuse would tame that red hair without resorting heavily to the use of pomade, her mouth was too wide and as for those freckles sprinkled liberally across her pert little nose and cheeks, any female with pretensions to fashion would have concealed them with a little powder. Having decided the freckles were a blemish, Alex found himself looking at them again. They did have a certain charm, he conceded. In fact, some men might find them quite attractive…

Diana's voice cut into his thoughts.

'No doubt you wish we still lived in your great-grandfather's time.'

With an effort he forced his mind back to the discussion.

'The fourth earl?' His brows rose. 'What has he to do with anything?'

'By all accounts he was a tyrant,' she told him cheerfully. 'He cleared whole villages to create the park and the views we now enjoy from the house.' She shook her head, saying disapprovingly, 'Positively feudal.'

'He provided a whole new village for his people.'

'Yes, because he needed to keep them close to work on his estate.'

'You are deliberately seeing the worst of my family.'

She laughed at that. 'The worst? Moving a few dozen villagers is nothing to the debauched and dissolute manner with which the Arrandales have conducted themselves over the years.'

Alex reined in his temper. Who was she to criticise his kin?

'The Arrandales are no worse than many other families,' he snapped. 'I would not contemplate displacing a whole village, but I *would* move two little girls! It is not as though I am throwing you on the streets. You may have the pick of my properties, if you wish I will even buy you a new house.'

'I do not want a new house,' she retorted. 'My sister thought it best for the children to be settled in one place and I agree with her.'

'I am not advocating that they should be constantly moving from house to house, Miss Grensham, merely asking that you settle them somewhere else.'

Alex reached across to refill her glass. By

heaven, but she was stubborn! He noticed that his own glass was empty. He might as well refill that, too. He had forgotten that the brandy in the cellars here was very fine indeed.

She sipped her wine before replying.

'No, my lord. Chantreys is an eminently suitable house for the children. Its proximity to London means that when they need dancing and singing masters we will be able to command the very best.'

There was the faintest suggestion of unsteadiness in her voice. His glance flickered over the half-empty wine glass. Was she intoxicated? He had intended that she should be at ease with him, but perhaps in the enjoyment of the dinner he had allowed her too much wine. After all, she was not used to society and possibly might not be used to wine-drinking either. He pushed his chair back.

'It is time I left,' he said abruptly.

She blinked at him, her eyes wide. 'But we have not finished our discussion, nor have I finished my wine.'

'I think you have had quite enough,' he muttered, walking round and putting his hand on her chair. 'Come along.'

With a tiny shrug of her shoulders she rose. She looked perfectly steady but he was taking no chances. He pulled her hand on to his sleeve and walked her out of the dining room. As they crossed the hall he barked out an order to a hovering footman.

'Ask Mrs Wallace to make tea and bring it into the drawing room, immediately.'

'Oh, are you staying for tea?' said Diana. 'That will be de—delightful.'

He felt the weight of her as she leaned into him. He had intended to leave her, but perhaps he should stay and make sure she drank something other than wine. She continued to chatter as he guided her into the drawing room and eased her off his arm and on to a sofa.

'Chantreys is most, most excellently situated,' she told him. 'We are close enough to London to visit the art galleries, and the famous Shakespeare Gallery in Pall Mall. Do you know it, my lord?'

'It is not somewhere I have visited as yet,' he replied, moving away.

'Then you should do so,' she said seriously. 'It has illustrations of Shakespeare's plays, commissioned from the finest artists.'

He watched her as she rose and began to walk about the room, idly running her hand along the chair backs.

'There is nothing to say you could not live further from town,' he said, 'You could bring the children to stay in London from time to time. Money is no object—'

'This is not about money, my lord.' She stopped and turned, fixing him with those large, hazel eyes. 'Chantreys has always been their home, they know it and love it. It would be cruel to up-root them now.'

The entrance of Fingle with the tea tray gave Alex time to consider her words and to admit to himself, grudgingly, that she was right. How could he even think of moving the girls at such a time? He could buy a house, or rent one. It might not be as perfect as Chantreys but there must be something suitable for entertaining. For some reason he found it difficult to concentrate on the matter. Or on anything very much. Perhaps it was not only Diana who had been drinking a little too freely.

When they were alone again he said, 'Come, take a cup of tea.'

'I do not think I want anything just yet.' She wandered over to the open window and gave a loud sigh. 'Is it not the most beautiful view from here?'

He crossed the room to stand behind her, but it was not the rolling acres of parkland that he was thinking about, it was the way the western-ing sun set her red hair aflame. Without thinking he reached out to touch it, but quickly snatched his hand back when she turned suddenly to face him. She was glaring at him, the light of battle in her eyes.

'Do you know what the problem is, my lord Davenport? You are spoiled. You have never had to struggle, to fight for anything. Is it any wonder if you are dissolute and irresponsible? Whatever you desire you only have to click your fingers.' She held up her hand, frowning in concentration as she tried to fit the action to the words. After a moment she gave up and turned her rather misty gaze upon him once more. 'You only have to click your fingers and your wish is granted, your wealth has always bought everything you want.' She stabbed at his chest with her fingers. 'Well, you shall not buy *me*.'

His eyes narrowed. 'Don't do that.'

'Why not?' She looked up, a challenging gleam in her eyes. 'Are you afraid I might sully your exquisite tailoring? Or do you fear I shall disturb the perfection of your cravat?'

Her fingers began to slide up over the embroidered waistcoat, but before she had reached the black linen neckcloth he clamped his hand over hers.

The effect was shocking.

A bolt of desire shot through Alex. It was no longer an annoying little governess standing before him, rather a creature of fire, a flame-haired siren who tantalised his senses. Her eyes widened, as if she was aware of the effect she was having. Hardly surprising since he was still holding her fingers against his chest, where she must feel the drumming of his heart. His free hand slid around her neck and cupped the back of her head. He almost expected those flaming locks to burn him but her hair was cool as silk against his palm. She made no move to resist and gently he drew her closer. As he lowered his head to kiss her he saw her eyelids flutter. Soaring elation overwhelmed him. His mouth came down upon hers in a bruising kiss.

Diana's senses swooped and spun. He teased her lips apart, his tongue flickering, demanding access and she could not deny him. She knew she should be outraged but instead she was exultant, revelling in the taste and smell of him, an exciting mixture of wine and spices plus something unfamiliar but very male. Her bones turned to water but it did not matter, because he was holding her so close, his arms strong as iron bands. Her hand was still trapped against his chest and she struggled to move and slip it around his neck, to push her fingers through the thick dark hair that curled over his collar.

She had never been in a man's arms before, no man had ever so much as kissed her cheek, but she felt no fear, only a fierce, primal pleasure when Alex's teeth grazed her lip before his tongue was once more dipping and diving into her. She gave a small moan of pleasure before returning his kiss and when she felt him withdrawing she clung tighter, instinctively pressing her body against his, wanting to prolong the hot, intimate embrace.

The blood was pounding through her veins, her senses were swimming, but she was aware that his arms were no longer around her, he was easing himself away, gently but inexorably. The frantic, heated kisses came to an end.

Dragging in a breath, Diana put her hands behind her, thankful to find the window frame was within reach. She leaned against it, trying to work out just what had happened. Alex was staring at her, frowning from beneath those heavy brows, his deep chest rising and falling with every ragged breath.

'I beg your pardon,' he muttered, his voice unsteady.

Her body cried out in agony at the distance between them. They were leaning against opposite sides of the window frame, only inches apart, but it was too much. She dug her fingers into the wood at her back to stop herself from cupping her breasts, which felt so full and hard they ached. She shook her head.

'I do not—' she began, when she could command her voice. 'That is, I have never—'

'No, you haven't, have you?'

A wry smile curved his mouth and Diana felt embarrassment replace the heat of passion. She should move away but her legs would not support her. There was a throbbing ache between her thighs, so intense that she wanted to throw herself at Alex, instinct telling her that only he could assuage it.

He stepped sideways, away from her and into the room.

'Let us blame it on the wine and think no more about it,' he said, walking to the door. 'I must go now.'

Diana did not want him to leave. She tried to drag her reeling thoughts into some kind of order.

'What—what about the children?'

He stopped at the door and bent another frowning look at her.

'I do not think either of us is in the mood for more discussion, Miss Grensham. I bid you goodnight.'

He was gone. Diana closed her eyes, breathing deeply and leaning heavily against the window frame at her back. She was not sure if she was most in danger of fainting or bursting into tears. Perhaps the earl was right, it was the wine. She had certainly taken more than usual, and she had felt very relaxed by the time dinner was over. Relaxed enough to tell Alex that she thought him a rich, spoiled nobleman for whom money could buy everything.

Her hands crept up to her cheeks. She had told him he could not buy her and he had punished her by showing that he did not need riches to reduce her to a trembling, incoherent wreck. He had done that with nothing more than a kiss.

She heard a soft scratching at the door and Fingle came in. Diana turned away quickly, pretending to look out at the gardens, deep in shadow now and with the moon rising in the distance.

'I beg your pardon, Miss Grensham. I heard his lordship leave and thought—but you haven't touched the tea. Would you like me to ask Mrs Wallace to put the kettle on again?'

'No, thank you, Fingle. I, um, I am going up to say goodnight to the children and then I think I shall retire.'

'Very well then, miss, shall I take the tray away?'

'Yes, please do.' She remained in the shadows and watched him depart with the untouched tray. No, she thought wretchedly, it was not tea that her body craved this evening.

* * *

'What in the name of all that's wonderful were you about?' Alex demanded of himself as he drove through the darkened lanes.

The cool night air had cleared his brain sufficiently for him to think straight again. The brandy had momentarily clouded his judgement. Thin redheads had never appealed to him and neither did headstrong, opinionated women. Diana was a lady, and his sister-in-law, to boot. It had been reprehensible of him to ply her with drink. True, she had annoyed him when she had called him irresponsible. Who was she to criticise him, to accuse him of trying to buy her? He had merely offered her the pick of any of his houses. By heaven, many a man would not even have given her a choice in the matter.

His mouth tightened. If he hadn't written her that letter assuring her she could stay at Chantreys, then perhaps he might now have ordered her and the children to leave, but he could not in honour do so. And he was not without honour, however dissolute she might think him. He gave a little grunt of frustration, knowing he had not acted honourably this evening. Her responses had been passionate but inexpert. Why, he would wager on it that she had never been kissed before. He recalled her look when he had put her away from him, her eyes huge and dark, regarding him with a mixture of wonder and apprehension.

It was not his habit to pursue innocent virgins and she was most surely an innocent. A veritable Sleeping Beauty, whose passion he had awakened with a kiss. His mouth twisted. But he was no Prince Charming. He had been on the town long enough to know what happened to men of experience who married innocent young women. They were bored within a month and within two they had set up a mistress, leaving a wife distraught at the desertion.

His hands jerked on the reins at the thought and he was obliged to give his attention to the greys, who objected strongly to his unaccustomed treatment. No, he thought, when the team was once more running smoothly, he had no intention of entering into such a marriage. He had determined to marry for convenience, a woman who understood what was required, who would make no demands upon him emotionally.

His mind wandered back to the memory of Diana, chin up, eyes challenging. He recalled the sudden stirring of interest, a flicker that had become irresistible when he had caught her fingers. He had only meant to prevent her from committing an indiscretion, but with her tiny hand clasped against his heart he had felt an irresistible urge to pull her into his arms. She had felt it, too, that connection between them. He had read it in her eyes, along with an invitation that he had accepted far too readily.

So there was another reason to remove Diana Grensham from Chantreys. She was governess to his wards and could not risk the loss of reputation that would result from an affair. And for himself, he would not want that on his conscience. Diana Grensham was no drab from the stews, willing to indulge in a quick tumble. When he had kissed her he had recognised her passionate nature and it had drawn a response from him. He knew that these attractions were never long lasting, but Diana was not experienced in flirtations—what if she were to develop a *tendre* for him?

He reached the outskirts of London and bowled through the town, his mind made up. Whichever way one looked at it, the best thing would be for Diana and the children to remove from Chantreys and preferably a good distance from London, well out of harm's way. The problem was how to achieve it? The devil of it was that so far Diana had proved surprisingly stubborn. She was determined not to capitulate. His jaw tightened. Well, he could be stubborn, too. This was no longer about the children, it was a battle of wills, and he was not about to lose.

Chapter Three

The following day brought word from Chantreys, the letter arriving at Alex's lodgings just as he was about to set off for Jackson's Boxing Academy. With a faint sense of satisfaction he broke the seal. Perhaps his lapse yesterday had not been such a bad thing. Diana was probably so mortified that she wanted nothing more than to remove as far away from him as possible.

His hopes were short lived. The missive was brief and to the point. Miss Grensham sent her compliments—*hah!*—and wrote to inform him that she had decided the children should remain at Chantreys for the next year at least.

'*She* has decided!' he exclaimed, resisting with an effort the temptation to crush the paper between his hands. He forced himself to continue reading to the end.

Miss Grensham therefore considers further discussion of the children's future would be

*of little benefit. However, if Lord Davenport
wishes to call upon the children a message
to Chantreys ahead of his visit would be
appreciated, in order that Lady Margret
and Miss Florence might be ready to receive him.*

Alex swore explosively. Nothing would persuade him to make an appointment to visit his
own property! He threw the letter on the table,
snatched up his hat and gloves and set off for
Bond Street.

Striding through the crowds brought some relief and after an hour in Jackson's Boxing Academy, sparring with the great man himself, he was
able to view Diana's letter more dispassionately.

She had made it clear that she did not wish to
move from Chantreys, but it was equally obvious that she was reluctant to meet with him again
after their last encounter. That was the reason
she wished for prior warning of his visits to the
house, so that when he called she could arrange
for Nurse to bring the children downstairs. For
a moment he recalled that impromptu game of
battledore upon the lawn and felt a tinge of regret
that they would not do it again. But that could not
be helped. She must be persuaded that it would
be better for her and the girls if they moved out
of Chantreys altogether. If only he could think
of a way to do it.

* * *

A week later Alex was still no nearer solving the dilemma and such was his distraction that he almost walked past Gervase Wollerton in Jermyn Street without a word.

'By Jove, Alex, I don't know when I last saw you looking so blue-devilled,' observed his friend, when Alex had stopped and begged his pardon. 'Something amiss? I was going to look in at White's, but if you want to talk...'

'No, I don't,' said Alex. 'I am on my way to see Lady Frances, if you want to give me your arm.'

Mr Wollerton lifted his eyeglass and surveyed Alex.

'Thing is,' he said slowly, 'not sure I can do that, my friend. Not with you in that coat. In fact, if it wasn't growing dark, I would hesitate to acknowledge you.'

Alex's lips twitched.

'Gammon,' he said rudely. 'Have you been listening to Brummell again, Gervase? What is it this time, are the buttons too large, is my coat not plain enough for the Beau's taste?'

'No, no,' Mr Wollerton assured him. 'It ain't the buttons and the coat's plain enough. It's the cut. Shouldn't be surprised if you can shrug yourself into it.'

'Of course I can shrug myself into it.' Impatiently Alex took his arm and urged him on. 'I am happy to follow Brummell's lead when it comes to clean linen and simple, dark coats, but I'm damned if I'll spend hours each morning letting my man dress me.'

'Which is why the Beau will never be seen in the street with you, dear boy.'

Alex gave a bark of laughter. 'I shall live without that privilege.'

'I think you will have to,' murmured his friend. 'But at least you have come out of the sullens.'

'I was not in the sullens,' Alex objected, preparing to cross Piccadilly. 'Are you coming with me to see Frances, or would you rather retrace your steps and go to White's?'

'Happy to call upon Lady Frances.' Mr Wollerton coughed delicately. 'If I won't be *de trop*?'

'Good God, no. What makes you think that?'

Wollerton gave a slight shrug.

'You seem to be getting mighty close, taking her out to Chantreys and all that.'

Alex frowned.

'I haven't taken her to Chantreys.'

'Well, she has seen it at all events.'

'What? How can she have done so?'

'She drove out to view the place recently, heard her telling Anglesey about it at the assembly last night.'

'The devil she did.'

Gervase brushed a speck of fluff from his

sleeve as he said, 'I think she aspires to be your countess, old friend.'

Alex scowled. 'I thought I had made it very plain I am not yet in the market for a wife.'

'So you are not meeting her tête-à-tête tonight?' asked Wollerton, looking relieved.

'Great heavens, no. She has invited all the world and his wife.'

Mr Wollerton protested mildly, 'The world might turn up, but not so sure about the *wives*. Not the high sticklers, at any rate.'

'Thank God for that,' muttered Alex. 'That's one of the main reasons I go there, to get away from the single females and their mamas on the hunt for every eligible bachelor. This Season has been particularly grim, having been obliged to escort Lady Hune and her protégée to just the sort of parties that I most abhor.' He quickened his pace. 'Come along, it's starting to rain.'

Lady Frances's soirées were comfortable affairs where one could expect good conversation and excellent refreshments. The company was predominantly male but at least a man could relax and enjoy himself without falling prey to a matchmaker. Alex and Gervase stepped indoors before the rain had sullied their coats and since they were familiar with the house they went directly to the card room set up in one of the spacious salons. Their hostess appeared in the doorway as they approached and held out her hands to Alex, smiling.

'Welcome, my lord, and to you, Mr Wollerton. You are set upon cards, I see. What will it be for you this evening?'

'Whist,' said Alex. 'If you and Wollerton will join me.'

He noted the little flicker of surprise and wondered if Frances wanted to keep him to herself. If Gervase's observations were correct, Frances had aspirations Alex had no intention of fulfilling for a long time yet. It was reassuring to see her smile without any hint of disappointment.

'Of course,' she said smoothly. She looked about her. 'We will need a fourth...Sir Charles, you are free? Do join us for a rubber of whist.'

Alex had no great opinion of Sir Charles Urmston and when they moved to an empty table he chose to sit opposite Gervase, leaving Lady Frances to partner Urmston. As they made themselves comfortable Alex glanced up and surprised a look pass between Urmston and the lady. It was fleeting, but there was an intimacy that made him wonder if they were more than friends.

The first rubber went to Frances and Urmston. Alex threw down his cards.

'I beg your pardon, Gervase. I was not concentrating.' He glanced at Lady Frances. 'You did not tell me you had seen Chantreys. When was this, ma'am? When did you go there?'

Her eyes widened but her smile did not falter.

'I did not exactly *go there*, my lord. I was on my way to Upminster to visit friends and I glimpsed it from the road.'

'You must have driven a long way around the perimeter,' he said sardonically. 'As far as I am aware there is only one spot where you have a clear view of the house.'

'I was curious to see the place that holds such happy memories for you, Alexander.' Her fingers touched his arm. 'I am now in a rage to visit Chantreys in the summer.'

'That will not be possible. My wards will be in residence.'

She looked up at him, her finely arched brows rising.

'But you were looking forward to holding a party there for all your friends.'

'*You* were looking forward to it, Frances.' His glance was mocking. 'As I recall the idea of a ball to shock the *ton* was yours.'

The lady brushed this aside with a smile.

'Nevertheless, my lord, I thought you had decided to send the children to school.'

'The decision is not solely mine to make.' The admission rubbed at his pride. 'Miss Grensham is also their guardian and she is against the idea.'

He continued, deciding it would be best to get the whole thing over with. 'She is also against moving from Chantreys for the next twelve months at least.'

'And have you no say in the matter?' murmured Urmston, unwrapping a new pack of cards.

'We discussed it,' said Alex shortly.

Lady Frances put her hand on his arm. 'My dear Alexander, you should have left her in no doubt of your wishes in this matter. I thought we were agreed that the girls would be better off at school.'

'Unfortunately when it comes to the girls' education, my brother decreed that the final decision should belong to Miss Grensham, as the… er…"most fit and proper person to attend to it".'

Gervase laughed. 'James certainly had your measure, then, my friend!'

'It seems odd that she will not give up the place,' murmured Sir Charles. 'I believe the ladies generally find your charms persuasive.'

Alex felt his lip curling in derision. 'It is my money and my title that they find persuasive.'

Lady Frances tensed and Alex wondered if she thought the barb was directed at her.

'You are probably right, old boy.' Wollerton nodded, enjoying his wine and oblivious to the tension around the table. 'Not that you ain't charming when you want to be,' he added hastily. 'It's just that most likely you didn't think it necessary to charm a servant.'

'Miss Grensham is not a servant,' retorted Alex, unaccountably annoyed. 'She is the children's guardian.'

'But that does not give her the right to monopolise your property,' objected Lady Frances.

Alex might agree, but something compelled him to put Diana's point of view. 'She considers Chantreys the most suitable place for the children at the present time.'

Sir Charles was about to deal, but he hesitated as if a thought had struck him.

'Perhaps, my lord, you should demonstrate that the lady is not a…er…*fit and proper person* to have responsibility for your wards.' He sat back, smiling in a way that made Alex dislike him even more. 'How difficult can it be?' he drawled. 'Wollerton here says you have charm, when you wish to use it. Seduce the wench and send her packing.'

'Miss Grensham is no *wench*, Urmston,' Alex retorted coldly. 'She is a lady.'

'But Sir Charles has a point,' remarked Lady Frances, her tone smooth and reasonable. 'Perhaps not seduction,' she said quickly, observing Alex's frown. 'But if some gentleman were to take her fancy, if she wanted to *marry*, she might be more willing to compromise over the little girls' education. And consider the advantage to the lady; she could exchange the drudgery of being a governess for a much more respectable station. She would be a married woman and have a man to protect her.'

Alex watched Urmston deal out the cards, but his mind was on Frances's words.

'That might be possible,' he said slowly. 'If she were to marry she could no longer look after the girls. And why not school rather than another governess? My brother's will provided Miss Grensham with a handsome sum, so she would not be a penniless bride.'

And she was not unattractive, if one liked dainty, red-headed women, he thought, regarding Lady Frances's voluptuous form.

'Yes,' he mused. 'It might just work. I know several fellows in want of a wife.'

'Well, there you are then,' murmured Sir Charles. He finished giving out the cards and turned over the last one. 'Hearts,' he declared. 'Hearts are trumps.'

The second meeting with Lord Davenport had left Diana angry and unsettled. She was appalled at her own behaviour in encouraging the earl to kiss her; just the thought of it sent a shiver running through her. She was even more appalled to realise how much she wanted him to do it again. Quite reprehensible! Clearly in future he must not call unannounced. She decided, therefore, that she would write to him, telling him as much. The letter was written and despatched before she broke her fast the following morning, but even before it could have reached its destination she was regretting the rash impulse. Her tone had not been at all conciliatory and she was sure the earl would take offence. However, when the timorous side of her nature suggested that she should write again and apologise her spirit rebelled strongly. Lord Davenport must acknowledge that he was as much to blame for the lapse in decorum.

Why should he? He is an Arrandale, after all.

The thought came unbidden and Diana was obliged to acknowledge the truth of it. Even the late earl, for all his staid and respectable nature, had possessed the famed Arrandale arrogance. They went their own way, convinced of their superiority, and she had no reason to think Alex Arrandale was any different from the rest of his family.

The thought remained with her for the next few days, contributing to her mood of restless anxiety. It became so bad that one evening, after saying goodnight to the children she did not go immediately downstairs but instead went to the schoolroom, walking around and idly touching the familiar objects.

Was she being unreasonable to keep the children at Chantreys? It was perfectly understandable that the new earl would wish to make use of his properties and since he was an Arrandale, she was in no doubt that any party he brought to Chantreys would be far from respectable. The society pages of the newspapers she read often mentioned his name in connection with the more notorious of society's hostesses. She had a shrewd idea that he considered Chantreys would be the perfect place to bring his latest flirt.

That he refused to do so with the children in residence showed he had some sense of honour, but Meggie and Florence were not his children and it was clear he saw them as an inconvenience. She had learned a great deal about the family since becoming governess to the late earl's children. James and Alex had been brought up to want for nothing, an army of servants to obey their every whim, but their parents had been shadowy figures with little time to spare for their offspring. Margaret had always said it was a blessing James had turned out as respectable as he had done, but was it any wonder if his younger brother had grown up to consider nothing but his own pleasure? No, Diana was sure he would not give up the fight to remove her and the girls from Chantreys.

Well, perhaps she would write to him again and suggest a compromise. She would offer to take Meggie and Florence away for a few months. The earl had offered her the use of any of his other properties, or perhaps they might remove to the coast. A spell of sea bathing might prove beneficial, as long as Meggie and Florence knew they could return to their home afterwards.

'It is certainly worth pursuing,' she murmured as she blew out her candle that night. But her encounter with the new earl of Davenport had roused her spirit and she was reluctant to capitulate too easily. No, she thought as she settled down to sleep. She would not write immediately. It would do the new earl no harm to savour his defeat for a little longer. However, a little over a week after the earl's visit, a letter arrived from him that sent all thoughts of compromise from her head.

Chapter Four

'How *dare* he?'

Diana screwed the paper into a ball and threw it into the corner. She paced about the morning room, hands clenched and muttering angrily, thankful that she was alone and could allow her temper full rein. The letter had been waiting for her when she returned from a walk with the girls and, recognising the seal, she had sent the children off with Nurse as soon as they had all removed their muddy boots and outdoor clothes.

She had braced herself for the earl's response to her letter, expecting at best a suggestion for another house where they might reside, or at worst an angry condemnation of her presumption in opposing his will, even an ultimatum, but not this missive couched in the politest terms, telling her that he intended to bring a party of friends to the house and was giving her a month's notice of the visit, that she and the children might be prepared.

'How very considerate of you, my lord!'

Her words echoed around the morning room, but although her indignation remained, her anger was cooling. She picked up the paper and smoothed it out, then she sat down on a chair to read it again.

Perhaps he expected her to panic at the thought of his visit, to demand that he find another home for his wards immediately, but what if she did not do so? She nibbled her finger. He might be selfish and hedonistic but she did not believe he would hold a truly outrageous party while Meggie and Florence were living in the house. Diana made a quick mental survey of the building. The nursery and schoolroom were on the top floor, there would be no reason for visitors to venture so far. The children would not be able to have the run of the house, as they did now, but it would be May, so they would be able to spend much more time out of doors. She glanced at the clock. There was no time now to reply, but once she had concluded the children's lessons she would compose a letter to the earl. A polite note that would leave him in no doubt that she would not allow the children to be chased out of their home.

The cavalcade of carriages rattled through the park and swept around the curling drive that snaked towards the front door of Chantreys. Alex was leading the way in his curricle, with Lady Frances beside him. As he drew his team to a halt she placed her hand upon his leg, saying with a laugh,

'My dear Alexander, it is quite, quite charming!'

He had to admit it was looking particularly well in the late-spring sunshine, a perfectly proportioned little confection of a building. Rather than ruin the aesthetics by extending the house itself, successive generations had added two pavilions to flank the house and provide extra accommodation.

Alex glanced upwards. The rooms under the eaves had once been the servants' quarters but his parents had moved the staff outside into one of the pavilions and converted the whole top floor into a nursery. He wondered if Diana and the children were looking out for their arrival. Or perhaps they were waiting just inside the wide door, which was now thrown open as the servants came spilling out to welcome Lord Davenport and his guests.

Alex jumped down and walked around to help Lady Frances alight. He led her past the row of wooden-faced servants and into the hall, cool and light with its pale marble floor and white-painted walls. He paused there, waiting for the rest of the guests to follow them inside. It was a small party, only six guests, as many as the house could hold without opening up the south pavilion to accommodate them. Gervase Wollerton was the last to come in, looking about him in appreciation.

'You are right, Alex,' he declared, 'it is a very pretty place. Is this where you plan to put the Canova, opposite the stairs? The plainness of that wall would be the perfect foil for it.'

'Yes, but not while the children are in residence,' murmured Lady Frances. 'One dreads to think of what might happen to such a precious statue with little ones running riot through the house.'

'Quite,' replied Alex. He beckoned to a hovering servant. 'And talking of children, where are the girls, Christopher?'

The footman gave a little bow. 'Miss Grensham begs that you will advise her what time you would like your wards sent to the drawing room.'

Alex felt a hand on his arm and heard Lady Frances softly laughing beside him.

'Dear me, I hope you will allow us time to change out of our travelling clothes and rest awhile, my lord.'

'If you wish it,' he replied, 'although I had thought this an easy distance from town.'

'It is, of course,' she returned smoothly. 'But I should like to refresh myself and look my best when I meet your wards.'

'Then I shall hand you over to Mrs Wallace.' He beckoned to the housekeeper, who was hovering expectantly. His glance swept over the guests now assembled in the hall. 'She will show you to your rooms while Fingle and Christopher deal with your baggage. If you will excuse me.'

With a brief smile he left them and ran up the stairs two at a time, a pleasurable anticipation speeding his steps as he made his way to the schoolroom. He opened the door on a particularly domestic scene. A sofa had been placed beneath one of the windows and Diana was sitting there with Meggie and Florence on each side of her while she read to them from a large, leather-bound book.

At his entrance all three rose, the young girls' faces breaking into smiles of delight, while Diana's conscious look and sudden blush told him she had not forgotten their last meeting. Neither had he, Alex thought ruefully as he stifled a sudden rush of desire at the memory of that one, sizzling kiss.

'Uncle Alex!' Margaret ran forward and he scooped her up in his arms, laughing.

'Yes, I am here, Meggie.' He hugged his niece, then set her down and turned to greet Florence, who had followed more slowly. That gave him a few moments to compose himself before he looked up and acknowledged Diana with a friendly nod. 'Miss Grensham.'

She dropped a slight curtsy to him.

'Lord Davenport.'

He surprised a slight, puzzled look in her eyes.

'Is anything amiss?'

'Your neckcloth…you are no longer in mourning?'

He put his hand up to the froth of white linen at his throat.

'I shall always mourn my brother, but I decided it was time for a change.' He wanted to say more, but the words would not come. All he could think of was how her simple cream gown enhanced her flame-red hair, which was pulled back from her face into a knot, almost tamed, save for a few silky curls that had escaped and now kissed the back of her neck. His eyes regarded that neck, noting the elegant way it rose from the folds of the muslin fichu covering her shoulders. Demure as a nun. Was that for his benefit?

'Look, Uncle Alex, we have new gowns.' Meggie was pulling at his sleeve. 'Diana ordered them. Do we not look well?'

'As fine as fivepence,' he told the girls as they twirled before him.

'They are ready to meet your guests, my lord, as soon as you wish me to send them downstairs.'

'I wish you to *bring* them downstairs, Miss Grensham,'

'There is no need for me—'

There is every need,' he interrupted her. 'You are as much their guardian as I am. In fact, more so,' he added, 'since you are in charge of their education.'

A mischievous gleam put to flight the rather anxious look he had seen in her eyes.

'I think that rankles with you, my Lord Davenport.'

Alex's lips twitched.

'I am not deceived by your demure tone, Miss Grensham,' he growled. 'You revel in your superiority in this matter.'

'That would be ignoble of me, sir.'

She was smiling, clearly more comfortable when they were teasing one another. As was he.

'It would indeed,' he replied gravely. He glanced down at his dusty boots. 'I beg your pardon for appearing in all my dirt. I wanted to come up immediately to see the girls.'

The faint blush was on her cheek again but she spoke calmly enough.

'Not at all, Lord Davenport, your eagerness to see your charges does you credit.'

Diana hoped he could not see how he discomposed her. From the moment she had heard his booted tread outside the door her heart had been racing. She would have liked to say it was from anger, or indignation, but she had to acknowledge the *frisson* of pleasure that ran through her at the thought of seeing the earl again. And when he had appeared, she had thought for an instant how much less severe he looked, but that might have been merely the fact that he was no longer wearing the black neckcloth, which had certainly heightened the glowering effect of his heavy black brows. Really, she must be desperate for adult companionship if she had been looking forward to this visit! That is what she told herself, but in her heart she suspected it was specifically Lord Davenport's company she enjoyed. The verbal sparring. The kiss.

No!

As the children took their visitor to the table to show him their drawings she busied herself with gathering up the books and slates and putting them away. The kiss had nothing to do with it. That was a mistake, the result of too much wine, nothing else. She had been alone too long at Chantreys. Since the death of her sister and brother-in-law she had shut herself away too much with the children. That was all.

'I must go and change.' The earl's voice broke into her thoughts. Diana turned to see that he was moving towards the door. 'You will bring the children to join us after dinner, Miss Grensham.'

Diana would have preferred to send the girls downstairs with Nurse, but there was something in the earl's tone that told her he would brook no defiance. She would not argue. At least not in front of her charges.

'As you wish, my lord.'

The hard look he gave her suggested he was surprised by her meek acquiescence, but after regarding her silently for a long moment he gave a little nod and was gone. The girls ran about, chattering excitedly. For Meggie and Florence the hours could not pass quickly enough but it was quite the opposite for Diana, who could almost wish for a disaster to save her from the forthcoming ordeal.

At the appointed hour Diana accompanied her charges to the drawing room. There were seven persons awaiting her, three ladies and four gentlemen, including Lord Davenport. He had a voluptuous blonde at his side but it was not the lady's striking beauty that drew Diana's attention, it was the fact that she was standing rather closer to the earl than was necessary and had one hand resting possessively on his sleeve.

Resolutely Diana turned to the other two ladies in the room. The younger one was Miss Prentiss, a single lady with all the poise and confidence Diana lacked. She also had a rather strident voice and a harsh laugh that grated upon the ear. Her companion was considerably older. The young lady addressed her as Mrs Peters, not her mother then, but Diana guessed she was here to act as chaperon.

So, thought Diana, she had been right about the earl, he would observe the proprieties while the children were at Chantreys. Considerably relieved, she turned to consider the gentlemen. They were all of a similar age and all fashionably dressed, but it was Lord Davenport who caught and held her gaze.

She was surprised. With his broad deep chest and craggy features she had not thought the earl would look so well in the plain dark coat and pale pantaloons that Mr Brummell had made *de rigueur* for evening wear, but she saw now that it enhanced his powerful frame and the lithe, athletic grace of his movements as he walked towards her. Hastily she looked away and forced herself to concentrate upon Meggie and Florence.

Diana had prepared them well. They accompanied Lord Davenport around the room while she followed, hoping that everyone would be so charmed with the little girls with their pretty dresses and glossy ringlets that they would not notice the ungainly creature in the lavender gown following them with her awkward, dragging step. Any thoughts she had of retiring unheeded to a corner disappeared when the earl took her arm and led her forward. She was puzzled when he introduced her as his sister-in-law but she recalled their conversation, when she had told him that governesses were of no consequence and she realised, with something very like gratitude, that he was endeavouring to give her some standing amongst his guests.

That thought and the earl's presence steadied Diana as the introductions continued. The guests showed little interest, although she felt their stares upon her as she crossed the room. As always when amongst strangers Diana was painfully aware of her shortened leg and found herself limping even more. She was relieved, however, when the introductions were over and she could at last sit down upon a vacant sofa and watch the proceedings. The girls were received kindly, no one petting them so much as the blonde, whom Diana now knew to be Lady Frances Betsford. However, the novelty of having children in the room soon palled and Diana called them back to sit with her while the ladies exhibited their skill upon the harpsichord. When Lady Frances was begged to take her turn at the harpsichord she modestly declined at first, but when the earl added his entreaties she capitulated.

'Very well,' she said, casting a melting look up at him. 'But only if you will sing a duet with me.'

The suggestion was met with such approval that Diana knew it was not the first time they had performed together. She folded her hands in her lap and fought down the uncharitable hope that Lady Frances might prove inept and tone deaf.

As if in punishment for her ungraciousness Diana knew Lady Frances would excel as soon as she began to play. The earl stood behind the lady, his rich baritone harmonising with her voice in a love song that they had clearly sung together before. Diana looked down, surprised to see that her hands were tightly clasped and she made a conscious effort to relax. It should not matter at all to her that they were so at ease with one another.

When the duet was over she applauded and praised the performance to Meggie and Florence, who were clapping enthusiastically.

'You enjoyed that, did you, brats?' The earl was smiling as he came away from the harpsichord with Lady Frances on his arm.

'We did, very much,' exclaimed Florence. 'Will you sing again for us, sir?'

He laughed and shook his head.

'Perhaps later. We must let the others have their turn.'

'Diana is teaching us to play,' Meggie announced. 'And she plays for us to sing and dance, as well.'

'Does she?' Lady Frances was smiling, but Diana thought there was more speculation than warmth in those blue eyes as they rested upon her. 'Perhaps you would like to play for us this evening, Miss Grensham.'

Quickly Diana disclaimed any desire to perform but the lady persisted, finally turning to the earl.

'Alexander, my dear, will you support me? Insist that she plays for us.'

Diana froze and struggled to utter a protest from a throat that had suddenly dried.

'I assure you, my lord, I—'

'I will do nothing of the sort, Frances,' the earl said, as if she had not spoken. 'Miss Grensham shall play for us when and if she chooses to do so.'

Lady Frances was not pleased with his response and an awkward silence descended.

'I wish I could play well enough to take a turn.' Meggie sighed, oblivious. 'Or I could dance for you!'

Her comment broke the icy restraint. The earl reached out and patted her hair, saying, 'I have

no doubt you could, but it is your bedtime now.'
He added, when her face fell, 'You may dance
for us another night, brat.'

'Mayhap Miss Grensham will help you to prepare a little concert for our next visit,' purred
Lady Frances. 'Then we may see the accomplishments you have learned.'

Diana's spirits swooped in dismay at the
thought of another party at Chantreys.

'Good idea.' Lord Davenport agreed absently,
but it was clear his thoughts were elsewhere. 'Off
you go now. Miss Grensham shall take you upstairs.'

Diana rose and encouraged the children to
make their curtsies before she led them away.
She was aware of the earl's unsmiling gaze as
they passed him.

'Goodnight, my lord.'

'You will come back, Miss Grensham, once
you have settled the children.'

She inclined her head, acknowledging that he
had spoken, but she said nothing. She had en-
dured enough for this evening. She would not
return.

Alex wandered about the room, a word here,
a smile there, but the evening dragged intolerably. When Diana did not appear after an hour he
realised she would not be coming back. He was

not surprised, she had not wanted to appear in the first place, but at least she should be proud of her charges. Their manners and deportment were a credit to her teaching.

'My lord, you are not listening to me.'

Lady Frances shook her head at him as he quickly begged pardon.

'I was merely saying that I cannot wait for this evening to be over, so I may have you to myself.' She moved closer, smoothing her fingers over the lapel of his coat. 'You could come to my room, Alexander, or...'

He had a fleeting memory of Diana in his arms, her little hand pressed to his chest and his heart thundering against it. Madness. To be forgotten. He stepped away from Frances, out of reach.

'I do not think that would be wise.' She looked at him with a mixture of surprise and disappointment and he sought to explain. 'I would not have any hint of impropriety attached to this visit.'

'Nor I.' She added softly, 'But I can be very discreet.'

'I am sure you can, Frances, nevertheless we will have to restrain ourselves while we are at Chantreys.'

Anger flashed in her eyes, almost instantly replaced with a smile.

'As you wish, Alexander. But I shall not lock

my door. Oh, and I have had my maid's truckle bed moved into the dressing room. She is a *very* heavy sleeper.'

With another alluring smile she moved off and Alex watched her walk away. Every sway of her hips was an invitation but, strangely, he was not tempted to follow. He castigated himself as a fool. What difference did it make that the girls and their governess were lying abed on the top floor? They need never know what was going on below, yet he could not be easy. He signalled to Fingle to bring him another brandy. Hell and confound it, he was developing a conscience. The sooner he moved the children to another house the better.

Diana sat on the edge of her bed, slowly dragging the brush through her hair. So that was the first evening over. Mrs Wallace was disappointed that Lord Davenport and his guests were staying for no more than a se'ennight, but Diana wished he was staying only half that time. The freedom she and the children had enjoyed at the house was severely curtailed and she could only pray that the weather would remain fine and she would be able to take the children out of doors for a good part of every day.

The next morning, at least, her prayers were answered and she sent a message to the stables to have the old curricle brought to the door. She was just making her way down the stairs when the earl came out from the dining room. At the sight of her in her walking dress he looked seriously displeased.

'Why are you not joining us for breakfast?'

'I broke my fast with Meggie and Florence,' she replied evenly. 'I am now taking them out for an airing.'

'Yes, Uncle Alex,' piped up Meggie. 'Diana is taking us out in the curricle.'

'Oh? And who is driving?'

'I am.' Diana's chin went up. 'The late earl had perfect confidence in my ability to handle the ribbons.'

'Did he?'

The speculative look in his eyes roused Diana's spirit.

'You need not worry, my lord, Meggie and Florence will be perfectly safe with me.'

She shepherded her charges out of the house, but to her annoyance the earl strolled out after them and nodded to the old groom who was standing at the horses' heads.

'Well, at least you will have Judd with you in case you have trouble,' he said. 'That relieves my mind.'

The old groom chuckled. 'Now then, my lord, you've no reason to worry about Miss Grensham handlin' the ribbons. Besides, I'd be hard pressed to do anythin' from that rear seat.'

Diana was grateful for Judd's support, but she maintained her silence as she helped the children into the curricle. The girls were excited, regarding a drive in the antiquated vehicle as a high treat. Diana had just finished tucking the rug around their legs when Florence invited the earl to join them.

'Don't be silly,' said Meggie. 'There wouldn't be room for all of us.'

'No indeed.' Diana saw an opportunity for retaliation and turned to the earl, fixing him with a bright smile. 'Perhaps Lord Davenport would like to take you out today?' She glanced at the two elderly horses harnessed to the pole. 'Salt and Pepper are not quite such a, a *bang-up* team as you are used to, sir, but I am sure you will be able to manage them.'

A sudden bout of coughing affected the old groom. Diana and the earl ignored it.

'Thank you, Miss Grensham, I am sure I should, but I would not deny you the pleasure.'

The look in Lord Davenport's eyes promised retribution, but Diana met it with a bland smile before she limped around to take her place beside the girls. She knew him to be an excellent whip, but the temptation to tease him had been irresistible. Would he make her suffer for it? She thought not. He might be arrogant and selfish, but he had a sense of the ridiculous and she had seen the gleam of humour in his eyes on more than one occasion. She bade the girls to hold on as she flicked her whip over the horses' ears, relieved she did not make a mull of it with the earl's critical eyes upon her.

Alex watched them drive off in grand style, an appreciative grin tugging at his mouth. So she still had spirit enough to make fun of him. She drove well, too, he noted, although he wondered if she would have set off at such a smart pace if he had not been watching. He found himself wondering how well she would handle his racing curricle with its fast-paced greys.

The smile died and he turned and went back into the house. Not that he would ever know. The less he and Diana Grensham saw of one another the better. In fact, the sooner she was away from Chantreys the better. Not that he wished her any harm, far from it, but she was a thorn in his side where the children were concerned. What she needed was something to think of other than the children. A husband, perhaps, as Frances had suggested. Well, there were three single gentlemen at Chantreys, excluding himself, so perhaps one of them would take her fancy. Not Gervase, of course, he was a confirmed bachelor, but Hamilton and Avery were perfectly eligible. He had made it clear to them that his sister-in-law had funds. Not a fortune, perhaps, but an easy competence. Enough to tempt a gentleman of modest means, so he was not unhopeful that one of them would make a play for her.

Chapter Five

The old curricle was no longer smart, and the horses definitely not fast goers, but Diana enjoyed tooling it through the lanes surrounding Chantreys. By the time they returned to the park the sun was at its height in the cloudless blue sky. The day was very warm and Diana wished that it were possible to drive to the secret lake. Of course it wasn't really secret, but it was hidden deep amongst the trees on the south side of the park with only a narrow, little-used path leading to it. No time to walk back there today either, Diana decided. The children had been out of doors all morning and once they had had nuncheon they would spend the afternoon in the schoolroom, at their lessons. She hoped to avoid Lord Davenport for the rest of the day, but although he did not come in person to the top floor, he did send a message requesting her to accompany the children to the drawing room after dinner.

Diana was not deceived. It was not a request but a command and one she could not ignore, however much she disliked the idea of going into company. To her relief no one paid her much heed when she entered the drawing room. She was allowed to retire to a corner while the guests made a fuss of the children and, apart from a nod when she came in, the earl did not speak to her. She was a little disappointed when he did not repeat his request that she return to the drawing room once the children had retired. Not that she wished to return, of course, but she was piqued that he did not ask her.

Rain pattered against the window of Diana's bedchamber as she dressed the next morning. The weather was responsible for her dullness of spirits, she decided, eyeing the leaden sky. That and the frustration of having a house full of visitors. She kept the children in the schoolroom after breakfast, but the lessons did not go smoothly, for the girls were fractious and disinclined to sit still. However, by the afternoon the weather had improved sufficiently for Diana to take them out of doors.

After walking in the park they went into the formal gardens, where they were soon joined by Lord Davenport and one of his guests, a Mr Avery. The girls ran to the earl, delighted to see 'Uncle Alex'.

'Well, brats, are you destroying my flower garden?' he demanded, observing the plants they were clutching in their hands.

'Of course not.' Meggie giggled. 'These are wild flowers and leaves from the park. We are going to take them upstairs to paint them.'

'Really? Avery here is quite a botanist,' the earl remarked, drawing his guest forward.

The young man coloured slightly and disclaimed.

'I wouldn't say that, I have a mild interest in flora, that is all.'

'I was about to show him around the garden but I think you would be a much better guide, Miss Grensham,' the earl continued, all affability. He held out his hands to Meggie and Florence. 'Come along, girls, I believe Cook has made some gingerbread so let us go to the kitchens and see if it is ready yet!'

Diana was so surprised by his actions that she could think of nothing to say. Mr Avery gave a little laugh.

'It appears Lord Davenport is more interested in cake than flowers, Miss Grensham. I hope you do not object to showing me about the gardens?'

'N-no, not at all,' she stammered.

'I fear Lord Davenport has exaggerated my knowledge,' he confided, offering her his arm. 'I have only a mild interest in botany, as I told the earl when he mentioned it just now, but he immediately insisted upon bringing me out to look at the roses. He must be very proud of them.'

Diana blinked. As far as she could remember the earl had never shown the least interest in the rose garden, but she could hardly say so. Perhaps he wished to spend a little time with his wards, she thought as she set off along the gravelled path with her companion. If that was the case, who was she to prevent it?

Mr Avery was in no hurry to quit Diana's company and it was late in the afternoon when she finally caught up with Meggie and Florence, who told her triumphantly that Uncle Alex had agreed to play a game of cricket with them. Diana accompanied the girls to the lawns, where she found the earl had already brought the small bat down from the schoolroom. Everyone else had come out to watch and some of the gentlemen had even been persuaded to join in. When Mr Wollerton asked Diana if she was going to play she quickly made her excuses and limped back into the house. The thought of hobbling around in front of an audience was too mortifying to be considered.

* * *

Diana looked longingly out of the window as she took the children downstairs after dinner. If it were not for the visitors she would have left the girls in Nurse's care and taken an evening stroll through the park, but such luxuries were at an end, at least until she and the girls had Chantreys to themselves again.

'Ah, here come your little charges, my lord,' Lady Frances called out as Diana followed the girls into the drawing room. 'Good evening Lady Margaret, Miss Arrandale.'

Meggie and Florence ran across the drawing room to join the party gathered about the harpsichord and Diana tried not to resent the fact that Lady Frances had ignored her in her greeting. She was a governess, little more than a servant and of no interest to Lord Davenport's guests.

As if to prove her wrong, Mr Wollerton and Mr Avery acknowledged her entrance with a bow, and Mr Hamilton stopped to talk to her for a few moments. She answered him briefly before she excused herself and limped across to a distant sofa where she could enjoy the music and her own company until it was time to take the children upstairs again.

Her solitude did not last long. As Miss Prentiss took her turn at the harpsichord Lord Davenport broke away from the group. Diana felt her pulse quicken as he approached her.

'I trust you enjoyed your time in the gardens, Miss Grensham.'

'Thank you, yes. The girls spent a happy hour sketching the flowers we collected.'

'I was referring to your walk with Mr Avery.'

'That was very pleasant.'

'But you could not be persuaded to play cricket.'

She shook her head. 'You did not need me, my lord.'

'It is not a question of need, Diana. I thought you enjoyed the game.' When she did not respond he gestured towards the group gathered around the harpsichord. 'Will you not join us? Meggie tells me you sing very prettily.'

She bit her lip.

'I would rather not sing in company, my lord. Not amongst strangers.'

'If you spent more time with my guests they would not be strangers.'

She inclined her head.

'True, but they go on very well without me and I prefer to sit here quietly.' She was aware of his disapproval and added quickly, 'This is the only evening gown I possess, I would not wish to draw attention to the fact.'

They would despise me.

She did not say the words but he would understand. It would be cruel of him to insist and he was not cruel. At least, she hoped she was not wrong in her judgement of him. After a tense moment he gave a little nod and walked away. Diana let her breath go, slowly. Another ordeal averted, at least for the moment.

'Look, Diana, Uncle Alex is waving at us!'

The two girls were standing at the schoolroom window, their noses pressed against the glass. At Florence's excited exclamation Diana glanced out at the drive below where Lord Davenport was mounted upon his powerful chestnut hunter, waiting for the rest of his guests to ride round from the stables to join him. A day's riding, Nurse had explained when she came upstairs from the servants' hall that morning. Everyone was going and Fingle had been told not to expect them back until dinnertime.

'So we have the house to ourselves for the whole day,' murmured Diana, relieved. The children might run up and down stairs as much as they wished and she need not fear bumping into Lord Davenport. Or any of the other gentleman, who seemed to have a knack of being present whenever she ventured into the library or the garden or the morning room. Diana thought that if she were vain and had an inflated notion of her own worth, she might suspect that they were lying in wait for her.

Florence sighed. 'I *wish* we were going riding with them.'

'Uncle Alex likes to travel hard and fast,' said Meggie, ever practical. 'Our little ponies would not be able to keep up.'

'Quite true,' agreed Diana, smiling. 'But that does not mean we cannot take a little ride of our own in the park. And after that we will go to the drawing room for a singing lesson. What do you say?'

After a full day's riding Diana expected the house party to be a little subdued, but when she entered the drawing room with Meggie and Florence that evening they discovered that the floor had been cleared for dancing.

'Ah, Miss Grensham, you are just in time!' Mr Wollerton greeted her cheerfully. 'You see we are about to dance.'

'Oh, and may we join in?' asked Meggie eagerly. 'Uncle Alex, please say we can join in.'

'Of course,' he declared. His hard eyes glinted as they rested upon Diana. 'In fact, I insist upon it!'

She had been quelling the familiar tingle of nerves she always felt when she saw the earl, but his words turned the flutter into full-blown panic. Meggie gave a little squeal and Florence clapped her hands in excitement as they ran off and Diana found herself abandoned. The earl came a little closer.

'Miss Grensham, you will dance, too.'

'N-no. That is, I—'

'Of course she will not, Alexander,' said Lady Frances, coming up. 'It is unkind of you to ask her when you know she has an infirmity.'

'I know nothing of the sort,' he declared repressively.

Diana's face flamed and she quickly moved away before anything more could be said. She walked across to the harpsichord, feeling the drag of her left leg even more acutely than usual.

'Oh, do you not mind playing?' asked Mrs Peters, who was standing beside the instrument. 'I have to say I dearly love to dance, but one should not deny the young people their sport.' Her eyes dropped, as if she could look beneath Diana's lavender skirts to the scarred limb beneath. 'However, if you are sure...'

'Perfectly, ma'am.'

Diana sat down and began to play, concentrating upon the music. Her fingers flew over the keys as she rattled off a succession of familiar dance tunes. Lady Frances's comments were forgotten and as her confidence grew, Diana felt herself equal to anyone. The room became full of laughter and movement. When Diana would have stopped and taken the children away there were cries of protest.

Meggie and Florence were clearly enjoying themselves and Diana gave in to the entreaties to play for one more dance. At the end of it Fingle came in with the tea tray and Diana called the girls to her, surprised to find herself almost regretting her decision to make her escape. She was bidding them say goodnight to everyone when she heard Nurse's cheerful voice at the door.

'Come along, Lady Margaret, Miss Florence. His lordship has asked me to put you to bed tonight, so that Miss Grensham can stay and take tea.'

'Oh, no—that is, I do not—'

'Pray do not be shy, my dear,' Mrs Peters interrupted Diana's floundering denial. 'We should be delighted to have you join us. Mr Wollerton, would you be kind enough to set another chair for Miss Grensham here, by me? She may help me by handing round the teacups.'

It was no longer her decision. Diana saw that it would be impossible to withdraw without seeming impolite. She sent a look towards the earl, who was standing a little apart from the rest, but his response was merely an unsmiling nod.

'B-by J-Jove Miss Grensham I thought you p-played extremely well,' exclaimed Mr Hamilton, when she handed him a cup of tea.

'Miss Grensham does play well, Hamilton,' the earl called across the room. 'I believe she sings, too, and I know you have a fine voice, sir. Perhaps the two of you will entertain us with a duet.'

'D-delighted to do so, my lord.' Mr Hamilton beamed. 'What do you say, Miss Grensham, shall we look for a song to suit us?'

'Perhaps another time, sir.' Diana went back to her chair, but before she could sit down Mrs Peters gave her a cup to carry to Lord Davenport. She approached him, frowning.

'You flatter me, my lord,' she said quietly. 'I sing only with the children.'

'It was not my intention to flatter you,' he returned. 'It was Meggie who told me how well you sing. And having heard your performance upon the harpsichord I am in no doubt that you are very musical.'

'Why should that surprise you? Do you think your brother would have entrusted the children's education to me if I had been lacking in any of the accomplishments?'

'No, you told me as much at our first meeting.' He took the proffered tea. 'You are an oddity, Miss Grensham, you puzzle me.'

'Why, because I am not afraid of you, my lord?'

He looked disconcerted and Diana felt a little shot of satisfaction.

'Is that what you think I want?'

'I think it is what you *expect*,' she replied, emboldened by her success in shaking him out of his complaisance. 'The rich and powerful Lord Davenport rarely meets with opposition, in any form.'

'That is hardly my fault.'

'No, but it is not good for your character, sir. It makes you think you can ride roughshod over everyone.'

She had gone far enough. The earl was frowning but for once she had the upper hand. It was a heady feeling. She waited, ready, nay, eager to continue the argument but Lady Frances interrupted them, laying a proprietorial hand upon the earl's arm.

'Alexander, are you not going to join us? Everyone is wondering what you are saying to poor Miss Grensham. I vow you look so thunderous I am in a quake.'

'If anything it should be poor Lord Davenport,' he replied with a wry grin.

'Really?'

Lady Frances did not sound very pleased, but Diana barely noticed. The earl had not taken his eyes from her and their glinting look acknowledged that she had won that encounter. A thrill of triumph ran through her, an elation that was not dimmed even when Lady Frances removed the cup and saucer from the earl and thrust it back at Diana before leading him away.

Diana regarded the half-empty cup in her hands. There was no doubting that Lady Frances considered her little more than a servant, but tonight she did not feel intimidated. She took her seat again beside Mrs Peters and listened to the conversation as it ebbed and flowed around her. A lively discussion developed between Mr Hamilton and Lady Frances about a scandalous play they had both seen recently. When Miss Prentiss asked about its content Mr Hamilton began to describe the play to her in all its salacious detail. Lady Frances tapped his arm with her fan.

'Have a care, sir, you will embarrass the governess.'

'I am not so easily shocked,' Diana responded, in no way discomposed. 'And I confess I have a fondness for the theatre.'

'I doubt you have had much opportunity to indulge in such pleasures,' remarked Mrs Peters.

'Not recently, but when my sister was alive I accompanied her regularly to the theatre.'

'Improving works, no doubt,' put in Lady Frances, the faintest curl to her lip.

'Not always. The performances varied enormously but I was always looking out for those that might be suitable for the children.' Diana's smile grew when she saw the surprise upon the faces turned towards her. 'The theatre can be very educational,' she informed them. 'I am a great believer in introducing children to the theatre at an early age. I took them to town to see one of Shakespeare's comedies, although I think they preferred the ballet that was staged between the performances, and of course the pantomime. They could talk of little else for days afterwards.'

The earl had come closer as she was speaking and now he said gruffly, 'You dragged the children to Drury Lane and back? I would have thought any benefit they might have gained would have been wiped out by their fatigue.'

'And so it would, my lord. That is why we put up in an hotel for the night. The girls thought it a high treat, I can tell you, and we were back at Chantreys before noon the following day.' She added with a hint of laughter in her voice, 'That is one of the advantages of being placed so near the capital.'

He regarded her through narrowed eyes.

'*Touché,* Miss Grensham, you have made your point.'

The earl spoke so quietly only Diana heard him. She looked away immediately, but she knew he would not miss the little smile of triumph that played about her mouth.

'Well, I must say, I have never heard of such a thing before,' declared Lady Frances. 'A governess taking her charges to the theatre. Quite, quite *novel*.'

Diana was still revelling in her victory over the earl and she was not at all daunted by the gentle malice in the lady's tone.

'You must remember, ma'am, that I am Lady Margaret's aunt and guardian to both girls. I also know my sister thought such visits could be beneficial.'

'Well, I wish *I* had had such a governess as you, Miss Grensham,' put in Miss Prentiss with her braying laugh. 'It sounds all high days and holidays for the children.'

'Not at all. They work very diligently most of the time.'

'But, forgive me…' Lady Frances approached, the icy glitter in her blue eyes at variance with her honeyed tones '…you are very young to have responsibility for Lady Margaret and Miss Arrandale. Surely you cannot teach them *everything* they need. Lord Davenport will tell you that an accomplished young lady requires more than mere book learning. A good school would surely be the best solution for them, there they would have masters to teach them.'

For herself, Diana might have shrunk away from the lady's patronising tone, but she was here as guardian to two little girls and that gave her the confidence to disagree.

'I beg to differ, Lady Frances, but the very best masters are all in London.' Diana's eyes flickered again to the earl. 'That is why I shall keep the children here at Chantreys, that they may have access to them.'

Anger flashed across the lady's face but Mr Hamilton was already moving the conversation on and Diana sat back in her chair, content to return to the role of passive listener. She had made her point, won the argument and she felt a small but satisfying sense of triumph.

The party broke up soon after as the exertions of the day caught up with everyone. Miss Prentiss was openly yawning and declared her intention to retire. Diana decided that she, too, had had enough and made her escape. Lord Davenport reached the door before her and held it open.

'I know your game, Miss Grensham,' he murmured as she passed him. 'You think your arguments in favour of remaining at Chantreys are convincing, but do not think you have won, madam. I am still determined that you will leave here. But I am also determined that the move will be in no wise detrimental to Meggie and Florence.'

She stopped.

'What makes you think you know what is best for them?' she challenged him. 'You have absolutely no experience of children.'

'Of course I have. I...' He paused and she waited. His hard eyes gleamed and she saw the smile tugging at one corner of his mouth. 'I was one, once, you know.'

For the life of her Diana could not hold back a gurgle of laughter, quickly stifled.

'I find that very hard to believe, my lord,' she murmured as she whisked herself out of the room and ran up the stairs, still chuckling.

Chapter Six

Diana could not sleep, her head, her whole body was buzzing with excitement. She was unused to conversing so much with adults and she had to admit she had enjoyed it, even the barbed comments of Lady Frances had not wounded her. It had still been something of an ordeal, not only because she felt awkward and ungainly every time she walked, but she had been painfully aware of the earl's presence. He had made little effort to include her in the conversation and when they had spoken it had only been to disagree. And yet… He had not patronised her and there had been a sizzle of excitement at being able to talk and debate with him as an equal.

She paced her bedroom floor, so full of pent-up energy that she felt she might burst. It was frustrating to have so many people in the house. Before, on the rare occasions when she could not sleep, she had wandered the rooms at will, but now she was afraid even to potter in the school-room for fear that the creaking floorboards would disturb the guests sleeping below.

The day had been unseasonably warm and her room was hot and airless. She threw open the window and leaned on the sill. A full moon was riding high above the park and gardens, bathing everything in a silvery-blue light. Everything was still, like a painted stage, waiting for the actors to make it their own. Suddenly Diana knew what she wanted to do. Five minutes later she was creeping down the back stairs, a dark woollen cloak covering her nightgown.

It was no good, after tossing and turning for what seemed like half the night Alex threw off the bedcovers and sat up. He pushed back the hangings and blinked a little as the moonlight flooded over him. He was wide awake and restless. He recalled Frances's invitation. He could still go to her room, he knew she would welcome him whatever time of the night he should arrive, but the idea did not appeal. He lay back down and put his hands behind his head, wondering why it was that he suddenly found the widow less attractive.

There was no doubt that Lady Frances Betsford was beautiful, clever and accomplished and she wanted to be a countess. Why should she not?

She was the daughter of a peer and would fill the role well, he had no doubt. The fact that she had had several lovers over the years had never worried Alex, yet now he was aware of a growing reluctance to make her an offer.

Why should that be, when Frances was so perfectly suited to the position? He knew it behoved him to marry at some point and beget an heir but he would not do so when society said he should, hence his intention to hold such an outrageous party that he would shock his world. But one day he must make his choice and why not Frances? He ran over all the things he required in a wife. Until recently he would have said that birth, breeding and beauty were sufficient, but now he knew he wanted something more. Just when he had changed his mind he knew not, but now he was convinced that there must be affection, too. His wife should love him for himself, not for his title.

'You are aiming too high,' he told himself, staring up at the inky black shadows above him. 'There is not such a woman in England. Go back to your original plan. Find an agreeable beauty for your consort. Someone who will not cut up your peace.'

With a sigh he slid off the bed and went to the window. The still, night-time scene beckoned him. Acres of land and no one out there to enjoy it. He resisted at first, but the insidious little voice in his head kept asking, why not? The full moon made it light enough to see and a walk might clear his head. Ten minutes later he was dressed and striding across the open park.

It did not take Diana long to reach the woods. She took a slightly circuitous route through the gardens, following a little-used path in the shadow of the high hedges, in case some other sleepless soul might be looking out of their window. Once she reached the park she headed for the thick belt of trees that stretched off to the east of the house, finally joining with the extensive woodland that bordered the estate. The branches overhead were not yet in full leaf and the moonlight filtered through, dappling the ground and giving ample light for her to see her way. At last the trees thinned and she could see the glassy surface of the lake ahead of her. She stopped, listening. The distant scream of a fox did not worry her, or the mournful cry of an owl. The lake was black and still, smooth as glass with the moon reflected perfectly at its centre. Nothing stirred. She was quite alone.

The rising ground and thick woods that surrounded the water had trapped the warmth of the day and Diana did not hesitate. She slipped off her cloak and nightgown and ran, naked, to the edge of the lake. She had been here many times before over the years and knew that this southern end of the lake was the deepest. That was the reason a small wooden landing stage had been built here. She took a breath, ran out along the jetty and jumped into the water.

The shock of the cold water forced a little cry from her lips before she sank down into the still depths of the lake. Silky fronds of weeds brushed her ankles and she felt the bottom beneath her feet. It was soft and muddy, but firm enough for her to push upwards again, arms above her head as she surfaced, turning up her laughing, gasping face to the moon before slipping back beneath the water. For the first time in a week she felt perfectly free.

Alex walked briskly and soon the house was out of sight. He began to relax, remembering the times he and James had spent here as boys. Only two years had separated him and his brother and they had been close in those far-off days. They had moved in different circles at school, but had always spent their holidays together at Chantreys. There was plenty to amuse them, the woods for hunting and climbing and they could swim or fish in the lake. By the time James went to Oxford, Alex's interests lay in more physical pursuits. James married early and settled down to his responsibilities, while the inheritance from his godfather allowed Alex to live in town and indulge his interest in sports and his taste for collecting beautiful works of art.

Over the past few years they had led very different lives, but the news of James's death had affected Alex profoundly. Outwardly he had gone on much as before, but his grief at the loss of his brother was deep and sincere. It was only now, six months after he had first heard the news, that Alex could remember their shared childhood without too much pain. Walking alone through the still, moonlit landscape, Alex found he could at last take comfort from the memories of the happy times he and James had spent at Chantreys.

A wall of trees rose before him, dark and shadowed, and he knew he had reached the edge of the park. He should turn back, but rather than retrace his steps he struck off at an angle, deciding to prolong the walk a little longer and return by the path that ran past the lake. His eyes soon grew accustomed to the gloomy shadows of the woods. Nothing was stirring and there was silence save for the occasional call of some night creature and his own soft footsteps. A glint of silver sparkled through the trees. He was nearing the lake's edge.

At that moment he heard simultaneously a cry

and a splash and he emerged from the trees to see the mirrored surface of the lake shattered. As he watched he saw one white arm emerge from the water, scattering diamond droplets. Another arm followed, then, briefly, a head and shoulders, then there was gasp and the body disappeared again beneath the water.

'What the—?'

Alex ran towards the lake, stripping off his coat as he went.

That brief glimpse of a shapely arm had been sufficient to tell him the figure was a female, but as the naked torso rose up, gleaming silver in the moonlight, he had had a perfect view of the creature's face and had recognised her instantly. Diana. He reached the landing and it was the work of a moment to remove his boots and dive cleanly into the water. Immediately he struck out for the place where she had disappeared.

Diana's feet touched the weed-cushioned bottom of the lake and she remained there for a moment, enjoying the sensation of weightlessness, but as she made to rise again she was buffeted by something large and powerful that forced the air from her lungs. In a panic she struggled as childhood fears of monsters and serpents invaded her imagination. She was gripped by strong arms and hauled upwards. As she emerged from the water, coughing and spluttering, she heard a deep voice commanding her to keep still.

'Don't struggle, I've got you,'

'Let me go!' She tried to prise herself free. 'Let me go,' she cried again, 'I don't need rescuing. I can *swim*!'

The vice-like grip eased, just a little, and she turned to face her assailant. She knew who it was, of course. There could be no mistaking that harsh voice, but it was still a shock to find herself only inches away from Lord Davenport, his white shirt clinging to his shoulders and gleaming like pewter in the moonlight. He gave a sudden toss of his head, to fling his wet hair from his eyes.

'Then prove it,' he said grimly. 'Get yourself out of the water. Now.'

Diana needed no second bidding. She struck out for the bank, heading for the spot where she had left her clothes. She felt angry and foolish at being caught out by the earl, that he should have come upon her naked, but it was impossible to swim in a gown. However, she felt sure she could acquit the earl of any amorous intentions towards her. Clearly he had thought she was drowning and when he had discovered that was not the case he had sounded quite furious.

Diana did not attempt to pull herself on to the jetty but found a spot on the bank where the plants were at their tallest and scrambled up between them, hoping they would give her some modicum of protection while she hurriedly donned her nightgown without making any attempt to dry herself.

'What the devil do you think you are doing out here at this time of night?'

The voice behind her told Diana that the earl had also reached the bank. The brusque tone also informed her that he was not a whit less angry. Well, that was hardly her fault. She had not asked him to spy upon her!

'I might ask you the same question,' she countered, swinging around to face him.

He was in the act of pulling off his wet shirt and her mind went blank. She was distracted by the sight of his naked body and could not drag her eyes away. The muscles in his powerful chest rippled as he drew the wet linen over his head, his ribcage expanded, throwing into sharp relief the narrow waist and flat stomach. There was a faint shadowing of dark hair covering his chest and descending downwards until it disappeared beneath the waistline of his breeches. She dare not allow her gaze to drop lower, for the material covering his legs clung so tightly it left little to the imagination. Quickly she turned away and picked up her cloth, rubbing her hair with hands that were not quite steady.

'I could not sleep,' he answered curtly. 'But I had no intention of taking a midnight swim!'

No, well, a midnight stroll would be enough for him, thought Diana bitterly. He walked, nay strode, with a lithe, effortless grace. *He* did not hobble in an unsightly fashion whenever he put one foot before the other.

'I did not ask you to rescue me.'

'How was I to know that? I saw you struggling in the water and thought, with your leg—'

'Water is the one place where my leg does *not* bother me!' Diana bit her lip. She had not meant to say that. She hated any reference to her lameness. With a sigh she spread her cloak on the ground and sat down upon it. 'Swimming is one of the few things I can do well.'

'I know that now.'

His voice had softened. There was even faint amusement in his tone. She tried to ignore him, pulling her hair over one shoulder and catching it in the towel. Too late, of course, her nightgown was already sodden where it had touched her wet body and the added water dripping from her hair made little difference.

The earl went to retrieve his own clothes from the jetty.

'Here.' He held out his coat to her. 'Put this on.'

She shook her head. 'Thank you, I am not cold.'

'Not yet, but you will be. I would not wish you

to catch a chill.' He dropped the jacket around her shoulders and she fought down a childish urge to shrug it off. It was a chivalrous gesture and she would be churlish to refuse.

Alex gestured towards the cloak. 'May I?'

Diana moved over, which he took for assent and threw himself down beside her. The flimsy nightgown clung to her curves, but thankfully with his jacket about her shoulders he could no longer see the swell of her breasts, nor the faint outline of dark nipples through the damp cotton. He could not forget the sight of her cutting strongly through the water as they swam to the lake's edge. He had deliberately stayed behind her, ostensibly to make sure she did not get into difficulties, but there was no doubting the pleasure of watching her naked body as she emerged from the water. It was a brief view, for she was quickly hidden by the tall grasses, but it was enough. She was petite but perfectly proportioned and scrambled effortlessly on to the bank. He noted that her shapely legs showed no sign of deformity and her soft white body looked like marble in the moonlight, very like the Canova he wanted to bring to Chantreys. But Diana was no cool statue, she was alive and hot-blooded. Hot-tempered, too, he thought as he watched her rub her hair with quick, angry movements.

'I beg your pardon,' he said peaceably. 'I see

now that you can swim very well. Where did you acquire such an accomplishment?'

He thought she might ignore him or snap his nose off, but she answered quietly.

'When I was young we lived near a river and Margaret and I often used to play there. Andrews, our old groom, taught us both to swim.' A sudden smile flitted across her features. 'He said it was in case we were taken up by the press gang, we would be able to jump overboard and swim ashore.'

'A wise man,' he said gravely and saw her shoulders lift in a tiny shrug.

'He knew swimming was something I could do as well as Margaret. I am no cripple in the water.'

She threw her hair back so that it tumbled down over her shoulders, the thick tresses hanging sleek and black against his jacket. She held out the towel.

'Would you like to dry yourself with this?'

'Thank you, no,' he told her. 'It is a warm night, my skin will dry naturally.'

He saw the corners of her mouth lift again.

'I would not wish to be the cause of *you* catching a chill, my lord.'

It was not a chill that she was causing him, he thought ruefully as his pulse quickened and the hot blood began to course through his veins. She was still rubbing at her hair with the towel. The nightgown was long, but with her arms lifted it barely covered her knees. He had an excellent view of her lower limbs and shapely ankles. He frowned slightly, looking hard at her dainty feet.

Diana felt his eyes upon her. The anger had evaporated and she was acutely aware that they were alone. She reached down to pull at the hem of her nightgown, but his hand shot out and caught her wrist.

'Wait.'

Suddenly the night air was no longer balmy. It was hard and sharp as crystal. Diana swallowed as the earl reached out and ran his free hand over her left foot.

'Where was the break in your leg?'

She should protest, pull away, but she could not do so. In alarm she realised that she did not *want* to do so. It was not just the iron grip on her wrist that immobilised her, the gentle touch of his fingers was equally compelling. She felt tense, fragile as spun sugar that would shatter at the slightest movement. She managed to run her tongue around her lips and answer him.

'J-just above the knee.'

His hand moved slowly up her leg. His touch was light as a feather but it left a burning trail on her skin and provoked an ache deep inside, an ache that brought back the memory of the punishing kiss he had bestowed upon her. The gentle fingers grazed over her skin in a tantalising caress. She did not move when he gently pushed her nightgown aside to reveal the jagged scar on her thigh. She trembled when his fingers touched the puckered skin where the gash had been badly stitched together. Even now she remembered the surgeon's words as she had slipped in and out of consciousness.

'A messy fracture and badly dealt with, but we can repair the damage and the leg will be as good as new, but she will need to work at it…'

Weeks of pain while the doctors argued over her, before her parents dismissed them all and consigned Diana to the nursery where she had been cosseted and pampered. Her old nurse had no truck with modern methods, with making children put weight on a limb if it hurt them.

The earl's fingers continued to move over her thigh, pressing lightly on the tell-tale bump beside the scar, on the outer edge of her thigh just above the knee joint.

'Is this the break?'

'Y-yes.'

He lifted his hand away and Diana felt the cool air on the spot where his fingers had been. Only then did she realise how her flesh had heated beneath his touch. He shifted and knelt before her, taking her feet in his hands and studying them intently. His thumbs moved slowly over the skin in an idle caress that left her breathless.

'There is no discernible difference in length,' he said at last.

'It...' She swallowed, her voice sounding strained and hoarse. 'It is very slight. An inch or so.'

'Not even that. The limb is strong, I have seen how you run and jump. Do you never try to walk normally? Perhaps the muscles need to be worked.'

'I cannot do so.'

'Who told you that?' He frowned, looking down at her feet, still cradled in his warm grasp. 'You have let such a little thing ruin your life, Diana.'

No! It was an anguished cry inside her head. It was *not* a little thing. How could he understand? How could he know the humiliation of being referred to as the little lame girl, of having her parents constantly apologising for her appearance. Her mother shaking her head and smiling sadly while she told everyone, 'It was an accident, you see. So tragic.'

Diana shivered. She must shut out those memories and she must be practical. She did not want sympathy, especially from this man.

'I have the life I want,' she said briskly. She

pulled her feet free and began to wipe them with the towel. They were perfectly dry, but she needed to rub away the memory of his touch, it disturbed her too much. 'We should go.'

Without a word he reached out and picked up her stockings and shoes, placing them beside her before moving away to put on his own boots. When they were both ready he held out his hand and pulled her to her feet. She shrugged off his coat and gave it to him.

'I have my cloak,' she explained as she wrapped herself in its voluminous folds.

It was a relief when the earl donned his coat and she was no longer obliged to see his naked chest. None of the statues she had seen at the British Museum had prepared her for the sheer beauty and power of a real, flesh-and-blood male. She wanted to stare at him, to reach out and touch the bare skin, to feel the steely strength beneath. Diana thought how fortunate it was that the path was barely wide enough for one person. He would have offered her his arm and she really did not think she dare walk that close to him. He picked up his wet shirt and stuffed it into his pocket as they turned to leave the lake, then he reached out and took her hand. Immediately she hung back.

'I can walk unaided—'

'The moon has moved on, the path is not so

well defined now. I do not want you tripping over a tree root.' He ignored her protest and tightened his grip. 'Come along, I will lead the way.'

Alex moved carefully through the darkness. Diana's little hand was secure in his grasp and it felt so right there, so perfectly at home. She followed him silently, uncomplaining and he made a conscious effort to slow his own pace so that she need not run to keep up. When they came to the edge of the woods she stopped him.

'I would rather use the path I followed to get here,' she said. 'The one over there. Through the trees.'

'Afraid of being seen with me, Diana?'

'Of course I am. There would be talk, if we were seen walking in the moonlight together.'

'But it is your natural *milieu*, is it not? You are named after the goddess of the moon.'

'Do not mock me, my lord.'

'I don't.' He pulled her closer, imprisoning her with one arm while the fingers of his free hand tilted up her chin. 'There must be some magic in the moonlight. Your limp has quite disappeared.'

She gazed up at him. In the gloom her eyes were huge and luminous and as dark as the lake they had left behind them.

'You, um, you were walking ahead of me, 'tis merely that you have not noticed it.'

'I notice everything about you,' he muttered.

Their faces were only inches apart and his body screamed at him to capture those lips that were parted so invitingly. His arm tightened. Was it her heart thundering against his chest, or his own tumultuous pulse? His fingers released her chin but only so they could trace the line of her jaw. Alex cupped her face and ran his thumb gently across her bottom lip. Her eyelids fluttered and his spirit blazed with the knowledge that she was not immune to him.

Her lips parted even before they met his own, her face turning up, straining to reach him and when they did kiss Alex felt it like a spark on dry tinder, an explosion of light and heat roared through his body. She trembled and leaned into him, her body surrendering, moulding with his as his arms slid around her back. His tongue darted, tasting, exploring, tangling with hers for a brief moment before she drew back, breaking off the kiss with a tiny sob.

'Ah, please, don't!'

Diana put her hands against his chest to push him away and he released her immediately.

'This is not right,' she said, averting her face so that he might not see her distress.

'It feels very right to me.' He had not intended

it to sound like a light-hearted quip, but he was struggling for control. 'Diana.'

He reached out to touch her and she flinched away.

'Perhaps it would be best if we made our separate ways back to the house, my lord—'

That he could not allow. Who knew what perils she might meet walking in the dark woods at night.

And what of the peril of being in your company?

He thrust the thought aside. There was no danger. His body was under control now.

Diana turned towards the woodland path, only to stop with a gasp as the earl caught her arm.

'Oh, no,' he said roughly. 'If you think I will let you wander about the grounds at night without an escort, you are very far off.'

'There is no need for you to come with me. I know my way.'

She knew she must be rational, even when she wanted so very much to throw caution to the winds and hurl herself back into his arms. His grip on her arm loosened, but only so he could slide his hand down and take her fingers again. How could something feel so comforting and so dangerous at one and the same time?

'I am sure you do,' he said, 'but I shall not rest until I have seen you safely back in the house.'

He set off and she was obliged to go with him, since he would not release her hand. In truth, she was glad of his support, for she stumbled occasionally over a stone or a tree root. The moon was low in the sky by the time they crossed the short stretch of open ground and slipped through the door into the kitchen garden. The path was narrow and Diana's skirts brushed against the plants lining the way, herbs in the first flush of new spring growth. Their delicate fragrances rose up to meet her: angelica and lovage, sage, thyme and rosemary. It filled her head with thoughts of fairy dells and magical meetings.

Ill met by moonlight...

With the house now in sight her fears of being alone with the earl were beginning to recede. She could even smile at the analogy. She was no Titania and he was certainly no fairy king, although the effect he had upon her defied her comprehension.

'I went out by the servants' door, over there,' she whispered when they reached a junction in the paths. 'I left my bedroom candle in the lower hall.'

He led her down the steps and into the house. Only then did he let her go and she felt achingly bereft. While the earl locked the door behind them Diana lit her candle from the single lamp burning on the wall. She had not realised just how much she was trembling until she tried to hold the wick steady in the burning flame. The passage ahead of her was in darkness and she waited until the earl was ready before setting off, holding her candle aloft so that he might see his way on the stairs. He walked close behind her and her spine tingled at the knowledge.

They soon emerged in the main entrance hall. No lamps burned there, but the darkness was alleviated by the faint moonlight streaming in through the windows and from the fanlight above the door. The earl touched her arm and the tingle ran up to her shoulder.

'Go on upstairs. I left by the front door, so I must lock it again. Do not worry,' he added, when she hesitated. 'There is sufficient light for me here to see my way.'

Diana hesitated.

'Sir, what happens in the morning, when we meet again?'

'What would you like to happen?'

Her mouth went dry.

'N-nothing,' she said at last. 'I would prefer to forget everything that has occurred tonight.'

For a moment he did not answer her. He reached out and touched her cheek.

'Is that truly what you want?'

Of course not! I would like you to take me to your bed and in the morning to declare your undying love for me, but I am not that much of a fool.

The words screamed in her head, but only the last one taunted her. Fool.

'Yes. Truly.'

She managed the words with admirable calm. His hand fell and he gave a little bow.

'Then it shall be as you wish,' he said lightly. 'It is forgotten.'

Without another word Diana slipped away, being careful to avoid the creaking stairs and floorboards. By the time she reached her bed-chamber on the top floor she felt as if she had climbed a mountain, her heart hammering against her ribs and her breath ragged and pain-ful. She climbed into bed and huddled beneath the bedcovers.

Tears were very close but she would not let them fall. Indeed, why should she be unhappy? She had enjoyed swimming in the lake, it had been invigorating, liberating and she had done nothing wrong. True, the earl's arrival had shocked her, but he had not really been angry with her. She shivered when she recalled the sight of him when he had first climbed out of the water. He had positively glistened in the moonlight, the damp shirt moulding to his form like a silver skin.

She remembered how he had examined her ankles and the shivering grew more intense until she could feel it deep inside her, but it was not unpleasant. She was already curled into a ball and her hands slid down her calves, wondering why his touch should cause such strange and unfamiliar sensations. He had said he could see no difference in her legs. He could not understand why she should limp so badly, and as he had led her away from the lake it was as if he had cured her simply by the force of his will. Not so, of course, but it had been less noticeable, just as it was when she played outdoor games with the children, running and jumping and forgetting the heavy, awkward drag of that left leg.

She had followed him silently to the very edge of the woods, lost in a moonlight world where nothing mattered save the fact that they were together. Even when he had taken her in his arms she had not resisted, even though he had seemed to envelop her in his huge, dark and powerful presence. It was only when she started to drown in his kiss that she realised her danger, Her treacherous body had responded to him, crying out for his touch, his kiss. She had never wanted him to stop, but some deeply ingrained sense of self-preservation had made her bring that kiss to an end. He had awoken a deeply buried longing within her, a yearning that she now realised had been building up during the long lonely years since her come-out. Years of self-imposed exile.

It had taken every ounce of determination to resist him, to beg him to stop and it had not been thoughts of impropriety that had made her do so, nor fear for her reputation. It was the knowledge, deep and instinctive, that if she allowed that kiss to continue she would crumble, as she had done before but this time, in this mystical moonlight world, there would be no escape. She would be lost, consumed by forces she could not control. She would give herself, body and soul, to a man who did not love her.

The tears scalded her lids as they squeezed themselves out and soaked her pillow. She was a governess, and a good one. If she gave herself to Lord Davenport, if she became his lover, even for one night, she would forfeit her position, most certainly lose her self-esteem and she suspected that the aching loneliness she felt now would be infinitely worse once she had tasted the happiness that he could give her. The tears flowed in earnest and she was racked by deep, wrenching sobs, but at least now she knew why she was so unhappy.

She was crying for what could never be.

* * *

Alex shot the bolts on the main door as quietly as he could and made his way up to his room. The house was silent, the staircase empty and grey in the faint moonlight that shone in through the windows, but in his mind he could see Diana ahead of him, her dark cloak billowing like smoke as she ran up the stairs. He could still remember the feel of her hand in his, the delicate, fragile fingers clinging to him as he led her back through the woods. His mouth twisted into a wry smile. She was aptly named, Diana, goddess of the moon. She had bewitched him. When he reached the landing he had to steel himself not to continue up to the top floor in search of her. She would not thank him for following, and in the morning he would regret it. Diana was not the perfect, comfortable wife he envisaged for himself, she was far too opinionated and would cut up his peace most dreadfully.

Yes, he thought as he turned and made his way to his bedchamber. In the morning he would see this night's work for what it was, a moment of moonlight madness.

Chapter Seven

By morning Diana had shed all her tears and was able to face the day philosophically. Lord Davenport and his guests were remaining at Chantreys for another two days and she must face them all. She trusted the earl not to tell anyone of their midnight encounter and therefore the best thing to do would be to act as if it had not happened. Indeed, the episode felt very much like a dream so it should not be difficult to pretend that is all it had been.

She decided to take the girls out for a morning walk. They met no one on the stairs, voices from the dining room suggesting that some people were still breaking their fast, but it was not until they were in the park that Diana realised how tense she had been, how nervous of seeing the earl.

An hour strolling through the park with Meggie and Florence did much to calm her and Diana

thought herself quite composed as they returned
to the house, until a footman relayed Lord Davenport's message that she and the children were
to present themselves in the hall at noon, when
they would all be setting off to picnic at nearby
Saxon Hill.

Meggie and Florence were with her when Fingle broke the news and they were so excited at the
prospect that Diana had not the heart to refuse
them. She tried to make her own excuses but she
discovered that the earl had anticipated that. Fingle smiled at her in a kindly fashion and told her
that Lord Davenport had specifically requested
that she should accompany them.

'I think his lordship feels he owes you a little
treat, miss, for all the inconvenience you have
suffered during his visit.'

'Oh, no, no…' she began, flustered, but the
butler interrupted her with a chuckle.

'No, it's been a pleasure to have the house so
full, hasn't it?' Fingle remarked, his faded eyes
twinkling. 'I tried to say as much to his lordship but he would have it that you and the young
ladies must attend.' Diana looked at him in dismay, but the old retainer took her silence for joy-
ous astonishment and his smile only grew wider.
'It's no wonder if you cannot find the words,
miss. Now, you and the young ladies had best

go upstairs and get yourselves ready, you won't want to keep his lordship waiting.'

Shortly after twelve the picnic party set off. Any apprehension Diana had of awkwardness between herself and the earl was soon allayed. He spoke to her only to suggest the girls should travel with him in his curricle, leaving Diana to ride in one of the two open carriages with the rest of the guests. Lady Frances elected to travel with Mr Wollerton and Mr Hamilton while Miss Prentiss begged Diana to accompany her in the second carriage with Mr Avery.

'Mrs Peters has the headache and is not coming with us,' explained Miss Prentiss, adding with an arch look, 'We will have to chaperon each other, Miss Grensham.'

The earl had sent his servants on ahead to lay out an array of rugs and cushions beneath a cluster of large and spreading trees, so when the party arrived at Saxon Hill all they had to do was to make themselves comfortable in the shade and enjoy the refreshments that had been provided. It was not a long walk from the carriages, but Diana felt the earl's frowning glance as she limped towards the picnic site. It made every step a struggle and she stopped at the first rug and called to Meggie and Florence to join her.

'Oh, do pray let them sit with me,' cried Lady

Frances, holding out her hands to the girls. 'I do so wish to become better acquainted with Lord Davenport's little wards.'

Meggie and Florence glanced uncertainly at Diana, but having received permission they ran off to sit beside Lady Frances. Miss Prentiss came up, saying gaily, 'Let us sit down here together, Miss Grensham, and the gentlemen shall wait upon us.'

'Yes, sit down, Miss Grensham,' murmured the earl as he passed her. 'This is your treat, remember.'

'But perhaps I should be with the girls—'

'You need not be anxious about Meggie and Florence. I am sure I can be trusted to look after them.'

He walked off and threw himself down beside Lady Frances. Diana was aware of a stab of something very like jealousy. She quelled it quickly and looked away. The other gentlemen had joined them and Miss Prentiss gave her loud, braying laugh.

'Three gentlemen and two ladies, Miss Grensham, I vow we should think ourselves very fortunate!'

It was an effort, but Diana forced herself to relax and join in the conversation. With the sun shining and everyone determined to be pleased, the time passed quickly. Diana was surprised to discover that she really was enjoying herself as they dined on dainty pastries and cakes washed down by wine, ale or lemonade. She glanced across only once to where the girls were sitting. The earl was reclining at his ease and Lady Frances was tempting Meggie and Florence with the choicest delicacies from the hamper. Diana quickly looked away. Lord Davenport had told her he would look after the girls, so she determined not to give them another thought. As the earl had said, this was her treat, she should enjoy it.

Alex watched Lady Frances as she cooed and petted the children, who giggled and chattered away as they helped themselves to the fancy cakes and sweetmeats Cook had prepared for their delectation. He would not look at Diana, even when he heard her laugh at something one of the other fellows had said. He realised how rarely she had laughed during this visit, so different from when he had called at Chantreys and they had played battledore and shuttlecock. Then they had both laughed almost constantly.

He heard Eliza Prentiss express a desire to pick a posy of spring flowers and from the corner of his eye saw the gentlemen scramble to their feet. Miss Prentiss skipped off across the grass with two of the gentlemen in attendance, but Hamilton paused.

'M-Miss Grensham, will you n-not come with us?'

Alex felt rather than saw Diana shrink away and he was aware of a ripple of irritation. Was she so ashamed to have people see her limping, or did she think her leg would prevent her from keeping up with the others? He had seen her playing games with the children, he knew it was not the case, but she did not believe it and that was what mattered.

Hamilton ran off and Alex scowled. The fellow should have tried harder to persuade her. He felt a light touch on his arm and looked up to find Lady Frances on her feet beside him.

'I am taking Margaret and Florence to collect flowers, too. Will you come with us, my lord?'

He shook his head and made his excuses.

Instantly Frances was hesitating.

'Well, perhaps the sun *is* a little hot…'

But Meggie would not hear of it. She and Florence were exhilarated by the attention they had received and they now jumped around Lady Frances, begging her to go with them. Alex grinned.

'You will get no peace if you do not go, Frances.'

Her smile became even more fixed and Alex bit back a laugh to see the spoiled beauty at a loss. He was well aware that her interest in the children was tepid, but it would do her no harm to exert herself a little more on their behalf.

'Off you go now,' he murmured wickedly. 'I will watch you from here.'

He did so, too, until they were some distance away, then he sat up and turned to Diana.

'You did not wish to join them?'

She shook her head. 'I collect flowers regularly for the house, albeit from the gardens.'

'The displays in the hall and the morning room are your creation?'

'Yes, they are.'

'Another of your many accomplishments, Miss Grensham.'

'A very minor one.'

'Not so. Your arrangements show you have a good eye for colour. Do you paint, as well?'

She answered in the affirmative and he began to draw her out, describing the exhibitions he had seen at the Royal Academy and telling her of the growing collection of paintings and sculptures squeezed into his London house. He did not say he wanted to move many of them to Chantreys, where they could be displayed to advantage, he did not wish to spoil the moment by reminding her of their dispute. Instead he moved the conversation on to include literature and the theatre. Gradually she lost her reserve and began to talk freely. Her eyes lit up and she waved her hands expressively when she talked of the plays she had enjoyed, the books she had read. It was a small step from there to politics, history and the recently resumed hostilities with France.

Alex found it was no hardship to talk to Diana. She had a lively mind and the questions she posed were intelligent, taxing his memory as he tried to satisfy her thirst for knowledge and find the arguments to refute her opinions, when they differed from his own. He found himself sitting forward, dragging up long-forgotten facts, debating subjects he had not even thought of since his student days, and he was thoroughly enjoying it.

All too soon Miss Prentiss's strident voice interrupted their conversation and Alex saw that the others were returning. He glanced across at Diana, who gave him a shy little smile.

'What a pity we did not meet and talk years ago, my lord. We might have become good friends.'

Friends! His brows contracted as she turned away to greet the others and he realised with startling clarity that her life so far had been—and still was—a very lonely one.

Meggie and Florence were the last to come up and Diana noted at once their over-bright eyes and flushed cheeks.

'Margaret wanted to pick a bouquet for you, Miss Grensham.' Lady Frances put her hand on Meggie's shoulder. 'Come along, my dear, give them up before they become too crushed to be of use.'

'Thank you.' Diana jumped up and took the proffered flowers, but she rested the back of her free hand against Meggie's brow. 'You are very warm, my love.'

Meggie's bottom lip began to tremble. 'I do not feel very well.'

'Nor do I.' Florence wound her fingers in Diana's skirts.

'Then you shall both sit in the shade with me for a little while,' said Diana, leading them to the empty rug.

'La, I am quite parched,' declared Miss Prentiss, collapsing on to a pile of cushions. 'I should be very grateful for another glass of wine, Mr Avery.'

'And for me, if you please,' called Lady Frances. She glanced down at the girls. 'Poor little dears, perhaps we can tempt them with a little marzipan—'

'No.' Diana put up her hand. 'I think they have had more than enough to eat. A few sips of lemonade might help, but nothing more, unless you wish them to be ill on the homeward journey.'

Lady Frances stepped back, staring in horror at the children as if they were infectious.

'They did have rather a lot of pastries,' Alex admitted.

'Oh, nonsense!' Lady Frances tossed her head. 'They are merely hot and tired. A little rest is all that is required. Come along, my lord, we will leave them to Miss Grensham while we enjoy another glass of wine. I vow I am quite exhausted by all the exertion.'

Diana kept the children with her while the others raided the hampers for the last of the refreshments. They leaned against her, uncharacteristically quiet, and she scolded herself for not keeping more of an eye upon them. Clearly they had eaten too many sweet things and were suffering the consequences. Diana was filled with remorse. It could have been avoided if only she had warned the earl, instead of giving in to the demon jealousy and studiously ignoring him and Lady Frances.

'I am so sorry, my dears,' she muttered, cuddling both little girls. 'I shall take better care of you in future.'

Her pleasure in the day was quite destroyed, the earlier discussions with Lord Davenport forgotten. She sat quietly with Meggie and Florence and could only be glad when it was time to return to Chantreys. The girls were still looking a little pale but she hoped they would make the return journey without mishap. However, when they reached the waiting carriages Lady Frances stepped up to the earl and took his arm.

'I will travel with you in the curricle, Alexander. The other gentlemen may travel in one of the landaus with Miss Prentiss, that will leave the final carriage for Miss Grensham and the little girls. That way they will inconvenience no one if they are unwell.'

The earl stopped.

'You would leave Miss Grensham to deal with the children alone?'

Lady Frances's finely arched brows rose.

'My dear sir, who better to look after them than their governess?'

'I will go with them,' offered Mr Wollerton. 'I have a young brother and sisters of my own, you know.'

He bent his kind smile upon Diana but she quickly shook her head.

'That is very good of you sir, but there is no need—'

'No, none.' The earl stepped forward. 'Gervase, you will go with Lady Frances in the curricle. *I* shall ride with Miss Grensham and the children.'

Diana's surprise was matched by that of Mr Wollerton, whose eyes fairly bulged in his head.

'D-drive your greys, Alex? Are you sure?'

The earl's hard eyes gleamed. 'Not up to it, Gervase?'

'Of course I am, it's just…you never let anyone drive your cattle.'

'I trust you not to ruin their mouths,' said the earl shortly. He turned to the girls. 'Now, let us get you two into the landau.'

'My lord, truly, I can manage perfectly well on my own,' said Diana as he lifted the children into the carriage.

'I have no doubt of it. Nevertheless I shall come with you.'

He held out his hand and silently Diana allowed him to help her into the landau. The carriages pulled away. The earl watched Mr Wollerton set the spirited greys in motion then he turned back to look at his travelling companions.

'Now, Miss Grensham, how shall we best divert ourselves on the journey home?'

There was no doubt that the hazy cloud covering the sky robbed the sun of much of its heat and made the drive much more comfortable for the girls, but Diana could not fault the earl's good humour as he sang children's songs with Meggie and Florence and entertained them with riddles and stories from his own childhood. At one point he surprised the thoughtful look in Diana's eyes and gave a rueful smile.

'You have a very low opinion of me as a guardian, do you not?'

'No, no,' she disclaimed quickly, then admitted with a twinkle, 'You have risen in my estimation enormously this past half-hour! Seriously, I am very grateful for your presence. You have left me with quite nothing to do.'

'You will have plenty to do if either of them is unwell,' he muttered. 'I doubt I will be of much help to you in that situation.'

She laughed. 'I do not fear that happening now. They may feel a little uncomfortable but they both look much brighter. Is that not so, Florence? Do you feel a little better now?'

The little girl looked up at her with a doleful stare.

'I still have a belly-ache, but I do not think I am going to be *sick*.'

'Nor me,' put in Meggie. She was sitting beside the earl with her hand tucked snugly into his. 'So, Uncle Alex, will you tell us again how you and Papa stole the plum pudding and ate it all in one go, and how you were both *disgustingly* ill afterwards?'

Diana met Alex's eyes and could not prevent herself from laughing.

* * *

By the time they arrived at Chantreys Diana had never felt so much in charity with the earl. Alex, she thought, recalling how he had invited her to use his name. He handed Diana out and then helped the girls down.

'Until dinnertime, then,' he said as she took their hands and prepared to carry them off to the nursery floor.

Diana shook her head.

'I beg you will excuse us. We have had enough excitement for today, I think. We shall spend a quiet evening upstairs.'

As she turned away he caught her arm.

'I will excuse Meggie and Florence, but you will join us after dinner.'

Startled, her eyes flew to his face. Immediately he released her and stepped back.

'That, of course, is an invitation, not an order.'

'Of course,' Diana said quietly.

She led the children into the house and handed the little posy Meggie had picked for her to Mrs Wallace to put in water. Then she took the girls upstairs. There was nothing she wanted more than to go down to the drawing room and see Alex again. To discuss the children, talk over the events of the day, continue their earlier discussions, but she knew it was impossible. Every time she saw Alex she was drawn a little further into the net. If she came to look upon him as a friend the pain would be so much worse when he went away again. And go away he would. His world was a bright, colourful one full of beauty and balls and, and *people*. Hers was the life of a recluse.

To go into society, to be laughed at, mocked, pitied—it would destroy her just as surely as the quiet domesticity of her existence would destroy Alex. And if they could not be friends, then what? Lovers? She shivered. It might amuse him to make her his mistress, but she knew enough of the world to be sure that when the new Lord Davenport married, his choice would not be an insignificant little cripple but an accomplished society beauty. Someone like Lady Frances Betsford. Diana prayed he would not choose Frances. She detected a coldness beneath that beautiful exterior. Alex deserved someone who would love him, someone who would love Meggie and Florence, too, and make them a part of their family.

And she would no longer be needed.

Suddenly the leaden weight inside her was almost too heavy to carry. Diana stumbled. Florence and Meggie looked at her in alarm.

'I beg your pardon,' she murmured, trying to smile. 'I am more tired than I thought. Thank goodness I have you two big girls to help me.'

Somehow she managed to get them up the last

few stairs to the top floor where Nurse was waiting for them.

'Well, well, my dearies, have you enjoyed yourselves?'

'I have the belly-ache,' Meggie informed her.

'Is that right, Lady Margaret? Well, that's no surprise. I am sure you are both so stuffed full of good things that you will not want your dinner tonight, is that not so, Miss Grensham?' Nurse's keen old eyes narrowed. 'And you look as if you are about to drop, miss, if you don't mind my saying.' She did not wait for Diana to reply but held her hands out to the children. 'Now, miss, you leave the little ones to me and you go and lie down upon your bed before you fall down. Blessed if I's ever seen you so pale afore.'

'I think I will go to bed,' said Diana. 'I informed his lordship that the children would not be going downstairs this evening.'

'I should think not,' Nurse agreed. 'Why, they will never sleep tonight if they has any more excitement. I shall give them a light supper and then put them to bed. Never you fret, miss, Nurse'll look after them, and you, too, my dear.'

The old servant's kindness was almost too much to bear. With a little nod Diana escaped to her room where she curled up on her bed and lay, unmoving, as the sun travelled across the floor and the day slid silently into night.

* * *

She was not coming. Above the chatter of the drawing room Alex heard the tinkling chimes of the ormolu clock on the mantelshelf. Dinner had been over for more than an hour and there was no sign of Diana. He prowled restlessly about the room, refusing to play cards and only pretending to pay attention when Lady Frances moved to the harpsichord and played a series of Italian songs with flawless precision. A dozen times during the long hours of the evening he almost sent word to the top floor with a message that Miss Grensham was to come downstairs, and when at last the party broke up and everyone made their way up to their bedchambers he was tempted to go and find her, to assure himself that she was not ill. But he did not.

He could not fool himself into thinking she had been taken ill and in need of him. Nurse lived up on the top floor and she had ruled the nursery since he and James had been young. Alex did not doubt that she was more than capable of looking after Diana and the children. He had to face facts. Diana had not come downstairs because she did not wish to do so.

Chapter Eight

The light pouring into the bedroom woke Diana. It was a glorious clear dawn and the rising sun reflected off the gilded plasterwork around the edge of the ceiling. She lay quietly, allowing herself to wake up slowly. One more day and the house party would be gone. Alex would be gone. She would have the house to herself again. She was relieved, but she was also aware of a vague feeling of depression. There was no doubt she had enjoyed some aspects of having adults in the house, in spite of Lady Frances's barbed comments and the uncomfortable feelings that the earl aroused in her. She had especially enjoyed the conversation. Not only with the earl, yesterday, although that had been exceptional, but in the drawing room each evening. She had spent most of the time listening but occasionally she had expressed her views, even though they must have thought her horridly unworldly. She would miss the conversation.

'But not so very much,' she said aloud as she scrambled out of bed. 'It will be a relief to be able to go where I want, when I want. In the meantime, life must go on and I must pick fresh flowers for the morning room.'

'Why did you not come downstairs last night?'

Diana jumped. She was in the rose garden, cutting the early blooms, and had not heard the earl approaching. Nerves made her clumsy and she winced as a thorn pricked her thumb. She replied without turning, 'I was fatigued, sir.'

'You are bleeding.' He reached out to take her hand and she was obliged to face him. He was too close, his presence too powerful and with an undignified squeak she pulled her hand away.

'I can deal with this!'

'Then do so,' he retorted irritably. 'Else you will have blood on your gown.'

She hesitated, uncertain. He was right, she had no wish to stain her cream-muslin gown. In desperation she put her thumb to her mouth.

A powerful wave of sheer lust surged through Alex. Did she not know how provocative she looked, standing there with that half-frightened, half-defiant look in her eyes and her thumb between those cherry-red lips? The children's presence in the house had damped his ardour for Lady Frances but it was doing nothing to quench his desire for Diana. He dragged a handkerchief from his pocket.

'Here, bind it up with this.'

'Thank you, but I think it has stopped.' She removed her thumb from her mouth and inspected it. 'Yes. It was only a little wound. Nothing serious.'

Her attempt at a smile made him want to take her in his arms. He harrumphed and stuffed the handkerchief back in his pocket.

'What are you doing out here so early?'

She waved at the basket on the ground beside her.

'The flowers in the morning room need replacing.'

'Do we not have gardeners for that? Or Mrs Wallace could do it.'

'Mrs Wallace is busy enough with a house full of guests.' She selected another rose to cut. 'I *could* ask the gardeners to fetch the flowers for me, but they do not know exactly what is required. It is not a chore,' she added quickly, anticipating his next objection. 'I enjoy arranging the flowers in the house. It is a task I have done ever since I came to Chantreys. Margaret…' She paused, as if struck with a momentary pain at the mention of her sister. 'Margaret never liked the task and was happy to let me do it.'

He watched her carefully snip off two more yellow blooms and lay them gently in the basket.

'What was the real reason you did not come to the drawing room last night?'

Diana's hand hovered over another rose while she decided on her answer.

Tell the truth and shame the devil, Diana.

She said quietly, 'The picnic was ordeal enough.'

'Ordeal? Was anyone unkind to you?'

'No.'

'Was the company not to your taste? I thought you enjoyed yourself.'

'I did, for the most part.' She put the final rose and her scissors in the basket and picked it up.

'So what was it you did *not* like?'

'I—' a heartbeat's pause '—I do not like being gawped at.'

She turned to make her way back through the rose garden towards the north front, where a solid wooden door gave access directly to the staircase hall. Alex fell into step beside her.

'I do not understand you.'

She waved a hand towards her skirts, saying impatiently, 'My leg. This horrid halting step.'

'I did not even notice.'

'You may be sure your guests did. And it is even worse indoors. I am aware of it every time I enter the drawing room.'

'Perhaps they did notice it, when they met you for the first time. By now I wager they do not even think of it.'

She felt the hot tears pricking at her eyes.

'You are very kind, my lord, but—'

'Kind! Why should I be kind?'

His response was so typical of the man she was beginning to know that she was surprised into a laugh, but answered bitterly, 'True. It is much more likely that you brought your friends here to laugh and ridicule me, so that I will give up all claim to Chantreys.'

With an oath Alex caught her arm and swung her round to face him.

'Do you truly think I would do anything so base?'

It was not his glare or his angry words that caused her to blush and look away, but her own shame at suggesting he might do such a thing.

She said quietly, 'No, I do not think it, my lord. I beg your pardon.'

'You are back to calling me "my lord"? I thought we were past that.'

When she did not reply he put a finger under her chin and forced her to look up at him.

'I do not deny I want you and the children out

of this house, but I told you at the outset that you would go willingly. Proudly,' he added. 'With your head held high.' His eyes narrowed, they bored into her as he said slowly, 'I do not see you as a cripple, Diana Grensham. I see you as an opponent worthy of my mettle. This will be a battle of wits, madam.'

Diana swallowed. He must be joking her, but there was no mockery in his hard eyes. It was a serious challenge, one adult to another. Equals. The thought was strangely uplifting. She replied cautiously, 'I have told you I have no intention of leaving Chantreys, Lord Davenport.'

'And I have every intention of changing your mind.'

His finger was no longer holding up her chin, she was meeting his gaze of her own accord and she did not feel at a disadvantage.

'How?' she asked, intrigued.

'That is my affair.' He released her and they began to walk on towards the house.

'But you promise the girls will not be distressed?'

'You have my word. By the end of the summer you will be agreeing with me that their best interests would be served by moving them elsewhere.'

She considered that.

'I do not see how that will happen, unless you trick me with some magic potion?'

'Something like that.'

She chuckled. 'Like Titania and Oberon in Shakespeare's play.'

'That ended very happily for everyone concerned.'

'So it did' she replied cordially. 'But that, Lord Davenport, was a play, a fairy tale.' They had reached the north front. Diana ran up the three steps to the door but stopped on the top one and turned to face him. For once she was looking down upon him. 'I think you will find real life will not work out quite so well for you.'

She held her ground, maintaining her smile even when she saw the disturbing glint in his eyes. He mounted the steps towards her and for one fearful moment she thought he was going to kiss her. Again.

She held her basket of roses before her like a shield with one hand while she reached behind with the other, scrabbling to find the door handle. She was trapped on the steps, the only escape was through the door and she could not open it! The menacing glint in the earl's hard grey eyes deepened and changed to unholy amusement as he observed her panic. He was on the top step now, towering over her, only the flimsy wicker basket was keeping them apart. Her pulse fluttered erratically and her heart was hammering so hard it threatened to unbalance her. A moment ago she had felt so strong and in control, but he had turned the tables on her. Nervously she ran her tongue over her lips and prayed that her knees would not give way. She was at his mercy as he leaned closer, a dangerous smile curving his lips.

'Allow me,' he murmured, his mouth so close she could feel his breath on her cheek. Her whole body froze.

He reached behind her and she heard the soft click as he opened the door.

'After you, Miss Grensham.'

If she had fallen from a tree she could not have felt more winded. He was *not* going to kiss her. She was *not* going to faint. Indignation rushed in. He had been teasing her, toying with her. She gave a little huff of anger but the gleam was still in those hard eyes and she knew it would be unsafe to remain. In fact, it would be positively hazardous. Without another word she turned and fled.

Alex watched Diana run off into the house. What a strange, jumbled mixture of parts she was. Shy and reserved, reclusive even, but he had experienced for himself her passionate nature. She was mentor and instructress to Meggie and Florence while little more than a child herself. She was not afraid to stand up to him, yet she was so painfully conscious of her slight impediment that she shunned company.

He shook his head as he went in and closed the door behind him. What had possessed him to invite her to engage him in a battle of wits over where the children should live? He should have told her instead to prepare to move out. Teasing her like that was only prolonging the inevitable but, confound it, he could not bear to see that wounded look in her eyes. It did not matter. When the time came, she would leave Chantreys and he would be able to get on with his life.

Diana ran directly into the morning room and quickly closed the door. She leaned against it, feeling much more weak and breathless than one would expect from such a short spell of exertion. It was Alex, of course. He was the cause of this heady, excited feeling. She did not believe that he deliberately set out to flirt with her, yet how else could she explain that wicked gleam in his eye, or the provocative things he had said to her? Perhaps he thought she knew how to play those games, but flirting was something she had never learned. No one had ever tried to flirt with her before, men were more inclined to avoid her, or turn away in embarrassment.

As soon as she thought her legs would move again she walked to the table where there was a pretty jug waiting to be ornamented with the roses she had cut. She began to trim the stem of each butter-yellow bloom and place it in the jug. She had to admit that Alex had never exhibited any embarrassment in her presence. Perhaps he was telling the truth when he said he did not notice her disfigurement. She had to admit she forgot it herself, when she was playing with the children, or in the company of good friends whom she had known for years.

She had even forgotten it in the earl's presence, more than once. Just now, for example, when he had called her an opponent worthy of his mettle. That was pure foolishness, of course. Alex was merely being kind. She slowly added another rose to the jug. He had said on more than one occasion that he was not renowned for being kind. But if not kind, what had he meant? She shook her head. The man was an enigma, she could not make him out at all. Yet there was no doubting that he made her forget that she was a cripple, that she had one leg shorter than the other.

But had she? It occurred to her that she had never questioned it before. Diana put down her scissors and placed her hands on the table top. She consciously adjusted her weight until it was spread evenly between both her feet. She was so used to favouring her left leg, keeping the weight from it when walking or standing, that she felt the strain immediately in her calf muscles, but both heels *were* on the floor. Perhaps the difference was not so great, after all...

'Oh! I beg your pardon.'

Diana swung around at the sound of the soft voice, blushing as if she had been caught doing something reprehensible.

'Do come in, Lady Frances. I was just replacing the flowers in here.'

'Pray, do not let me keep you from your work.' Lady Frances moved forward, the skirts of her pale-blue riding habit billowing slightly as she glided into the room. 'Lord Davenport is taking me driving this morning. He is gone to fetch the curricle but there is such a chill wind sprung up I thought I would wait here by the window until he brings it to the door.'

'Oh, yes, yes, of course.' Diana trimmed the final few roses and added them to the arrangement before placing it carefully in the centre of the table.

'How pretty,' remarked Lady Frances, in the same patronising tone she used for the children. 'I am sure the earl appreciates your efforts here, Miss Grensham. Alexander is a great lover of all things beautiful. He has acquired quite a collection of works of art, did you know?'

'Yes, I had heard that.'

'He is considered something of a connoisseur, I believe.' She sighed. 'Dear Alexander, he is quite intolerant of anything that is less than perfect. He has the most exacting standards, I vow I am almost afraid to go out in this wind lest it should pull my curls out of place.'

'I like blustery days,' replied Diana, adding with a smile, 'which is fortunate, since we have so many of them.'

'Ah, but you have the advantage of me, Miss Grensham.' Lady Frances replied in silky accents. 'The appearance of a governess is of little importance, is it? Ah—here is the earl now. I must go!'

She swept out of the room, leaving only silence and the faint trace of her heavy, cloying perfume in the room. Slowly Diana gathered up the abandoned leaves and trimmings from the roses and placed them back in her basket. She heard the thud of the main door and went over to the window. Alex's curricle was standing on the drive with Stark the groom holding the heads of the restive greys while Alex helped Lady Frances to climb up.

There was no doubt they made a handsome couple, Alex so large and rugged, the perfect foil for the lady's fair beauty. The final vestiges of the morning's happiness drained from Diana's spirit. Even if she could rid herself of that hateful, limp-

ing gait she would still be small, thin and freckled. No pretensions to beauty at all.

With something like a sigh she picked up her
basket and limped slowly from the room, her left
leg dragging more heavily than ever.

Chapter Nine

A day spent with Meggie and Florence restored Diana's cheerful spirits. Knowing the visitors would be leaving in the morning engendered a holiday mood in the schoolroom. The wind showed no sign of abating and by the afternoon the rain had set in, so they kept to the top floor all day, venturing downstairs only to join the house party for an hour after dinner. The girls were by now quite at home with their guests and when Mrs Peters invited them to come and sit with her they ran off happily, leaving Diana to retire to her customary sofa on the far side of the room. She was a little apprehensive when she saw the earl approaching, which he noted immediately.

'Lay those ruffled feathers, Diana, I have not come to quarrel with you.'

'That will indeed be a novelty,' she replied, unable to resist.

He grinned. 'Witch. I merely came to say that

if you were planning to bring the children to London again you need not put up at an hotel. I have rooms enough for you all at Half Moon Street.'

'Th-thank you,' stuttered Diana, surprised. 'I—'

'It is a bachelor establishment, but if you bring Nurse, or your maid, I am sure they will be able to make everything comfortable enough for you.'

'I do not have a maid,' she said, distracted. 'At least, not one that could be spared to come to London. Jenny, the head housemaid, does all I need.' She added, her encounter with Lady Frances not yet forgotten, 'My appearance is of little importance.'

He frowned, accentuating the ragged scar across one dark brow.

'Why the deuce should you think that? Meggie and Florence have no mother to guide them. You must set them an example, Diana. How will they learn to run their household if they have no experience of such matters?'

'Surely there is time for that later?' she responded, nettled. 'From your wife, perhaps.'

He said irritably, 'It may have escaped your notice that I have no wife.'

'Not yet, but—'

'You will appoint a maid, madam, with immediate effect. Take this Jane, or whatever her name is, if she suits you, and bring in another housemaid.'

'But—'

'See to it, Diana, or I shall do so.'

His tone and his look were implacable and Diana eyed him resentfully. His frown disappeared as suddenly as it had come and he laughed.

'I know, you think me overbearing and autocratic, do you not? But it is not only the girls' comfort I am thinking of. You are a lady, Diana, not a servant.'

His swift change disconcerted her but before she could say anything they were interrupted by calls for music.

'It is our last night here and we should dance with the little girls,' declared Lady Frances. 'And Miss Grensham can play for us again, since she does not dance.'

'Oh, but Diana *does* dance.' Meggie's young voice floated across the room. 'Very well, too. She never limps *then.*'

Diana's faced flamed. Alex was looking at her and she quickly excused herself, hurrying away to take her place at the harpsichord before anyone could press her to dance.

The carriages were at the door, the trunks and bags had all been loaded and now it was time for the guests to take their leave. Diana stood in one corner of the hall with Meggie and Florence while everyone bustled to and fro. Mr Hamilton dashed upstairs in search of Mrs Peters's lost gloves, Miss Prentiss tied and re-tied the strings of her cloak and no one seemed in any hurry to quit the house. Lady Frances came across to take her leave, acknowledging Diana with no more than a nod, but bending to say goodbye to the children.

'Your uncle has promised that we shall come to Chantreys again very soon,' she said, giving Meggie and Florence her dazzling smile. 'Then you will dance for me, will you not?'

'I am sure they will not disappoint you, Frances,' said the earl, coming up. He turned to Diana. 'When I come again the party will be much larger, the south pavilion must be opened up to accommodate my guests.'

'I am sure Mrs Wallace will take care of that, my lord.'

'And the orangery must be cleared. Meggie and Florence will need somewhere to show off their dancing skills. And, of course, we must have a ball.'

'A ball!'

'Why, yes, Miss Grensham.' Lady Frances straightened and sent a smiling glance towards Lord Davenport. 'Why should you be so surprised? It is time the new earl was seen by the local society, especially if we—if *he* is to spend more time at Chantreys.'

Diana had no doubt that the slip was deliberate. Her eyes shifted to Alex's face, but it was inscrutable. Lady Frances, however, was looking like a cat that had lapped up a bowl full of cream as she took the earl's arm.

'Of course, Alexander, for such a large party you will be needing a hostess.'

'I do not see that.'

'Oh, my dear sir, how can you be such a tease? You must have a hostess to look after your guests.'

The lady gave a soft, sultry laugh and threw a coy glance at him. Diana was aware of a very reprehensible feeling of satisfaction when the earl appeared unaffected by these blandishments, but his next words surprised her.

'Then Miss Grensham shall do it,' he declared.

'No!'

Diana's dismay was matched, if not surpassed, by that of Lady Frances. Her smile disappeared and her eyes positively snapped with displeasure. Alex, however, continued as if nothing was amiss.

'Since Diana will be here with the children she might as well make herself useful.'

Diana gave an uncertain laugh. 'How gallantly expressed, my lord.'

There was a glint of humour, but no remorse in his hard grey eyes when they rested upon her.

'You have lived at Chantreys for years. Clearly you are the best person to oversee the preparations for my visit. I also need a list of all the local families to be invited to the ball. Do you think the task too much for you?'

'Not that part of it, but I have no wish to be your hostess.'

'You are in effect the mistress of this house. By your own admission you do not wish to leave. It seems only fitting that you should fill the role. Unless you would prefer me to put one of my other properties at your disposal?'

So that was it, he was trying to oust her from Chantreys. Well, he should see that she would not be moved. Head up, she smiled, aware that her charges were listening intently to the exchange.

'Having promised Meggie and Florence the pleasure of another visit from you, I could not deprive them of it now, my lord.'

There was a flicker of appreciation in his eyes but he merely nodded and began to pull on his gloves.

'I will send you word of the dates for my next visit as soon as it is decided. I shall also have the invitations for the ball printed. How many people do you think we can get in the orangery, a hundred, two?'

'When the late earl held a ball there we had every family in the neighbourhood plus guests from London, so over a hundred.'

'Ah, so you *have* done this before.'

'I helped my sister with the arrangements, but your brother's secretary, Mr Timothy, took care of most of the work.'

'Then he shall do so again. He has been making his way around all the estates for the past few months, refreshing the inventories for me, but I shall write and ask him to come to Chantreys to help you.'

Lady Frances shifted impatiently at his side.

'My lord, everyone else has gone to the carriages.'

'Yes, yes, one moment, I have yet to say goodbye to my wards.' He bent to accept a kiss and a hug from Florence and Meggie, and as he straightened he addressed Diana again.

'I shall leave all to you. Write to me, tell me what you need. It shall be done.'

With a final nod he turned and went out with Lady Frances on his arm. Diana and the girls followed and stood on the drive, waving until the carriages were lost from sight.

'When do you think they will be back?' asked

Florence. 'How long will we have to learn a dance for them?'

'And will we have new dresses?' asked Meggie, skipping back to the house beside Diana. 'Oh, and shall we be allowed to go to the ball? When Alice Frederick's parents held a ball last year Alice said she was allowed to sit at the top of the stairs and watch the dancing.'

'But there are no stairs in the orangery,' Florence pointed out. 'And there is no minstrels' gallery either. Squire Huddleston has a minstrels' gallery at the Manor, and that is where the musicians sit to play. Where will they sit in the orangery, Diana? And what about—'

'Peace, peace!' Diana laughed, stopping and throwing up her hands. 'I have no answers for you. We must wait until Lord Davenport decides upon a date—indeed, by the time he reaches London he may have thought better of the whole idea!'

And I really, truly hope he does, she thought in silent desperation.

'So you have set the date for the Chantreys ball.' Gervase Wollerton ushered Alex into the box he had secured at the King's Theatre. 'Your grand ball will take place on the ninth of September.'

'Correct,' said Alex. 'I would have preferred

it to be earlier, but I was obliged to delay when I learned that peace with Bonaparte is at an end. Lady Hune believes her granddaughter is trapped in France. It was inevitable that the Treaty of Amiens would not hold and she had written to Lady Cassandra, urging her and her husband to return to England, but it would seem they remained just a little too long.'

'Dashed unfortunate. I believe there are a number of families caught up in that way. How is Lady Hune taking it?'

'You know my great-aunt, Gervase, she faces it with her usual sangfroid, but she is anxious and I want to be nearby to support her,' replied Alex. 'Having agreed to sponsor Miss Tatham in her first Season, Lady Hune is committed to remaining in town, but she would want to stay in any case, since if there is news it will reach here first.'

'Then let us pray there is some news, and soon, my friend,' said Gervase with unusual gravity. 'When do you intend to go to Chantreys?'

'Two weeks before the ball. I will be taking a party of guests with me, including you, Gervase.'

'And will your wards be in residence?'

'They will indeed,' Alex replied grimly, thinking of the letter he had received that very morning.

'So Miss Grensham hasn't panicked at the

thought of the house being overrun with your louche friends.'

'On the contrary, Miss Grensham has informed me that the children are looking forward to it. They are preparing a theatrical performance for us.'

Gervase laughed, but quickly turned it to a cough when Alex glared at him.

'I think she has your measure, Alex,' he said, keeping his eyeglass fixed upon the dancers who were now coming on to the stage. 'You are too fond of your wards to want to corrupt them. And she knows your guests won't be that disreputable. After all you are holding a ball to introduce yourself to the local society.'

'I am well aware of that,' replied Alex impatiently. 'I thought when I suggested the ball, the idea of acting as my hostess would have been enough to make her vacate Chantreys, for a few months at least.'

Mr Wollerton tore his eyes away from the stage long enough to cast a reproachful look at Alex.

'I have seen your guest list—it is hardly the sort of party we discussed holding there, old friend.'

'I am well aware of that fact, too!' Alex scowled. 'Dash it, Gervase, I had to invite my more respectable acquaintances. I can't take a crowd of rakes and lightskirts to Chantreys while Diana and the children are there.'

His scowl deepened. If he was honest with himself, the society of his more outrageous friends held little appeal for him these days. He would not have invited Lady Frances if he had not as good as promised her she should attend. However, she was entertaining company and would add a little leaven to the respectable party he had put together.

As the orchestra struck up for the opening melody he turned his eyes to the stage, wondering what had possessed him to arrange such an event. He could easily have found another property for his parties and his precious art collection, instead he had committed himself to what could only be a very tedious two weeks. The answer was clear, of course. He had told Diana he would persuade her to leave Chantreys of her own free will and he was not about to back down, not when the protagonist was a slip of a girl who showed no deference at all for his title or his social standing.

The dancers tripped on to the stage. Beside him Gervase raised his eyeglass to inspect them, but Alex was too lost in his own thoughts to give them more than a cursory glance. He had always been impatient of the sycophants who bowed and scraped and agreed with his every utterance, but Diana should show him some respect. He was after all several years her senior, as well as being a great deal more worldly-wise.

He shifted in his chair. It wasn't that he was conceited, puffed up in his own esteem, but it had become a matter of pride. Even as the thought formed he felt a grin tugging at his mouth. He had to admit he enjoyed pitting his wits against Diana. He wrote to her in the most high-handed manner regarding the arrangements for the house party and she always answered him graciously. She made no demur at his rapid and frequent changes to the guest list for the ball, and his outrageously flippant suggestion that she should invite the Prince of Wales was firmly but politely declined on the grounds that to have such an august personage at Chantreys would run the risk of at least two of his neighbours being carried off by apoplexy and seriously overpower the sensibilities of several local matrons.

'I am surprised you didn't invite Lady Hune and her young protégée,' remarked Mr Wollerton, when the dancers had finished their first performance.

'The marchioness has agreed to bring Miss Tatham to the ball, but they will stay only a couple of nights.' Alex grinned. 'Dash it, Gervase, I hope the two weeks ain't going to be *that* respectable. Besides, I am still hopeful of finding a husband for Diana and do not want my great-aunt's débutante getting in the way.'

'Your attempts to palm Miss Grensham off on Avery or Hamilton didn't work last time,' said Wollerton frankly. 'I had thought one of them might take a fancy to her, for she is sensible enough and passably good-looking, if one discounts the freckles.'

'Some men would think the freckles quite charming,' replied Alex, unaccountably rallying to Diana's defence. 'But I have to admit that she didn't appear to advantage. Her gowns were too plain and several seasons out of date.' His lips twitched. 'I have done something about that. I am confident she will be more fashionably dressed when you next see her.'

In a mood of devilry he had sought out the town's most notorious modiste and sent her to Chantreys, complete with enough silks and muslins to clothe the whole of the *ton* and instructions to supply Miss Grensham with all the dresses she would need to fulfil her duties as his hostess.

Madame Francot was famous for producing outrageously daring gowns for society's most dashing matrons and she also ranked amongst her customers many of the most successful courtesans in London. Since she made no secret of the fact and was herself always dressed in the most flamboyant style, Alex had expected Diana to turn her away at the door and write him a furious letter full of righteous indignation. Instead he had received a politely worded missive, thanking him for his thoughtfulness and informing him that not only was *madame* supplying her with the most delightful gowns, she had also conjured several very pretty dresses for Florence and Meggie, as well as providing some very useful lessons in dressmaking skills for them.

He said now, 'The next time you see Miss Grensham I hope she will be dressed in the very latest fashion. We shall see then if we can't find someone to take her to wife and get her out of the way. I have invited several fellows who might just do the trick.'

'D'you know, Alex, I am beginning to think this trip to Chantreys will prove devilish dull.'

'I know, but it can't be helped. This party will be comprised only of those I can rely upon to behave themselves.'

'What, no straw damsels?' asked Mr Wollerton, a note of regret in his voice. 'No opera dancers?'

'I'd have thought you get enough of your dancers here,' retorted Alex, grinning in spite of himself. 'Why, have you taken a fancy to one of the little beauties currently parading her wares before us?'

He raised his quizzing glass and ran his eye

over the line of dancers performing on the stage, their diaphanous skirts scandalously short.

'Certainly not,' retorted Mr Wollerton, affronted. 'I'll have you know we are watching a celebrated French ballet troupe. They have performed at the Paris Opera and are noted for their artistic interpretation.'

Alex gave a crack of laughter. 'Looking at the audience, I doubt many of them are here to admire the artistic interpretation.'

'These young ladies are extremely talented,' said his friend, spoiling the effect by adding, 'and extremely expensive.'

'Are they, now?' murmured Alex. He watched two of the female dancers leap and twirl across the stage, his mind racing.

'Yes, they are,' affirmed Wollerton. 'As you would know if you ever bothered to come backstage with me.'

'Well, Gervase, you have convinced me.' Alex grinned. 'When the performance ends tonight I *will* come backstage with you!'

'Diana, Diana, there is a carriage coming towards the house!'

Meggie's excited voice brought Diana and Florence to the schoolroom window to see an elegant travelling chaise bowling along the drive.

'Could it be Madame Francot with our

dresses?' asked Florence, her nose pressed against the glass.

'Not unless she has employed an army to finish them all in so short a time,' remarked Diana.

She smiled at the memory of the exuberant little Frenchwoman who had arrived at Chantreys with her entourage just over a week ago. Lord Davenport had given the lady quite the wrong idea of the kind of clothes required—quite deliberately, Diana suspected—but once they had resolved the misunderstanding Diana found Madame Francot most obliging. *Madame* was also enchanted by Meggie and Florence, said they reminded her of her own darling grandchildren and went out of her way to produce the most delightful sketches of gowns that would suit them. Diana had to check the voluble modiste only a couple of times for her rather colourful language and after that they proceeded very well indeed.

Madame had stayed two nights, entertained Diana with tales of her flight from France during the Terror, taught the children a little French as well as the secret of attaching a flounced hem to a gown, and left Chantreys in a cloud of perfumed silks and the promise to return *tout de suite* with all the gowns, cloaks, habits and dresses made up as they discussed.

Surely not even the indomitable Madame Francot would produce everything in so short a time? thought Diana as she ran down the stairs. A female voice talking rapidly in French floated up to her from the hall and she thought for a moment that she was wrong, but when she descended the last few stairs she found herself confronted by two young women she had never seen before in her life. They were both very pretty, very petite and wearing high-waisted walking-out dresses of the latest fashion. Fingle was goggling at them and when Diana arrived he cast an agonised appeal in her direction.

Before Diana could speak one of the young ladies came tripping over to her, taking off her bonnet and shaking out her golden curls as she said in her pretty, musical voice with a strong French accent, 'Ah, you must be Mademoiselle Grensham. Milord told us all about you and the *jolies filles*.'

'Did he?' said Diana warily.

'*Mais oui*.' The girl gave her a dazzling smile. 'He sent us 'ere to teach your leetle girls to dance!'

Chapter Ten

Diana blinked.

'Are you…' she paused, then continued slowly '…are you, perhaps, opera dancers?'

The second young lady approached. She was as dark as her companion was fair, but equally pretty.

'*Non, non, mademoiselle.* We are from ze Ballet de l'Opéra de Paris. They 'ave only the finest dancers in ze world, *je vous assure.* Monsieur Reynard, he brought us to *Londres* where Milord Davenport, he saw us perform, and he…er…*il a organisé avec* Monsieur Reynard that we should be…er…' She waved her little hands and looked to her companion for assistance.

'Zat we should come 'ere for two weeks to 'elp you with ze ballet your leetle girls are to perform.'

'*Bon.*' The brunette smiled and made a deep

and graceful curtsy to Diana. 'I am Chantal, *à votre service, mademoiselle.*'

'*Et moi*—Suzanne.' The blonde twirled about, as if to demonstrate her ability.

How dare he?

The two girls stood before Diana, smiling expectantly. She bit her lip. It was not their fault. Alex had sent them on purpose to outrage her. So far she had managed to turn to advantage his every attempt to put her out of countenance, but opera dancers!

I see you as an opponent worthy of my mettle.

Diana heard his words as clearly as if Alex was standing at her shoulder and it calmed her. She must not react in anger, that was what Alex expected. She took a deep, steadying breath and coolly invited Chantal and Suzanne to accompany her to the drawing room, where Fingle would bring them refreshments. They went before her, exclaiming at the view from the window, the pretty furnishings, the paintings on the wall.

'Thank you. Will you not sit down, ladies?'

As they made themselves comfortable she observed them. They were very young, not yet twenty, she suspected, and brimming with friendly good humour. One could not dislike them, there was no malice in their attitude, they were genuinely happy to be at Chantreys and seemed unaware of Alex's motive in sending them here. She waited until Fingle had brought in wines and sweetmeats before questioning them. She decided it would be easier if the conversation was conducted in French, then they could have no excuse for thinking she did not understand them.

'Lord Davenport sent you here to teach his wards to dance, is that not so?'

'But, yes, *mademoiselle*. He says they are to perform for his guests at the party he is arranging.'

'Are you well acquainted with Lord Davenport?' she asked them. 'The truth, if you please.'

'He came backstage, with his friend, Monsieur Wollerton.' Chantal's big brown eyes looked at her with not a hint of guile. 'Monsieur Reynard, he is very strict about the gentlemen he allows to visit us after the performance.'

'No doubt they have to be very rich.'

'Certainly, *mademoiselle*.'

'And Lord Davenport is exceedingly rich,' Diana continued. 'He is able to…er…pay Monsieur Reynard very well for your services.'

'But, yes, of a certainty. It is not at all convenient for us to leave the ballet at such a time, but milord, he was very exact about the dancers he required.'

'Ah.' Diana felt an inordinate amount of relief. 'So you are not…'

'We are not his lovers,' finished Suzanne with a frankness Diana wished she could emulate.

Suzanne clapped her hands and gave a little trill of laughter. 'I wish it might be so, *mademoiselle*, but, no. Milord Davenport, he comes to watch us dance, yes, but he has been backstage but rarely and he has never taken any of us for his mistress.' She looked at her companion and they sighed in unison. 'It is a great pity, for he is very 'andsome, do you not think?'

'No, I do not,' retorted Diana, rattled. 'His countenance is too rugged and his nose is not straight.'

'But he is so very big, *mademoiselle*,' murmured Chantal dreamily. 'Such a strong, shapely body. And when he smiles…'

Yes, well, Diana did not want to think about that. She rose abruptly.

'Very well. If Lord Davenport has gone to the trouble of sending you here then we must make use of you. I shall have rooms prepared for you immediately. And I shall take you upstairs to meet the children. It will be beneficial for you to converse with them in French, I think. They know enough now to follow you and it will improve their ability considerably. Now, shall we go?'

* * *

Lincoln delivered Diana's next letter to Alex when he brought up his hot water a few mornings later. The missive had been sitting on a silver tray in the hall and the valet recognised the neat, sloping writing. He had become familiar with it over the past few months and was intrigued to see its effect upon his master. So far the lady's correspondence had elicited a variety of responses. Sometimes the earl would burst out laughing as he scanned the lines, other times he would scowl and mutter ominously under his breath.

With his face devoid of all emotion, Lincoln handed the letter to Lord Davenport and then busied himself at the washstand. He heard a bark of laughter. That augured well.

'The little minx.'

Lincoln turned, a look of innocent enquiry upon his face.

'My lord?'

But the earl was in no mood to expand upon his utterance.

'Nothing.'

He waved Lincoln away, declaring he would shave himself. This was nothing unusual, but the valet would have dearly liked to remain a little longer in the bedchamber and try if he could see just what it was that Miss Grensham had written. However, his master had put the letter under his reading book and was even now preparing to get out of bed. Lincoln tenderly draped the folded towel over the rail and took his leave.

'So she is delighted with my choice of dancing teachers, is she?'

Alex brushed the soap liberally over his face and picked up the razor. He had really thought that Diana would take one look at those two little charmers and send them packing. Instead, her letter informed him that Meggie and Florence were not only enjoying the ballet steps they were learning, but they were also becoming most proficient in the French language. His eyes narrowed. He would wager Diana's first reaction was not as sanguine as her letter implied.

He had been most careful in his choice of dancers. Reynard had assured him that Chantal and Suzanne had been strictly reared and that he looked after them like his own daughters. Alex was not so sure about that, but he had interviewed them both and satisfied himself that they could be trusted to behave well during their stay at Chantreys. Indeed, if they wished to earn the enormous sum he had agreed with Reynard, they would make sure there was no hint of impropriety attached to their visit. Perhaps he should take a trip down there, just to make sure.

The idea took root. There was also his secretary to consider. He had sent John Timothy to Chantreys to deal with arrangements for the forthcoming ball, but it would do no harm for him to go and see for himself just how things were progressing. He cast his mind over his engagements. His great-aunt was bearing up well, despite her worries over her granddaughter's incarceration in France, and he need not dance attendance upon her and her protégée every day. Lady Frances would expect him to attend her party that evening, but he could send his apologies for that. No one would wonder at it if he wished to assure himself that everything at Chantreys was in readiness for his guests.

His ablutions complete, Alex dried his face and considered the matter. He was honest enough to admit that none of these points was the real reason he wanted to drive into Essex. It had cost him no little effort to keep away from Chantreys these past weeks and with every letter he received from Diana the temptation grew. He wanted to see her, to talk to her. He wanted to know what she really thought of Madame Francot and if she was truly pleased to have the dancers at Chantreys or if she was merely trying to pay him back in kind.

She haunted his thoughts, with her stubborn refusal to move out, her continuous opposition to his plan to find her and the children a new home. And why had he challenged her in that foolish way? He enjoyed teasing her, but there was little enjoyment in remaining in London, unable to see for himself just how she was reacting to his taunts. A smile tugged at his mouth. Her countenance was so expressive, he could read it like a book. That is what he missed. Her letters amused him, but it was not the same as a face-to-face confrontation. His duties to his great-aunt had filled most of his summer, but even when he had got away from town for a short time the horse-racing had failed to divert him.

With sudden decision he threw down the towel and set the bell pealing for Lincoln. Within minutes a message had been sent to the stables to prepare his curricle and he was changing his town dress for something more suited to a drive into the country.

'My lord, this is a pleasant surprise. Miss Grensham and the young ladies are in the orangery, taking a dancing lesson.'

There was a twinkle in the butler's eyes as he welcomed Alex into the house.

As if the old man had detected a blossoming romance, thought Alex in alarm.

'I have come to see my secretary.' Alex stripped off his gloves and put them on the hall table beside his hat. 'Is Timothy in the office?'

His cold tone had its effect. Immediately Fingle became the perfect butler, inclining his head a little as he answered in the affirmative. Good, thought Alex, as he strode away. He didn't want anyone getting the wrong idea about his visit here today. Diana was co-guardian of his wards. He would have to see her in that capacity, naturally, but he had no interest in her as a woman. She was small, thin, freckled and confrontational. A nuisance. She had no place in his hedonistic, well-ordered life. None at all.

His business with John Timothy was soon concluded. Arrangements for his visit were well in hand, the south pavilion was cleaned out and all the rooms made fit for guests while the orangery roof had been repaired and extra staff from the village would be recruited in time for the arrival of the earl and his guests in two weeks' time.

'I have ordered a covering over the path from the house to the orangery, my lord, just in case the weather should be inclement for the ball.'

'Good idea.' Alex nodded absently, wondering how Diana would react when she saw him. Would she be pleased, or would she rip up at him for his high-handed behaviour?

'Miss Grensham thought of it, my lord,' said John Timothy, tidying the papers on his desk. 'She is an excellent manager, if I may say so.' He smiled. 'She really has left me very little to do.'

'I had hoped your being here would take some of the work from her shoulders, John.'

'And I have, my lord, but she had most of it organised before I even arrived. She knew exactly what was required and how to obtain it. I suppose it comes from living in the house for several years, she is well acquainted with all the local tradespeople. Very efficient, she is, but in no way *managing*, if you know what I mean, sir. It has been a pleasure to work with her.'

'I am glad you have got on so well.' Alex was a little taken aback by this fulsome praise from his usually laconic secretary. He spent a few more minutes discussing business before going off to find Diana.

The orangery was situated at some distance from the house itself, behind the south pavilion. It was a large structure, its southern wall consisting entirely of glass and was built originally to house and protect citrus fruits during the winter. It had been enlarged considerably during the early years of the last century in an unsuccessful attempt to cultivate the highly fashionable pineapple, but the very size of the building had made it impossible to heat successfully. Since then the building had returned to its original function, with a few pieces of furniture added so that guests might take their ease on sunny days, and on rare occasions it was used as a ballroom.

As Alex followed the path to the south front of the orangery he saw that the long windows had been opened and sounds of much merriment and childish laughter drifted out to him, overlaid by the melodic sounds of a pianoforte. He remembered Diana writing to tell him that she had asked John Timothy to hire an instrument for the musicians to use at the ball. Perhaps she thought he would baulk at the expense. Perhaps that was her way of paying him back in some measure. Well, let her think that. He had been considering replacing the old harpsichord at Chantreys with a more fashionable keyboard, so if she thought to upset him with her extravagance she would be disappointed.

Alex entered by the side door that led into a small anteroom. It was filled with the odd pieces of furniture that had somehow accumulated in the orangery over the years. They had obviously been moved in preparation for the ball and were swathed in new holland covers. He smiled. That would be Diana's doing, no one else would have thought it worthwhile to protect the old sofa that had been relegated to the orangery in his father's day. He slipped quietly into the main room and stood for a moment, enjoying the scene. The orangery had been emptied of all but a few decorative citrus trees in their pots. The walls were freshly painted and the candle sconces had been polished until they shone. The hired pianoforte stood in one corner of the dais at the far end and a woman he had not seen before was playing a lively tune that echoed around the large room, but Alex paid scant heed to the music or the pianist, for it was the little group in the centre of the dais who held his attention. The two French girls, his wards and Diana were all dressed in gowns of gossamer-thin white muslin that stopped well short of the ankle.

He was immediately aware that of the three ladies, Diana's ankles were by far the most shapely. Meggie and Florence were sitting on the edge of the dais with their backs to him, watching as the two dancers helped Diana to rise on tiptoe. There was a great deal of giggling and laughter as she wobbled and collapsed and tried again, encouraged by her companions. On her last attempt she achieved a very creditable attitude.

Alex could not help himself.

'Well done,' he declared, coming forward.

The lady playing the piano stopped suddenly and everyone turned to see who had spoken. Their differing reactions caused him no little amusement. His wards shrieked joyfully and ran towards him while the two French dancers followed, beaming. Only Diana held back, her hands creeping to her cheeks as if trying to cover up the deep blush that had risen to her face. His amusement grew. She would find it difficult to rip up at him now, at least until her confusion had died away.

'Ah, milord Davenport, welcome, you are just what we need!' The blonde, whom he remembered was called Suzanne, clapped her hands in delight and gestured him to join them. 'We are teaching Mademoiselle Grensham to stand *sur le demi-pointe*, as we do now in ze ballet. Come, come, milord, we need you to play the part of the great Monsieur Vestris.'

'But I am no dancer,' protested Alex, laughing as he stepped on to the dais.

'*Tiens*, we do not need you to *dance*,' explained the brunette, with an impatient toss of her head. 'Only to 'elp the lady to balance.'

Diana gave a little gasp.

'No, Chantal, we were not seriously trying to—I do not think—'

'Stand 'ere, milord,' Chantal commanded him, ignoring Diana's breathless protest. 'You must be behind *mademoiselle* and place your hands *comme ça. Bon*.'

Alex was aware of Diana's alarm but she made no further demur as he took his place behind her. No, she wouldn't, he thought, not with Meggie and Florence watching, and the two dancers acting as if there was nothing the least unusual in what was happening. He guessed Diana and he were thinking the same thing at that moment, to get this over with and move on with the least possible fuss.

Smiling to show he thought there was nothing amiss, Alex allowed Chantal to take his hands and place them on Diana. Immediately his throat dried and he lost all desire to smile. Her waist was so tiny his fingers almost spanned it. He could feel the soft flesh of her body through the thin layer of fine muslin. With a jolt he realised she was not wearing stays. Of course, he should have known it the moment he saw those diaphanous gowns, they would not be able to dance so freely if they were restricted by stiff linen and whalebone.

It had become very hot and his neckcloth felt far too tight, but he dared not lift a finger to loosen it. He kept silent as the dancers encouraged Diana to rise on tiptoe again. He supported her lightly, but he could feel the smooth curve of her waist as it narrowed beneath her ribcage and his fingers rested on the hard bone of her hips. He wanted to tighten his hold, to pull her close, feel that soft body yield against his own. The mere thought of it sent a jolt of pure lust through him and he struggled to suppress it as everyone applauded Diana's graceful rise.

'Very good, *mademoiselle*. You are *très naturelle*.'

Diana came down off her toes, Alex removed his hands and she quickly stepped away him.

'Thank you, Suzanne, but I think you flatter me.'

He heard the slight tremble in her voice and saw her shoulders pull back, as if she was trying to regain her composure.

'That is enough for today,' she continued. 'We should return to the house and change. I have asked Mrs Wallace to prepare a light nuncheon for everyone in the dining room.'

Her voice was much firmer but she was taking all her weight on her right leg, the left foot lifting very slightly. He had not noticed her doing that when he came in. When she was not aware of his presence.

'You will eat with us, will you not, Uncle Alex?' said Meggie, coming up.

'Yes, of course.' His own voice was a little less sure than usual. He cleared his throat. 'You had best run on ahead and make sure Fingle has laid a place for me.'

Laughing and chattering, Meggie and Florence set off with the dancers while Diana moved towards the pianoforte where the unknown lady had risen and was packing away her sheet music.

'Mrs Appleton, thank you for playing for us

again today. I am most grateful.' She cast a fleeting glance towards Alex but did not meet his eyes. 'Do you know Lord Davenport, ma'am? He is the girls' guardian. Mrs Appleton lives in the village, my lord, and kindly agreed to play for us.'

Alex murmured a polite response, his attention still distracted by the memory of Diana's waist beneath his hands. Mrs Appleton blushed and murmured something incoherent, clearly discomposed to be facing an earl and when Diana invited her to remain for nuncheon she accepted with a few more disjointed sentences, then hurried away to the house.

Diana realised her mistake as soon as Mrs Appleton had left the orangery. She should have accompanied the lady back to the house rather than remain alone with Alex. Why was it that whenever he was near her wits disappeared? He did not look to be best pleased and was no doubt going to rip up at her for something. She eyed him resentfully.

'I do wish you would give me notice of when you intend to call at Chantreys, my lord.'

His frowning look disappeared.

'But it is my house, Diana. Besides, if you had known I was coming you might have cancelled your dancing lesson.'

'I would certainly not have been dressed thus,'

she replied frankly, colouring a little. 'I did not expect to have an audience.'

'Evidently.' He grinned. 'Pray do not feel embarrassed on my account. Shall we go back to the house?'

He held out his arm and Diana placed her fingers upon it. Her body was still thrumming with the memory of his hands on her waist. He had behaved with perfect propriety, his hold had been light, impersonal, just enough to support her, but it had sent excitement fizzing through her blood. Suzanne and Chantal had been perfectly at ease, they saw nothing wrong in being so lightly clad and having a gentleman stand so close, but they were dancers and accustomed to such things. She could only hope her face had not been as red as a beetroot!

'So,' said the earl, 'will our guests have the pleasure of seeing you dance with Meggie and Florence?'

'Heavens, no. I would not dream of—that is, I was merely...' She tailed off, wondering miserably how she could explain to him that when she saw them all dancing so freely, not restricted by a corset, she was eager to experience it for herself. And then Chantal had offered to lend her one of her gowns and there had seemed no harm in it... 'I did not intend for anyone to see me dancing.'

'I am not just anyone.'

'Quite true,' she replied with false sweetness. 'I have no doubt you are quite accustomed to consorting with dancers and are not at all shocked by their scanty dress.'

'Oh, I have seen dancers much more scantily clad,' he replied cheerfully.

Diana bit her lip. He was laughing at her. She wanted to laugh, too, and to retort, but she knew it would be unwise to challenge him further. She must maintain a dignified silence until they reached the house. Instead of thinking of Alex and his teasing ways she would concentrate upon walking, as she had been doing for the past few weeks, trying not to favour the left leg, but to put each heel to the floor with equal weight and prevent the halting, dragging step that has become such a habit.

They entered the hall just as Suzanne and Chantal came skipping down the stairs, their dance dresses replaced by demure muslin gowns. They informed her that the 'leetle girls' had gone upstairs with Nurse to be made tidy in readiness for their nuncheon.

Diana nodded. 'Thank you. If you would all like to go into the dining room I will fetch Meggie and Florence and join you shortly.'

'What,' Alex murmured wickedly as she released his arm, 'you would leave me alone with these charming young creatures? Is that wise?'

'I shall have to trust you to behave yourself.'
Diana stepped over to the dining-room door and
threw it open, adding with a mischievous smile,
'And in case you forget yourself, my lord, we
have Mrs Appleton and Mr Timothy here to keep
you in order.'

When their repast was finished the party broke
up. Mr Timothy offered to drive Mrs Appleton
back to the village while Chantal and Suzanne
took the girls off to the gardens. Diana was about
to leave the room when Alex stopped her.

'I thought we might go through the guest list
for the ball.'

'I sent you the full list last week, my lord.'

'But you will have had more replies to the invitations since then.'

Bowing to the inevitable, Diana led him to a
small room that had been furnished as a study.
She pulled a large ledger from the desk. Alex
walked over to the window, which gave a good
view of the flower gardens.

'My wards appear to be on the best of terms
with the *mademoiselles*.'

'I told you as much in my letter, sir.'

'I thought you wrote that merely to punish me
for my impudence in sending them here.'

Diana laughed. 'I confess I was at first nonplussed that you should do so, but they assured

me they are not opera dancers, but respectable members of the French ballet.' She added shrewdly, 'I also suspect they are being paid very well.'

'True, but you have promised my guests theatricals and I would not have them disappointed.'

'Meggie and Florence are learning a ballad to sing and they have a very pretty dance to perform. They will not let you down.'

Alex turned from the window. 'And what will you be doing?'

'Me? Why nothing. I am merely their governess.'

'You are my hostess,' he reminded her. 'And while I think of it, I hope you now have sufficient new gowns for the occasion?'

Diana thought of the cupboards and the linen press in her room, all full to overflowing.

'More than sufficient, sir, as Madame Francot's bills will attest. There is only the ballgown yet to be delivered. *Madame* was dissatisfied with the colour and had to order more material.'

'And are they very daring? Madame Francot is renowned for her dashy dresses.'

She saw the teasing light in his eyes and it was an effort not to reply in kind, but that was a slippery slope. It was better to keep him at a distance, to keep her dignity.

'I think you will find they are appropriate to the occasion.'

He was smiling at her and, oh, how she wanted to give in, to confess how much she had enjoyed looking at the silks and muslins with the modiste, who had insisted she choose gowns for all occasions, for dancing, walking, riding or merely looking elegant. Very much like a débutante preparing for her first Season. At least she assumed that is how it must feel, although she had never been in that position herself. If only she could tell Alex, but it was not possible. He might laugh at her. Worse, he might pity her. Quickly she thrust the open ledger at him.

'Here is the list of everyone invited to the ball, my lord, and you will see there is a mark against those who have accepted. There are very few replies still outstanding.'

She sat down in the window while Alex took a seat at the desk and perused the list. It gave her an opportunity to look at him, to observe the unruly dark hair that fell forward as he leaned over the page. Chantal and Suzanne had said they thought him handsome. She did not consider him so, but she was forced to admit there was something attractive about him. Perhaps it was a combination of his strong, rugged features, the mobile mouth that would curve suddenly into a smile and those slate-grey eyes that could pierce her soul.

She dragged her eyes away and realised she had almost let out a sigh. If she *had* been a débutante, young and naïve, she might have pined for his good opinion, tried to win his regard, but she was a woman of two-and-twenty, governess and guardian to two young girls. Such dreams were pointless. Alex knew her flaws, he had seen the ugly scar on her leg and he found her small and unattractive. She could not possibly compare with all the beautiful ladies he knew. Beauties like Frances Betsford.

Diana felt a sudden chill and rubbed her arms. He had seen her naked when she had climbed from the lake and now he had seen her dressed in the short skirts of a dancer. If it had been possible to enflame him then one of those scenarios should have done the trick, but they had not. On both occasions he had acted with humour, with kindness, but never with passion.

No? Then what about the kisses?

She fixed her eyes on the far horizon. The first time had been the result of much wine. It was well known that men could not control themselves when they had been drinking. It was a lowering thought that a man could only find her attractive if he was drunk. She thought of that second, searing embrace in the moonlight. He had broken away as soon as she had resisted.

Very commendable, but it clearly showed he only thought of her as a passing fancy.

'Hmm?' Alex looked up. 'Did you say something, Diana?'

'N-no.' She shook her head. 'I said nothing. I beg your pardon if I disturbed you.'

'It does not matter, I have finished with this.' He closed the book. 'So, you have everything arranged. Is there anything you need me to do?'

'I do not think so. The ball is organised, the musicians engaged, Mrs Wallace is already turning out all the guest rooms. Mr Timothy is on hand to help with any last-minute crises.'

'And you have allocated the rooms?'

She nodded. 'As you instructed.' She threw off the last shreds of melancholy and allowed herself a small smile. 'You have nothing to do but to arrive with your guests, my lord.'

'Excellent. John Timothy told me you managed everything very well.'

'Yes, in spite of your attempts to throw me into a panic.'

'You gave me my own again on every occasion.'

'I shall take that as a compliment, my lord.'

'Yes, do so!' He hesitated, looking as if he would like to say more, but after a moment he seemed to change his mind. He pushed himself out of his chair. 'I must go.'

'Yes.'

Diana wished she could find some way to keep him there longer, but what good would that achieve, save to delay the inevitable parting? She rose. 'Will you find Meggie and Florence? They will be unhappy if you leave without saying goodbye.'

'Yes, I'll find them. I hope all this planning will mean you are able to enjoy yourself once the guests arrive.'

'Of course, although you must understand that I will not neglect the girls.'

'I would not expect you to do so, but Nurse is perfectly capable of looking after them while you fulfil your duties as my hostess.'

'I trust I shall not disappoint you, sir.' She said, unable to resist, 'But tell me the truth! Did you suggest this whole thing—the house party, the ball and the idea of my being your hostess—was it all done in the hope I should take fright and remove from Chantreys?'

'Do you think me capable of such a thing?'

'Why, yes,' she said frankly. 'I do.'

He smiled.

'I said you were a worthy opponent, Diana. Very well.' He shrugged. 'I admit that was my intention, to intimidate you with the idea of a large party and a ball. It was reprehensible of me and I beg your pardon.'

She chuckled. 'But it is a large and *respectable* party, sir. I do not think that is quite your usual style.'

'No, it is not.' He grimaced. 'I admit I was caught out there, but having committed to it I cannot go back. And, do you know the strangest thing of all? I find myself quite looking forward to it now.'

'I am delighted to hear that.'

A smile spread through her and burst forth as she held her hand out to him. All restraint was forgotten, so much so that she did not recognise the warning signs, did not hold back as he pulled her closer, into his arms. It seemed the most natural thing in the world to accept his kiss, to close her eyes and forget everything except the warm, enveloping embrace.

When at last he raised his head she remained in his arms, her head thrown back against his shoulder, eyes half-closed while he stared down at her. It took a few moments for Diana to bring his face into focus and when she did the warm contentment that had wrapped around her was stripped away. She gathered her strength and pushed herself out of his arms, turning away that he might not see the hurt and disappointment in her eyes.

'Diana, I beg your pardon—'

She put up a hand. 'Please, do not say anything. I realise you had no intention of kissing me.'

'No. I forgot myself.'

The knife in her heart twisted.

'I quite understand.' Her voice was calm, controlled. She gripped her hands together. She could do this if she did not look at him. 'Please leave me now, sir. You have a long drive back to town.'

'Yes. Diana, I—'

His voice was harsh. What right had he to be angry with her? He had already admitted he was at fault. She whipped up her own indignation to protect herself.

She said coldly, 'There is no need to explain your reprehensible behaviour, my lord. Just leave me, if you please.'

Diana stood with her back to him, tense, head held high, straining her ears for any sound behind her. At last there was the faintest noise, like a sigh, then a firm step, the opening of the door, the soft click as it closed. He was gone.

She kept her eyes fixed on the window but all she saw was the look she had seen in Alex's eyes when he had raised his head from that kiss. Bewilderment. Consternation. Horror.

Chapter Eleven

It was just over a week until Alex was due to
take his party to Chantreys. He had not had any
word from Diana since that last, calamitous visit.
He had tried to write and apologise for his behaviour, but every attempt ended with the paper
being torn to shreds. How could he explain what
had happened when he did not understand it himself? When she had smiled up at him his response
had been pure instinct. He had taken the hand
she was holding out to him and drawn her into
his arms as if they had done it a hundred times
before. Afterwards she had been so calm about
it, so understanding, but she must now think him
a hardened rake who would take every opportunity to steal a kiss.

His lip curled in bitter self-derision. Perhaps
that is what he was. He had grown so accustomed
to being courted by every woman he met, perhaps Diana's resistance had attracted him. What a

courtcard he must be, if he must pursue a woman simply because she did not pursue him!

London was white-hot, baking in the August sun, and Alex did not want to venture out but he could no longer put off a visit to his tailor, or to his bootmaker. It was just past noon and he was crossing Piccadilly when he saw Diana and her charges emerging from one of the shops. For one wild, foolish moment he thought he had conjured her from his imagination, because she was constantly in his thoughts these days.

She looked very fetching in a new sage-green pelisse and with a chip-straw bonnet fixed over her glossy red curls. He recalled her comment that no one noticed governesses. No one would think of her as a governess today, several gentlemen turned their heads to take another look as they passed her. She was busy handing a neatly wrapped parcel to her footman and did not see Alex until he called out to her.

She looked around. There was no mistaking the dismay in her face. Meggie and Florence immediately ran up, holding up their purchases for Alex to admire. Diana let them chatter on for a few moments before she shushed them and drew them back to her side.

'Good day to you, Lord Davenport,' she greeted him without meeting his eyes. 'We have come to town to do a little shopping. Madame

Francot's new clothes made it necessary to buy matching gloves and slippers and all kinds of little extras.'

He glanced at the shop behind them.

'And books?'

His teasing question brought only the ghost of a smile.

'One cannot come to town without visiting Hatchards, my lord.'

'Where do you go next?'

'I am not quite sure.' She glanced back at the footman. 'There are more purchases to make, but poor Christopher has about as much as he can carry already.'

'I have a suggestion,' said Alex. 'Let Christopher take your parcels to the carriage while I take you all to Gunter's tea shop for ices.'

The idea found instant approval with Meggie and Florence and he was pleased to see that Diana's hesitation was very brief before she nodded her agreement and dispatched her footman, with orders that he was to meet them later in Berkeley Square. Piccadilly was particularly crowded and it was impossible for them all to walk together. Diana invited Alex to lead the way and he found himself with Florence at his side. She slipped her little hand into his.

'Is this not quite delightful, Uncle Alex?'

'Yes, delightful,' murmured Alex.

He spotted George Brummel strolling in the centre of a group of fashionably dressed gentlemen on the other side of the road. One of their number was Gervase Wollerton and Alex touched his hat to him, hiding his grin as the rest of the party glanced across the road, several of them raising their quizzing glasses to stare at the sight of the noted Corinthian hand in hand with a chattering child. That would give them something to talk of in the club today, he thought and he had no doubt that Gervase would quiz him mercilessly when they met up at Feversham House later that evening. Surprisingly, Alex found he did not care.

There was no opportunity to talk until they were seated in Gunter's and the girls were enjoying their ices. Diana had declined the treat, but had been persuaded to take a cup of coffee. Alex waited until they had all been served before he spoke.

'Do you go back to Chantreys tonight?'

'No, we are booked into an hotel.'

'I told you to come and stay in Half Moon Street.'

'That was very kind of you, my lord, but I did not think it wise.'

She kept her eyes lowered and it did not need the faint flush on her cheek to tell him why she had not brought the children to his town house. She did not trust him.

'Diana is taking us to the theatre!' announced Meggie.

'We are going to see *The Frozen Mountain,*' Diana hurried to explain. 'I have studied it thoroughly and taken advice from acquaintances who have already seen it. I am content that it is quite suitable for young minds. And there is a ballet, too, which they will enjoy.'

She gave him a bright smile, but it was a professional one, it did not warm her eyes. She had put him at a distance.

And that was what he wanted, Alex told himself, nettled. The woman was a confounded nuisance, she distracted him, made him act out of character. And she was standing in the way of all his plans. The best thing would be to marry her off, give her something to think about apart from the children. They could then be moved off with a new governess to another house, or sent to school. That way everyone would be happy. A movement at the window caught his eye.

'Ah, Christopher has arrived,' said Diana, looking up. She pushed away her empty cup. 'And in excellent time, as we are ready to go.'

When they emerged into the sunshine Diana gathered the girls to her.

'Meggie, Florence, thank Lord Davenport for his kindness and we will be on our way.'

'Have you more shopping to do? I could come with you,' offered Alex.

'Thank you, my lord, but we have taken up more than enough of your time today. Your way lies towards Piccadilly and we have a few purchases to make in New Bond Street. We shall look forward to seeing you at Chantreys next week.'

Alex watched, silenced as she walked away, Meggie and Florence on either side. She had dismissed him and with such confidence that he had been quite unable to argue. He felt a reluctant admiration for Miss Diana Grensham, who was proving to be a very worthy opponent. His eyes narrowed as he watched the little group disappear around a corner. Diana's awkward, halting step had almost completely disappeared.

Alex turned and made his way back to Piccadilly. The day was almost gone and he had much to do before this evening, when he was promised to join his friends at the Fevershams' rout, but the thought of a riotous evening of cards and drinking was surprisingly unappealing. He thought he would much prefer to watch an innocuous play at Drury Lane.

Chantreys was alive with activity. The guests were due at any time and Diana was as apprehensive as her wards were excited at the thought of having so many visitors. Not that it showed when she and the girls made their way to the drawing room shortly before the dinner hour. She had left Fingle and Mrs Wallace to greet the earl and his party and deal with the bustle and confusion of settling everyone into their rooms. She had continued with the girls' lessons in the schoolroom, but ever since she had heard the first scrunch of wheels on the gravelled drive she had been expecting a curt summons. It had not come and she took the girls downstairs at the appointed hour, steeling herself to appear calm and composed as she entered the room.

She was wearing one of her new evening gowns, a moss-green silk that Madam Francot had said would enhance her beautiful eyes. Diana had dismissed her words as mere flattery, but when she tried on the gown she was surprised to see that her eyes did look larger, brighter and it brought out the tiny green flecks in them. It gave her confidence. She might never be beautiful, but in this gown she did not look *dull*.

Diana breathed slowly, steadily and forced herself not to drag her left leg as she led the girls forward. Alex had called her a worthy opponent and worthy opponents did not cower or walk with a halting step, not if they could do anything about it.

A memory flickered. She was a child, crying,

while across the room Mama and the doctor were locked in fierce debate.

'Madam, the child must try to put her weight on the leg. It will hurt at first, of course, but if she *persists*—'

'It is no good. She is a cripple and we must face the fact. Good day to you. Your services are no longer required. Send in your bill...'

And Diana had been left to her own devices, favouring the left leg, allowing the muscles to waste, accepting the fact that she would always walk with a limp. Until Alex had questioned it.

The earl appeared, imposing, breathtaking in his dark coat and white linen. His rugged countenance was impassive. Had he noticed the effort she was making to walk normally? Did he care? It would appear not, she thought as he gave her a little bow. His frowning gaze rested on her neck.

'Is that the only jewellery you have?'

'It is.' She put her hand up to the single string of pearls clasped around her throat. 'Are they not suitable?'

'Oh, eminently.'

His attention was claimed by the children and she observed how his hard look softened at their effusive greeting. She might have told him that governesses had little need of trinkets but he was already taking the girls off to meet his guests.

He indicated by a look that Diana should accompany them.

The introductions began. Diana recognised some guests from the first house party, including Mr Wollerton, whose friendly greeting she returned with a grateful smile, but there were still a dozen faces she did not know. Exchanging greetings with so many strangers was a struggle for one who had spent the past few years avoiding society but everyone was very polite. It was clear that Alex had already informed them all of her position at Chantreys as the girls' governess and guardian and no one questioned her right to be hostess, although when Alex led her past Lady Frances Diana felt those blue eyes boring into her like daggers of ice.

When dinner was announced Nurse came downstairs to collect the children, leaving Diana free to join her guests. It needed every spare leaf inserted into the table to accommodate all the diners and as she took her place Diana felt very alone, for she and Alex had the full length of the table between them. Her glance moved to Lady Frances, who was sitting on Alex's right. If he had appointed Frances as his hostess then she would have been sitting here, as far away from the host as it was possible to be.

Diana concentrated on her duty, making sure

those around her had everything they required. At one point she looked up to find Alex was watching her. He raised his glass and her chin went up. What did it matter if he wanted Lady Frances by his side? It was nothing to her. She smiled and returned his salute. Alex might not admire her as a woman, but he did consider her a worthy opponent.

Throughout dinner Alex cast frequent glances down the table. Diana was conversing quite happily with her guests, whereas the company around him seemed dull and lacklustre. Even Frances's barbed wit failed to amuse him. At the appropriate moment Diana rose and invited the ladies to follow her into the drawing room, leaving the gentlemen to enjoy a glass of brandy. The conversation moved on to politics and gambling and, inevitably, women. Sir Charles Urmston leaned forward to address his host.

'I understand you wish your guests to act with decorum this week, Davenport.'

'Discretion was the word I used,' replied Alex coolly. 'I expect my guests to behave with discretion while they are under my roof. I hope Lady Frances made that clear to you?'

He had not been pleased when Frances had told him this morning that her cousin Simonstone could not come and she had invited Urmston to take his place. However, at that point it was too late to do much about it. He signalled to Fingle to charge the glasses again and sat back, his brow slightly furrowed.

'She did, my lord, and I must say I was a little surprised.' Urmston gave the superior smile that never failed to grate upon Alex's nerves. 'Your wards are quite delightful, my lord, but I had not thought you the sort to turn prudish.' He stopped, raising his head as though some shocking thought had struck him. 'You ain't taken to religion, have you, Davenport?'

'No, of course he hasn't,' exclaimed Wollerton, laughing. 'He's just trying to protect his wards from corrupting influences such as yourself, Urmston!'

A ripple of laughter went around the table and the conversation moved on, but Alex found himself regarding Urmston with growing dislike. Why had Frances invited him? Did she think he hadn't heard the rumours about the two of them? Surely she knew Urmston was not the sort of bachelor Alex wanted to foist upon Diana. Simonstone now, the cousin who was meant to have come, he was a different proposition. A respectable fellow of independent means, very much like Avery and Hamilton. Dull dogs, all of them, but any one of them could be relied upon to make a good husband for Diana. That was why he had invited them to Chantreys.

Alex's gaze strayed back to Urmston. Most likely Frances was trying to make him jealous by flaunting Urmston before him and in his own house, too. Alex's mouth thinned. Such tactics would not work with him. Quite the opposite, in fact.

The decanters were empty and Alex decided not to send for more. Instead he suggested they should join the ladies. As they all rose and moved towards the door, Sir Charles waited for Alex and fell in beside him.

'You know, that governess of yours is a taking little thing, Davenport. I'd be happy to give her a tumble, if you want her discredited.'

Alex stopped. The others were already crossing the hall and he detained Urmston in the now-empty dining room, closing the door upon them.

'I never wanted her discredited, as you put it,' he said in icy tones. 'Let me tell you now, Urmston, that I should take it very badly if anyone were to seduce Miss Grensham. Very badly indeed.' He met and held the older man's gaze. 'I hope we understand one another.'

For an instant he saw a flash of something in those hooded eyes. Anger, dislike, he could not be sure, then it was gone and Sir Charles was smiling and spreading his hands.

'Why, of course, Davenport, I was just trying to be of assistance.'

'I think I can do without your assistance in this matter, Urmston.' Alex opened the door. 'Shall we go?'

Diana tried to keep the conversation lively and interesting, but it was clear that the ladies were not enamoured of their own company, for when the gentlemen came in the atmosphere changed immediately. Only Mrs Peters appeared not to be affected and continued to rattle on inconsequentially to whoever would listen to her. One of the gentlemen suggested music and the ladies were delighted to oblige.

'It is a pity you do not have a pianoforte, my lord,' remarked Lady Cranbury, a dashing matron with roguish eyes. 'It is all the rage now, you know.'

'I am aware,' returned Alex. 'I intend to install one here before the year is out.'

'The children will like that,' observed Diana. 'Our neighbours, the Fredericks, have one and they have been allowed to try it.'

'And who will teach them?' asked Lady Frances. 'Are you trained upon the pianoforte, Miss Grensham?'

'We have one in the orangery,' said Diana. 'A Broadwood, hired in readiness for the ball. I have been practising upon that. And if the children show an aptitude then I shall hire a music master from London to drive out and give them lessons. That is one of the advantages of living near town.'

'Point taken, Diana,' murmured Alex as he passed her chair.

She smiled. *Point won*, she thought.

She went off to bring the children down to spend an hour in the drawing room, but conscious of her role as hostess she arranged for Nurse to collect them and put them to bed. She knew Alex would not allow her to slip away early this time. They were like two cats, she thought, as the evening wore on. They prowled around each other, perfectly polite but wary.

Or perhaps it was just her imagination. She was so conscious of Alex, his voice, whenever he was speaking and where he was in the room. He might not be thinking of her at all.

Towards the end of the evening as the guests began to retire, Alex crossed the room to stand over Diana, who was sitting a little apart.

'You are very quiet. Are you tired?'

'No, sir, I was thinking of the ball. I would like to move some paintings to the orangery, to brighten the walls. Would you object? They would mainly be from the servants' passages and the top floor. I would not leave conspicuous gaps that your guests would see, I promise you.'

'You may move what you please, Diana, you know that. You are mistress here.'

'Thank you, then I shall begin to make a list of the pictures I need.'

'And your first day is over. I hope it was not too much of an ordeal?'

'No, thank you. Your guests are all very kind.'

Everyone had treated her with courtesy and she had soon begun to relax and enjoy herself. Even Lady Frances, dazzling in a daringly low-cut gown and with a collar of diamonds and sapphires around her neck, had not daunted her.

'Your step is much improved.'

She blinked. 'I thought you had not noticed.' She could not read his look, but was heartened by the fact that he had seen the change. 'I have been practising. Working the muscles, as you suggested.' She was glad of the candlelight to hide her blush as she recalled the circumstances of that conversation. 'When I concentrate I find I limp hardly at all.'

'I am glad I was of some use to you. Even if I could not save you from drowning.'

His tone made her cheeks burn even more.

'And you are not regretting your decision to stay?' he continued. 'Even if I decide to hold parties such as this frequently?'

The teasing note was back in his voice. She could cope with that so much better than when he was being serious.

'I have told you, my lord, Meggie and Florence will remain here for at least the next year, whatever you choose to do. They are at home here, they feel safe and comfortable. And talking of drowning has reminded me of another reason to remain at Chantreys.' She rose. 'I want to teach them to swim this summer. You said yourself it was a useful attribute.'

With a slight curtsy and a mischievous smile she said goodnight to the remaining guests and made her escape.

'So, the little hostess has gone to bed.' Frances stood at his shoulder. 'Should we do the same, Alexander?'

'Of course, but not together.'

'Oh, my dear, are we still preserving your little foible about respectability?'

Her laugh was soft, smoky, and once he would have found it seductive, but he had heard her use it too often and with too many men. He turned to face her. The last few remaining guests were gathered at the far side of the room. There was no one to overhear them.

'No, I mean that our little flirtation is at an

end. It should not come as a surprise, we have seen so little of each other recently.'

'You have been busy with your plans for the party,' she replied. 'And then you have been running around after Lady Hune and her heiress.'

'True, but we could have found time to see one another, had we so wished.' He said gently, 'A little light-hearted flirtation, Frances, that is what we agreed.'

'At first, perhaps—'

'I hope you won't pretend to be heartbroken,' he continued, a hint of steel entering his voice. 'You may not have been able to get me into your bed recently, but I know there have been plenty of others.'

She stared at him, biting her lip. Anger was smouldering in her eyes and he wondered what it cost her not to rip up at him. After a moment she lifted her white shoulders in a shrug and gave a small, rueful smile.

'Why should it end? If we still amuse one another—'

'It is over, Frances.'

She touched the jewels at her throat. 'Is that what you were trying to tell me with this?'

'I think perhaps it was.'

'Then why did you not say so, when you gave it to me?'

'Then I had not quite decided. We might have

gone on a little longer, if you had not invited
Urmston to join us here.' His eyes narrowed. 'A
mistake, my dear, to bring your lover here.'

She did not deny it, he noticed.

'Sir Charles and I have been…friends…for
many years.'

'Then he will be able to console you now our
liaison is at an end.'

The smile grew and she moved closer.

'I may yet change your mind.'

'I doubt it.' Alex stood his ground. Her perfume filled his senses, but it did not move him.
He saw her beauty for what it was: a thin veneer
over an ice-cold heart. Eventually she realised
he was not going to succumb to her charms and
she moved away, giving him one final, regretful
smile before she left the room.

It was a novel experience for Diana, to leave
the children with Nurse and go downstairs to
break her fast with the guests. Alex was right,
Nurse was more than capable of looking after
Meggie and Florence, and Jenny, who had been
promoted to be her full-time maid, was the eldest
of a large family and was only too pleased to add
the care of the two young ladies to her duties.

Without exception everyone attended morning worship on Sunday. As hostess, Alex demanded that Diana should enter the church with

him, but she insisted that they should have Meggie and Florence walking between them. The rest of their guests filed in behind and Diana knew that her neighbours were watching everything with the liveliest curiosity. The invitations to the Chantreys ball had all been accepted, no one would miss the opportunity to attend such a grand event. She was grateful to receive an encouraging nod from Squire Huddleston's lady and smiles from Mr and Mrs Frederick, kindly people who had often deplored Diana's solitary existence at Chantreys, and as everyone went out into the sunshine after the service Diana knew there were many introductions to be made before she could return to the house.

Strangely Diana was undaunted by the prospect. She kept her head high as she left the church, concentrating upon her steps, not scurrying away to the carriage but walking slowly, putting equal weight on each foot. Her left leg ached with the effort but her reward was in her smooth, almost gliding progress. And the smile she received from Alex.

The first week passed uneventfully and much more agreeably than Diana had envisaged. Even Lady Frances showed her no more disdain than she displayed for the rest of the party. It was clear that with the exception of Sir Charles Urmston,

Lady Frances found the company at Chantreys beneath her. Diana had seen the pair exchanging looks full of mockery and deplored their ill manners, but she said nothing. They were the earl's friends, not hers. Alex himself proved to be an affable host, there was little ceremony and the guests were left to amuse themselves as they wished. If Diana could fault the earl it was that he was very eager she should not be left out, even though she would have happily remained in the background. He asked her to assist Mr Johnson in seeking out a particular book from the library, encouraged Mr Avery to accompany her when everyone strolled in the gardens and he even persuaded her to play the harpsichord for Sir Sydney Dunford when he entertained them with a song in the evenings.

It was all very enjoyable, but Diana wondered why Alex should be putting himself out for her, when he still maintained he wanted her and the children to leave Chantreys. She watched him as he moved about the drawing room each evening after dinner, laughing and talking with his guests. She had the strangest feeling that she had known him all her life and yet it was not true, she knew almost nothing of him. When she saw Mr Wollerton sitting a little apart from the rest one evening she took the opportunity to join him. Wine and brandy were available as well as tea and she knew the gentleman had been imbibing freely, so she felt confident he would answer her questions. They spoke idly for a few minutes and then she plucked up her courage.

'Mr Wollerton, you know Lord Davenport better than anyone here, I think. Will you tell me something of his life, how he lived before he became earl?'

Mr Wollerton looked a little hesitant.

'I would have thought you would know most of it, being his sister, so to speak.'

'We have been in company together very rarely,' she explained. 'I was still in the schoolroom when Margaret married his brother and after that, when he visited Chantreys, my duties as a governess kept me in the schoolroom.'

It was not the whole truth, but the gentleman did not question it.

'You knew him at school, I think,' she prompted him. 'Was he a scholar or a sportsman?'

He considered the matter as he settled himself more comfortably in his chair. As Diana had hoped, having been well fed and supplied with ample quantities of drink, Mr Wollerton was in an expansive mood.

'Oh, a sportsman, most definitely,' he said at last. 'But he always had a taste for the arts.'

'I know,' she said wryly. 'He wants to house his collection at Chantreys.'

'Ah, yes.' Mr Wollerton coughed and looked a little embarrassed.

Diana laughed, begged pardon for discomfiting him and gently drew him out to talk of Alex's schooldays. She built up a picture of a lively, vigorous young man but with a serious side, one that few people but his closest friends ever saw. She did not doubt that Gervase Wollerton was a good friend and a loyal one, too. He showed a reluctance to talk about the wild young Alexander Arrandale, who had burst upon the *ton* with a fortune in his pocket and no responsibilities.

'Was he a typical Arrandale?' she asked him. 'I have only heard about the family from my sister. She told me that James was the exception, quiet and studious and nothing like his wayward brother, with his sports and gambling and women.'

She realised Mr Wollerton was looking uneasy.

'Should I not have mentioned it? It is the truth though, is it not? You may tell me, sir, for I am not easily shocked, I assure you.'

'Well, yes, Alex was very wild when he first came to town, but nothing serious, you understand. He did not run through his fortune, like many young hotheads might do. He used his money to develop his sporting prowess and to indulge his passion for art. He likes collecting beautiful objects.'

'And beautiful women, Mr Wollerton. Is London littered with broken hearts?'

'No, no, not at all—Alex ain't like that,' he said quickly. 'There are females aplenty on the hunt for a husband, London is full of 'em. But Alex is a great gun and he is not one to raise false hopes. Believe me, his liaisons have always been with females who understand what he is offering them. And he's very generous, too, he always makes sure they have some pretty but expensive gift when it's time to part. Diamonds and the like. That's what the ladies seem to like most, jewellery!' He stopped, then added ruefully, 'By George, Miss Grensham, I should not be telling you all this, I beg your pardon.'

'No need, Mr Wollerton. I am glad to learn so much about the earl.' She laughed. 'And you have my word I shall not tell him you have, um, opened the budget!'

Across the room Alex watched them with growing irritation. What the deuce was Gervase saying to keep Diana at his side for so long? And laughing so freely. She had not appeared so much at ease with any of the other fellows. He straightened in his chair. Do not say that Diana was forming a partiality for Gervase! Everyone knew Wollerton was a confirmed bachelor.

An unpleasant doubt shook him. There was no denying Diana looked very well in the new gowns Madame Francot had made for her. Last night's creation in teal-coloured silk had enhanced the flames in her red hair, while the green silk she was wearing now made her eyes shine so that he was reminded of the seasons, of hazelnuts and spring moss. His eyes fell on the pearls around her neck. They were very fine, but she needed something warmer on that fine skin of hers.

He was aware of a sudden change in the conversation. Lord and Lady Goodge were preparing to retire. Alex walked to the door with them and called to the footman dozing in the hall to light their bedroom candle. When he returned to the drawing room he wandered across and stopped beside Diana's chair. She was laughing at something Gervase had said to her and when she turned her face towards Alex it was still alight with mischief, her eyes dancing. His breath caught in his throat at the beautiful picture she presented.

'Go away. Alex, can you not see that Miss Grensham and I are enjoying a tête-à-tête?'

For once Alex was not in the least amused by his friend's humorous quip. His scowl deepened.

'Miss Grensham—' he stressed her name '—must not neglect her duties as hostess.'

Her brows rose but she responded mildly enough.

'No, of course not. The party is breaking up, I must go and speak to Mrs Peters again before she goes to bed. If you gentlemen will excuse me…'

Gervase jumped to his feet as she walked away.

'You are rather cross-grained tonight, old friend,' he observed, his eyes on Diana's retreating form. 'If I did not know better, Alex, I would think you were jealous.'

'Jealous? What rot!' Alex gave a short laugh as he walked away, but he was uncomfortably aware of his friend's thoughtful gaze following him across the room.

Chapter Twelve

Another day, another new gown. Diana felt the smile building inside her. She had never before had so many new clothes. There was no doubt it lifted one's spirits to have so many to choose from. Or perhaps it was just to have so much adult company. She hummed quietly to herself as she allowed Jenny to help her into the embroidered lemon muslin. The girl had also proved herself adept at dressing hair, and when Diana went downstairs her wayward tresses had been tamed and confined upon her head by a wide yellow ribbon. She felt fresh and cool, which was an advantage when the day was promising to be very humid.

It was so warm that Diana ordered all the windows in the reception rooms to be opened and had cushions, chairs and rugs placed out of doors in the shade of the trees on the lawn so that everyone might wander freely out of doors. It proved a popular idea and by noon most of the party were gathered under the trees, sitting or reclining as their mood dictated.

Alex strode out to join them.

'Fingle is bringing refreshments for us.'

'Oh, well d-done, my lord,' stammered Mr Hamilton. 'That is just what is required.'

'Pray do not thank me, Hamilton. Our hostess arranged it.'

'Then Miss Grensham has our undying gratitude,' declared Sir Charles Urmston. He directed a little bow at Diana, but there was mockery in the gesture and she chose to ignore it. He was lounging very close to Lady Frances, who murmured something that made him smile. Diana could not help wondering if that was the reason Alex did not sit down beside the lady.

'Is that John Timothy going off?' remarked Mr Wollerton, observing a solitary figure riding away from the house.

Alex threw himself down upon a spare rug. 'Yes. He is gone to town to fetch something for me.'

'Poor man, to be obliged to ride out today, when it is so very warm,' declared Miss Prentiss, fanning herself vigorously.

'Yes, indeed,' agreed Mrs Peters, closing her book. 'I vow it is a day for doing nothing at all.'

'I do not think Miss Grensham would agree

with you,' murmured Alex. 'Did I not see you in the grounds with Meggie and Florence before breakfast this morning?'

'Why, yes.' Diana nodded. 'I thought it would be wise to take them out early, before the day became too hot.'

'Dear little girls,' murmured Lady Frances with an insincere smile. 'And what are they doing now?'

'Giving Nurse a headache, I shouldn't wonder,' murmured Alex.

Diana chuckled, but shook her head at him.

'Nothing of the kind. My maid is looking after them and when I left they were engaged in painting pictures for her. When that is done I expect they will take up their sewing. Jenny is an excellent needlewoman and is helping them to make clothes for their dolls.'

'How admirably well organised you are.' Alex stretched out and put his hands behind his head. 'You think of everything, Diana.'

Diana started slightly at his use of her name in company, yet there was no reason why he should not do so. They were brother- and sister-in-law. She was his hostess. Yet she was aware of the knowing glances that passed between some of the guests and the cold stare Lady Frances bestowed upon her. Diana was thankful she was wearing her rose-green spencer or she would have shivered at the iciness of that look.

Fingle provided a welcome diversion when he led out a small procession of servants with various jugs of wine, ale and lemonade, plates piled with tiny baked fancies, plus a large and colourful bowl of fruit. She was gratified by the exclamations of delight, the little crows of pleasure from the ladies as they picked out a delicate pastry, the satisfied sighs of the gentlemen as they quaffed the cool ale or sipped a glass of wine.

When everyone had been served the servants withdrew, leaving the remainder of the food and drink on a small table placed beneath one sturdy tree. Conversation became desultory as everyone relaxed, enjoying the food and drink. Only Diana remained alert, observing her guests closely and getting up to hand round more cakes or refresh the glasses when necessary.

Sir Sydney Dunford beamed up at her as he held out his wine glass for refilling. 'As Davenport says, you think of everything, ma'am.'

'I suppose one in your position must be organised,' observed Lady Frances, her voice dripping with insincere sweetness.

'I am afraid I do not understand you, ma'am.'

'You will not wish to be moving around any more than you have to, not when each step is such a struggle for you.' Too late did Diana realise she had walked into a trap. The honeyed words continued. 'Your poor leg. A childhood accident, I believe. Although I fancy you do not limp as badly as you did in May, Miss Grensham.' Lady Frances looked pointedly at Diana's skirts. 'Has the doctor suggested a metal brace for your leg, perhaps?'

The air was charged with embarrassment. Diana heard someone gasp. Mrs Peters, she suspected.

Miss Prentiss stifled a giggle. 'Lady Frances—!'

Those blue eyes widened. 'What have I said? I beg your pardon, Miss Grensham, but we have all been getting along so famously, I thought there could be no harm in mentioning it. Not when we are all such good friends now.'

Diana felt her left leg stiffening, the heel beginning to lift. She must concentrate upon standing straight. These barbs could only hurt her if she let them in. Alex, she noted, had not moved. He was still lying on the rug, his eyes closed. She supposed it was possible he was asleep…

'Oh, my dear…' Lady Frances put her hands to her cheeks in mock horror '…have I offended you? I would not for the world have drawn attention to your little—infirmity if I had realised it would upset you.'

Diana kept her head up and gave a smile every

bit as false as Lady Frances's. 'No, indeed, why should I be offended? I am very happy to tell you that there have been no doctors involved in my recovery, merely my own hard work and persistence.'

'Indeed, Diana works harder than anyone I know.' Alex scrambled up. 'More wine, anyone?'

So he had not been sleeping. But he had not rushed to her defence, either. Had he enjoyed her humiliation? Having her affliction brought to everyone's attention? She felt a sudden surge of anger. She had misjudged him.

Dismayed at the prickling of tears in her throat, Diana moved over to the table full of food and tried to look busy, pointlessly moving things around. Even there she could not escape, for Lady Frances followed her and murmured in a low voice.

'Oh, my dear, I *do* beg your pardon. I am mortified to have embarrassed you, but indeed, *indeed* we are all very pleased to see you walking so well. It must have been very disagreeable for you to appear in public with such an ungainly step. Alexander was very aware of it—'

Diana's hands stilled. 'The earl mentioned it to you?'

Lady Frances looked coy.

'We are very close, you see. And he is so keen to find you a husband.'

'I beg your pardon?'

'My dear, have you not seen how he has gone out of his way to present you in a good light to the gentlemen he has invited here? Of course it will be much easier now there is no longer that ungainly walk to worry about.'

Diana stared at her. There was malice in those sky-blue eyes, but her words made sense. Alex had been throwing her in the way of the bachelors in the party. She moved back towards the main group, forcing a smile.

'If you will all excuse me, there is something I must attend to.'

Alex watched Diana hurry away. She was favouring her left leg again. Not as much as before, but he noticed it. She was making an effort, he thought, but she was distracted. He looked suspiciously at Frances.

'What did you say to her? I thought you were going over to make peace.'

'I did.' Frances smiled at him, all innocence. 'I even begged her pardon for mentioning that ugly walk of hers. I am sure Diana and I will be very good friends now.'

Diana went quickly into the house, but she was only halfway up the stairs when she slowed and finally came to a halt. The children were in the schoolroom, all the doors and windows there would be open to allow in what little air there was. She needed to be alone, to think, and she did not want the children to see her distress. She went back downstairs, but going through the empty rooms she realised that none of them was really private, she might be disturbed at any moment. The orangery. No one would question her going there. She slipped out of the house and made her way along the winding path, relieved that there was no one in sight, not even a servant.

Why should Lady Frances launch an attack upon her now and why did Alex say nothing to defend her? Close upon that question came another—why should he? They were combatants, after all. Perhaps it was his plan to humiliate her, to force her to remove from Chantreys. She had not thought that of him. She had thought him… honourable. A bitter laugh caught in her throat. Alex was no knight in shining armour, prepared to fight for her honour and shield her from every unfavourable wind.

But he could be and I wish he was.

The thought caught her unawares and a wave of longing crashed over her, so strong that she actually stumbled. Diana rubbed her temples, feeling the beginnings of a headache. It was the weather, it was hot and sultry, no wonder she was feeling low. She forced her mind to concentrate upon the forthcoming ball. It was Wednesday already and she had done little yet to prepare the orangery for the ball on Friday. Tomorrow evening Meggie and Florence would perform there and in the morning a team of men were coming to fit a canopy over this very path, to shelter the guests as they made their way from the house to the orangery. She was glad they were not there now to see her dashing an angry tear from her cheek.

The orangery was empty but stiflingly hot. The few potted plants that had been placed around the walls were wilting from the heat and Diana made a mental note to have them watered. She went from window to window, throwing them wide. The curtains she had ordered had been put up, hanging over the pillars between each window in soft folds of butter-coloured muslin, but even with all the windows open there was no wind to stir them.

'I thought I might find you here.'

Alex was walking on to the terrace. Diana turned and went back inside.

'Please go back to your guests, my lord. There is nothing for you to do here.'

'You are right,' he said, following her into the room. 'The walls are too bare.'

So they were to ignore what had occurred in the garden. Very well.

'I do not want to move the paintings from the house until the last minute,' she replied. 'The heat in here might damage them.'

'Have you chosen the ones you want?'

'I have. I will give you a list for approval.'

'I have already said you may do as you wish.'

Diana turned away from him. She began to rearrange the curtains—it was an idle, useless occupation but it meant she did not have to look at him.

'I am very sorry if Lady Frances upset you.'

She felt the tears pressing against her eyelids and fought them back by summoning up her anger.

'Why should you be sorry? Perhaps you think her animosity will make me wish to quit Chantreys.'

'No, of course not—'

She rounded on him.

'Oh, do not lie to me, my lord. You want this place to show off your works of art and to hold your, your riotous parties. You find this sedate gathering all very boring, you and Lady Frances and Sir Charles Urmston, yawning behind your hands at the decorous conversation. Nothing like your usual racy style, is it, my lord?'

'Nonsense! And stop calling me my lord.'

'Well, that is what you are, is it not? Lord of all you survey. Except me, of course. And Chantreys. That irks you, does it not, that your brother's will gives me the right to remain here?'

'No! 'Pon my honour, Diana, I will not force you from this house, I have already told you that.'

'Oh? And what of your plans to m-marry me off?' she threw at him. 'Can you deny you invited Mr Hamilton, Mr Avery and the other single gentlemen in the hope that I might fall in love with one of them?'

He glowered at her. 'Who told you that?'

'How I learned of it is not important. It is perfectly obvious that that is what you have been doing.'

'Was it Frances? She was making mischief, Diana.'

'Oh, I am well aware of it. She wishes to humiliate me, that is very clear.' She brushed a rogue tear from her cheek. 'And since you do not stop her I can only conclude you are happy for her to do so.'

'You are wrong.'

'Hah!'

She went to turn away but he grabbed her arm.

'You think I should have jumped to your defence when she suggested you had fitted a brace to your leg?' He shook his head. 'You are wrong, Diana. I believe your family—even my brother—defended you far too much, with the result that you have come to see yourself as some ugly, deformed creature. Can you not see now that it is not true? It is time you took your place in society, Diana, you do not need to remain hidden away. And as for Lady Frances, you did not need me to defend you. You answered her very well for yourself.'

'Yes, well—' she snatched her arm free '—I have grown up having to look after myself.'

'You have grown up hiding away from the world!'

Suddenly she could stand no more. If he did not leave her soon she would dissolve into tears and she could not bear to show so much weakness before him. She threw up her arms.

'Just go away!' she shouted. 'Leave me alone, *Lord* Davenport. I do not need you. I do not need *anyone*!'

'Diana, stop!'

His words followed her as she dashed out of the orangery and away through the gardens.

She ignored his call. She had lost her temper and needed to be alone with her misery and her anger until she was once more in control. Tears of rage and frustration streamed down her face. She could not go back to the house looking like this, the children would want to know what had upset her. She ran through the gardens and across the grass, away from the house and the guests. She would seek shelter in the woods.

* * *

Alex strode quickly after Diana, swearing softly when she veered from the path and headed for the trees. He should catch her, make her see that he had not intended for her to be hurt. Frances had been deliberately provoking, but Diana's response had been perfectly judged. She had not crumbled but had replied with her head held high. Even while he was supposedly lying at his ease he had noted that. It had been an effort not to jump in, but he was well aware of the dangers of publicly defending Diana. Frances was already smarting from his rejection. If he gave her reason to think Diana was the cause, she was quite capable of spreading rumours and lies that would be even more injurious than her barbed remarks today.

Diana disappeared from view and he stopped. He exhaled, long and slow, thinking of their guests lounging at their ease on the lawn. She was clearly not going back to them, so he must do so. Later, when she had recovered a little, he would talk to her. Explain.

As the afternoon wore on the clouds that had been building on the horizon moved in, a thick grey canopy that blotted out the sun and covered Chantreys in an ominous shade. Alex ushered his guests indoors to amuse themselves in the library or the drawing room while the thunder began to roll around the house. Frances and Sir Charles Urmston had disappeared but Alex gave it no more than a thought. Frances was no longer his concern.

When the rain started Alex moved restlessly from room to room. There was no sign of Diana, but it was possible that she had slipped up to the schoolroom. He was making his way upstairs to find out when he saw Diana's maid on the landing and stopped her to ask if Miss Grensham had come in.

'No, sir.' A loud thunderclap made the girl jump and look nervously towards the window. 'She said earlier that she was going to the orangery. I 'spect she's sheltering in there.'

Alex dismissed her and stood for a moment, irresolute. A lightning flash, followed by an even louder crash of thunder, decided him. He turned and ran swiftly back down the stairs.

The heavy rain was lashed by a gusting wind and Alex was drenched within moments of leaving the house. He gave a hiss of frustration when he saw the orangery was just as he had left it hours earlier, the windows thrown wide and long folds of yellow muslin billowing out into the rain. He began to run. He should have thought to send someone out to make sure it was closed up. But if Diana wasn't here, where was she? His heart went cold at the thought of her being out of doors in this storm.

Then, through the deepening gloom, he spotted a bedraggled figure in the first of the windows, pulling it closed. Alex reached the terrace and leaped in through the next window, dragging it shut behind him. Diana hurried past him and in silence they secured the rest. The storm was overhead now, an almost continuous roar of thunder while the rain lashed at the glass and rattled the window frames. A flicker of lightning flashed in through the glass and caught Diana in its brilliant glare. She was drenched to the skin, her hair plastered to her head and the skirts of her thin gown clinging to every curve. Alex's relief at knowing she was safe was so strong it confounded him, rocked him off balance and found expression in a sudden outburst of anger.

'What the hell do you think you were doing, leaving this place open to the elements?' He waved one hand. 'The new curtains are sodden and the floor is awash!'

Compared to his furious outburst her voice was low, controlled.

'It is a pity and I am very sorry for it, but we can wash the muslin and hang it out to dry once the storm has passed. And the stone floor will not suffer from a little water. I am sure everything will be in order for Meggie and Florence's little performance tomorrow evening. I have checked the Broadwood, it is well away from the windows and not harmed.'

'No thanks to you!' he raged at her. 'Of all the irresponsible acts, to go off and leave the place unattended.'

'*You* were here when I left, my lord,' she retorted angrily. 'I do not think you can put all the blame upon me.'

Alex was being unjust and he knew it, but he could not stop. Such was the raw emotion blazing through him he was almost shaking with it.

'I am only thankful you had not brought my paintings out here! Heaven knows what damage might have been caused by your thoughtlessness.'

She threw up her head, raking him with her angry glare.

'Yes, that is all you care about, isn't it, your precious works of art. Inanimate objects, but they are more important to you than any living, breathing creature!'

'Now you are being ridiculous.'

'Am I? You want to fill Chantreys with your paintings and statues, to make it a display case for beautiful things rather than a home for real people, with all their flaws and imperfections.'

She was standing very close, eyes glittering and her breast heaving. The air between them was so charged with emotion it was tangible. He could taste it, feel it. Alex clenched his fists to stop himself reaching for her, whether to shake her or kiss her he did not know.

Diana felt the first stirrings of alarm. She had allowed her temper to get the better of her, she had lashed out, wanting to wound Alex, and judging by his thunderous countenance she had succeeded. But it was not only murder she read in his fierce gaze, there was something else. A look, a primal gleam that she had seen there before. It burned into her, set her pulse racing and threatened to overwhelm her. She felt as if they were balanced on the edge of a precipice, one false step and they would plunge into some unimaginable peril. Surprise and apprehension flickered over Alex's countenance, gone in an instant, but she knew without a doubt that he too realised the danger of the situation. They must draw back. Somehow she dragged her eyes away and tried to speak calmly.

'I hope there will be no lasting damage. I came back as soon as the rain started.'

'Not soon enough,' he barked at her.

There was no placating him. Diana had the nonsensical notion that she had disturbed a slumbering dragon and she had no strength left to defend herself. She must get away. Quickly.

'No,' she agreed, determined not to antagonise him further. 'We had best get back to the house.'

* * *

She had stopped fighting him. Alex was aware of an irrational disappointment.

He said sharply, 'Do not be so foolish. You cannot go out in this weather.'

'But we are already wet through.'

'Only an idiot would go out in an electrical storm.' As if to reinforce his point, the air shuddered with another roar of thunder. In the accompanying flash of light he saw the dejected slump of Diana's shoulders. He had never seen her so defeated and it tore at his heart. He took her arm and said more gently, 'Come into the other room. We need to dry you off a little.'

The shadows were deeper in the anteroom, but at least its small windows faced away from the storm. Alex dragged the protective cover from one of the chairs.

'Here, use this. Not the finest linen, perhaps, but better than nothing.'

Diana took the cloth and wiped her face. The urgency that had consumed her when she saw the orangery windows standing wide had evaporated, now she felt cold and miserable. The day had been a disaster, the rapport that had been building between herself and Alex had gone. She had made him angry and shown herself quite ungrateful for all he had done for her. She felt as if she had lost a friend. Her only friend.

Alex had shed his coat and was vigorously rubbing his hair, but he stopped when he saw that she was watching him.

'Come, you need to dry yourself.' He took the cloth from Diana's nerveless fingers and dragged it over her hair, removing the worst of the wet. He briefly rested a hand on her shoulder. 'That spencer of yours has soaked up water like a sponge. It needs to come off.'

She reached up, but her fingers were shaking too much to do anything more than fumble uselessly with the buttons.

'Tsk. Here, let me.' He pushed her hands aside and dragged the sodden velvet from her shoulders. The sleeves were tight and had to be tugged off, but at last the spencer was discarded and he rubbed her bare arms with the cloth. Even through the coarse linen he could feel the chill of her skin. He gave an exasperated sigh, covering his anxiety with irritation.

'How could you be so foolish?' he muttered. 'If you catch a chill you would be well served.' He threw aside the sodden cloth and dragged off another chair cover which he arranged over her shoulders. 'You should have gone indoors as soon as the rain started.'

'I know it,' said Diana quietly. 'I am sorry—'

'Ah, don't!' He stopped her, exclaiming as if the words had been forced from him. 'You must not be sorry, Diana. Never sorry.'

She looked up, her misery forgotten when she saw the blaze in his eyes. Lightning flickered warningly. They were frozen in a moment of tense silence and Diana knew with sudden, frightening certainty that they were still on the edge of the precipice. She had not stepped back and had no intention of doing so.

There was an explosion of thunder as they crashed together. Diana raised her face and Alex covered it with kisses, finally finding her lips. They parted eagerly beneath the onslaught and his tongue explored her, plundered her senses, possessed her. She pushed herself against him, with only instinct to guide her responses. The kiss became more frenzied, the cloth slipped from her shoulders but she did not need it, she was burning and barely aware of the damp muslin that clung to her body.

His arms tightened. He lifted her as if she weighed nothing at all and laid her gently upon the sofa. Her loose wet hair pressed against her back and Diana trembled slightly. Alex paused, raising his head, and even in the dim light she could see the question in his eyes. Fearful he would leave her Diana threw her arms about his neck, dragging his head down towards her.

He obliged her with another searing kiss. She clutched at his shoulders, wanting him, needing him to continue his assault of her senses. Excitement rippled through her body, she moved restlessly beneath him, sighing as his hands began to explore her, tearing at her gown. When he uncovered her breasts she gasped at his touch, but made no attempt to stop him when he trailed a line of kisses down her throat. Her hands drove through his hair, feeling its silky strength as his lips travelled lightly over her skin. She arched towards him, offering up to him her full, aching breasts. He cupped one with his hand, his thumb circling, teasing while his mouth covered the other and his tongue began to flicker over its hard nub, drawing a response from deep within. A yearning hunger was unfurling inside. Her body was heavy with it, her skin so sensitive that she was aware of his every touch and impatient for more.

Her skirts were bunched around her hips and Diana felt his free hand moving over them and down to the juncture of her thighs where his fingers stroked and caressed and finally slid inside her. Urgent desire shot through her, heating her blood, making her moan with the exquisite craving that his touch unleashed. She did not understand it, only the need to go on, to finish this. She reached for him and, obedient to her touch on his face, Alex gave up pleasuring her breast and returned to kiss her lips, the sweep and thrust of his tongue matching the movements of his fingers deep inside her and rousing her to a frenzy. Somehow amidst the fury of their embrace he had unfastened his breeches and she exulted in the feel of his skin upon hers. He was hard against her, she should have been frightened but instead it only heightened her own need, even as the insistent rhythms of his tongue and his fingers carried her almost beyond reason.

She groaned into his mouth, her hips moving, pushing against his hand as new sensations took hold, rippling and growing, filling her like floodwaters rising against a dam. He eased himself over her and she slid her hands over his smooth, firm buttocks, urging him on, knowing there was more he could give her. She cried out as he entered her, not with pain but joy. He pushed into her again and again, up to the hilt. Her body tightened around him, she wanted this to go on for ever, but even as the thought formed she felt herself unravelling, bucking and writhing as the dam broke and she was carried away on a wave of heady, intolerably sweet sensations. She screamed, shuddered and clung to Alex, falling, drowning in sweet sensuous pleasure even as he gave a shout and a final, urgent thrust before collapsing against her, his own passion quite spent.

Chapter Thirteen

The storm was moving away, the lightning had all but ceased and the thunder was nothing more than an occasional, distant mutter. Alex shifted his weight to one side but kept his arms about Diana. In truth he never wanted to let her go. He felt dazed, confused and battered by the feelings that had raged through him. His anxiety for Diana's safety had thrown him off balance and he had hidden his confusion beneath a veneer of anger, but even that had been no proof against the wave of emotion that swept over him when she stood before him looking so lost and vulnerable. At first he had wanted only to protect her, but having her so close roused a strong desire to possess her. He had not intended to kiss her, he had wanted to turn away but his body had suddenly become a separate entity, answering only to the siren call of the woman before him. The woman who was now in his arms. The virgin he had deflowered.

That was not his way. What madness had come over him? He had not felt so out of control since his schooldays, when the love of his life, the stepmother of one of his school friends, had initiated him into the pleasures of the flesh. She had been much older than he and her protestations of love had been false and short-lived. Alex had soon been cast aside and he had never let himself grow so fond of any woman since. Looking back, he recognised that she had seduced *him*, taken advantage of his innocence.

And was that not what he had done now to Diana? She had been very willing, but he was the experienced one, he should have shown restraint. He closed his eyes, angered by his weakness, and yet he could not feel any real regret at what had occurred, it had been so natural, so right and it was as much as he could do not to roll her over and take her all over again. And again. To make her his own.

To make her his countess. The thought came suddenly, shockingly, but he knew now that was what he wanted. Not some barren, sterile, comfortable marriage of convenience, but to spend his life with this tempestuous, spirited woman who would infuriate and enchant him by turns.

What of Diana, what would she want? A sudden chill ran through him. He had always said he would not be coerced into wedlock so why should she, just because he had taken advantage of her? She had grown and blossomed since that first spring meeting. Alex felt a certain pride that he had somehow been instrumental in her transformation, but despite what they had just done he had no right to claim her as his bride. She might not wish to be tied down when she had only recently discovered her own strength. He buried his face in her wet hair and breathed in the unique scent of her. He had likened her to Sleeping Beauty, but just because he had awakened her did not mean they would live happily ever after. She needed to live in the world a little, to choose her own partner, whoever that might be. He would not rush her into a decision, she must be allowed to consider her position and that would take time, more time than they had now. With a long sigh he gathered her to him for one last kiss.

'We must go, sweetheart. We will be missed.'

He helped Diana to her feet then bent to scoop up the holland cover from the floor and place it once more around her shoulders.

'I would this were the finest cashmere,' he told her. 'But it must suffice. At least it will cover the ravages I have wrought upon the neck of your gown.' He ran one gentle finger along her cheek.

'You must go to your room now. If anyone sees you, tell them you were caught in the storm and took shelter in here, but with luck everyone will be changing for dinner.'

'And you?'

Her eyes were still starry and luminous from their lovemaking and he could not resist taking another kiss.

'I shall slip around the house as if I were coming in from the stables.' He smiled. 'Have no fear, Diana, I shall protect your reputation. No one need ever know of this.'

'Alex, we must talk—'

'I know, sweetheart, but there is no time now for all that must be said. If we are both late for dinner it will give rise to the sort of speculation we wish to avoid.'

The warm, beloved feeling that had enveloped Diana evaporated when Alex moved away. She wanted to remain beside him for much longer, to explore these new and delicious feelings. Was it love? She thought so, but how could she tell? Diana felt bemused, stunned by her own behaviour. He was right, of course, she must get back to the house and change, but there was so much unsaid, implied but never put into words. It was on the tip of her tongue to ask Alex if he loved her but she held it back.

She was afraid he might lie.

It was still raining when she ran back to the house, but only a light drizzle. The storm had spent itself and there were signs of a clear sky spreading from the west, promising a fine evening. Jenny was waiting for her in the bedchamber, and burst into relieved chatter when Diana came in.

'So there you are miss, I was beginning to be that worried about you! I guessed you'd stay in the orangery until the rain stopped.'

'Unfortunately I went for a walk and I was in the woods when the storm broke.' Diana was surprised that her voice was so normal after all that had occurred. 'I ran back to the orangery to wait for it to pass.'

'Very wise, mistress, I've heard stories before now of animals and people being struck down in an electrical storm.' The maid shook her head. 'La, but your gown is all ruined. That's the trouble with these very fine muslins, they're that flimsy they don't stand no wear at all. You should've put on an old dimity gown if you was going to be working in the orangery.'

'I should indeed, Jenny.'

'I've filled a tub for you, miss, in the dressing room. The water might be getting a bit cool now but I'm sure you will feel better for a bath—'

As the maid came forward to help her mistress

undress, Diana held out the wet spencer that she had carried back with her. 'Take this away, if you please, Jenny, it is dripping all over the carpets. Take it down to Mrs Wallace and see if this can be dried and restored. Quickly now.'

While the maid hurried away Diana drew off her gown, trying not to think about how the bodice came to be torn. She inspected the muslin skirts and her petticoats for evidence of her wanton behaviour in the orangery, but thankfully there were no telltale signs, so her secret was safe, for a little longer.

Her spirits swung between euphoria and despair, soaring when she thought of the way Alex had kissed her and swooping when she considered how reckless she had been, giving herself to a man in such a wild, abandoned manner with no thought for the future. She summoned up every vestige of courage to fight down her fears. Alex felt the same, she knew it, her very bones told her that he loved her. But what if she was wrong?

Jenny had looked out her moss-green gown and Diana put it on, allowing the maid to pin up her hair and thread a matching green ribbon through the curls which were damp and heavy about her head. Just before the appointed hour she made her way downstairs, but as she was about to enter the drawing room she heard Alex's voice from across the hall.

'Ah, well timed, Diana. If you could spare me a moment, there is something I wish to discuss with you.'

The sight of him, calm and immaculate in an evening coat of deep-blue superfine, almost turned her bones to water. She suddenly felt very shy.

'It—it is almost time for dinner, sir. I—'

'I am aware, but it will not take long.'

He was standing by the study door and after the briefest hesitation she preceded him into the room and heard the door shut behind them. Diana wondered if he intended to sweep her into his arms and knew a moment's disappointment when he moved away from her towards the desk. She stifled her regret and faced him with a calm that matched his own, but his first words came as a surprise.

'I am glad you are wearing green tonight.' He picked up a small leather case from the desk. 'I thought these might go well with it.'

Her brows went up when he opened the box and she saw the cluster of emeralds nestled against the velvet lining.

'Oh, how lovely.' She reached out to touch one finger to the gems. The set comprised a necklace and earrings of fine, dark emeralds in a heavy gold setting. 'You would lend these to me?'

'No, I am *giving* them to you, since you appear to have no ornaments of your own.'

'No.' She kept her eyes on the jewel case, fascinated by the sparks of green fire that flew from the gems as they caught the light. 'I have never purchased anything for myself.'

'Best not to wear jewels or too much finery, Diana my dear. You must not draw attention to yourself.'

Mama's voice, kind but firm, echoed in her head. Diana sighed. She had never questioned it, until now.

She said, 'Margaret left me her personal jewellery in her will, but of course she was carrying it with her when, when the ship went down.'

'I beg your pardon, I did not mean to distress you with that memory.'

She shook her head and gave him a faint smile.

'You did not, sir. But, are you sure you wish to give these to me?'

'Of course.'

'May I wear them now, tonight?'

He smiled at her eagerness.

'Of course, that is why I am glad you are wearing that gown. Turn around now and let me fix the necklace for you.'

Diana removed her pearls and stood very still

while Alex fastened the emerald necklace about her throat. The stones rested heavily on her collarbones, but she was even more aware of Alex's fingers at the back of her neck, brushing her skin and sending little darts of fire through her blood. She breathed deeply and slowly, resisting the urge to lean back against him. She closed her eyes for a moment, imagining herself turning and pulling his head down until their lips met in another sizzling, explosive kiss.

'There, it is done. Here, take the drops for your ears and put them on.'

Her eyes flew open. She could no longer feel his touch on her skin and she wanted to cry out, but instead she forced her reluctant feet to move away from him. She walked to the mirror and slipped the emerald drops in her ears. As Diana stepped back to look at herself the evening sun chose that moment to blaze between the dispersing rainclouds and she was caught in a shaft of golden light that enhanced the red-gold tints in her damp hair and made the green silk of her gown glow richly. It set the emeralds on fire, but they sparkled no more brightly than her eyes, which positively shone with happiness. She stared at her reflection in wonder.

I look beautiful.

She put her hands to her cheeks, shocked by the revelation. Margaret had always been the pretty one, Diana was the red-haired little cripple, to be hidden away, despised and pitied. But no longer. Alex had neither despised nor pitied her this afternoon. He had *worshipped* her! A huge smile burst from her as she turned back to Alex.

'Thank you so much.'

He looked slightly nonplussed at her gratitude.

'John Timothy collected the emeralds for me from the London today. They were in the family vault and you are…family. James would have given them to Margaret, but he told me once that she did not like emeralds.'

'No, she never wore green, she thought it an unlucky colour.'

But avoiding the colour had not saved her from drowning. Diana gave a little shiver.

Alex saw the shadows of sadness flitting across Diana's face and he longed to cross the short distance between them and take her in his arms, but he was very much afraid if he did so he would not be able to let her go until he had kissed her so thoroughly that she would be obliged to go upstairs again to tidy her hair, and possibly her gown.

There was no doubt that the emeralds were a good choice, they enhanced the creaminess of her skin and brought out those tantalising green flecks in her eyes. He had thought her quite splendid when she was angry, but now, glowing with happiness, she looked truly magnificent. If there hadn't been a room full of guests waiting for them he might well have ravished her again, here, over the desk…

He turned away so that she might not see how she affected him. He thought of the bachelors he had invited to stay. He had made it clear to them that Diana would be a good match. Well, he had vowed she might choose her own husband, but he knew now he would not promote anyone but himself for that role! Alex cleared his throat. Perhaps he was wrong to wait until they had time to discuss the matter. He should tell her now, make her an offer.

'We had best go to the drawing room,' said Diana. 'Fingle will be announcing dinner very soon.'

He closed his eyes. As he was thinking of marriage, so she talked of dinner. Clearly this was not the moment to propose. He dropped the pearls into the empty jewel case.

'I will send this up to your room later.' He went to the door. 'Shall we join our guests?'

Diana walked beside Alex across the hall, matching her step with his. She could walk with barely a hint of drag now and every day it became a little easier. And it was all Alex's doing.

He had called her a worthy opponent and encouraged her to believe in herself.

She was well aware that he had sent the dancers to her in a spirit of mischief but they had been very useful, not only teaching the girls to dance but they had shown her exercises to stretch her leg muscles even more than she had already done over the past weeks, convincing her that she would walk normally if only she continued to apply herself.

Even sending the outrageous Madame Francot to Chantreys had proved a success, for she had not attempted to dress Diana in gowns unsuitable for a respectable hostess, instead she had provided her with fashionable gowns in colours and styles that made the most of her slender figure and unusual colouring.

It had all given her confidence. The confidence to face a house full of guests. To stand up for herself. What advantages had come her way through tangling with the new Lord Davenport! She could not stop her thoughts going back to their encounter in the orangery. It seemed to her that their coming together had been inevitable. Her body tingled with excitement at the very thought of it and although it had been irresponsible, even foolhardy, she could not regret it. She had never before felt anything quite so glorious or exhilarating. It was the sort of feeling poets wrote about, or artists captured with their brushes and oils, but she had never expected to have such an experience. A chuckle escaped her and Alex glanced down.

'Now what has amused you?'

She clasped his arm, saying impulsively, 'Oh, Alex, I have so much to thank you for—'

He stopped her.

'Hush now, we must perform for our guests.' He lowered his head to murmur in her ear as the footman threw open the drawing-room door. 'We must talk tonight, once everyone has retired.'

Uncertainty returned. Alex had made her no promises, she had asked for none, but perhaps what had been for her a momentous occurrence had meant very little to him. After all, he was an experienced man of the world. He had had many lovers.

Almost everyone else was gathered in the drawing room when they went in. Mr Wollerton was standing close to the door and turned immediately to greet them.

'Ah, our host and hostess at last.' He put up his glass. 'New coat, Davenport? I like the cut, Weston's, I would wager.' He stepped closer. 'I would have said you were trying to outshine Brummell, but I see you have the Davenport arms on the buttons, and the Beau would not like that. Simplicity is his style, y'know.'

'He might like it more if he was an earl,' drawled Alex. 'The buttons were made for my father. James never wore them, but I thought they would look well on the coat...'

Not by the flicker of an eyelid did Diana show her dismay when Alex walked away with his friend. He was right, they had their duties to perform, but being in company brought home to her the fact that things could never be the same again. She was no longer a maid. She had given herself to Alex wholeheartedly, thrown herself at him. She could not even claim that he had seduced her, she had been quite aware of what would happen if they kissed. Had she not recognised the edge of the precipice? But in that moment of passion the feelings had been so strong, so overwhelming, that it had been impossible to deny them. The world would not see that as any defence, of course. *She* might not regret giving herself to Alex, but in the eyes of society, she was ruined.

Dinner taxed Diana to the utmost. Without Alex by her side she felt vulnerable, as if everyone could see how she had changed. She expected disapproving looks and cold stares but her reception was the same as always and that made her feel deceitful. Mrs Peters exclaimed at her misfortune in getting caught in the rain and Diana could not deny it, since her hair was still damp, but it was generally assumed that she had been soaked running back to the house from the orangery and she said nothing to contradict it.

Alex kept his distance. Not by a word or a look did he show that anything had changed between them. Her head told her he was being discreet, but that did not satisfy her heart. Then, when she returned to the drawing room after seeing Meggie and Florence to bed, Alex looked up and smiled at her, and everything was well again.

Lady Frances touched her arm. 'Do come and sit with me for a while, Miss Grensham.'

Before Diana knew what was happening Frances was leading her across the room.

'I vow I have not had the opportunity to tell you how much I admire your new gowns. You must tell me, who is your modiste?'

She guided Diana to a sofa at some distance from the harpsichord, where Miss Prentiss was playing a lively sonata.

'Ah, dear Madame Francot,' Frances exclaimed, when Diana had replied. 'Did Alexander send her to you? I told him she is a genius with a needle, and her creations can transform the most unpromising of subjects.' She put her hands to her face. 'La, pray do not take that amiss, my dear, I did not mean—that is, what I intended to say is that your colouring must be quite…*daunting* when it comes to purchasing new clothes.'

Diana was still basking in the memory of Alex's smile and the barb missed its mark.

'Red hair and freckles? I believe it is.' She laughed. 'However, *madame* was quite delighted with the challenge of finding fabrics and styles that were a little less *ordinary* than those suitable for her usual clientele.'

The blue eyes snapped and Diana was pleased to think she had given the lady a taste of her own medicine. She would have risen but Lady Frances put a hand on her arm to stay her.

'There is something about you today, Miss Grensham, a certain air,' she hissed. 'I hope you do not think that these new gowns of yours will entice the earl. He is far too much of a connoisseur to be taken in by a few pretty clothes—' She broke off, her eyes narrowing. 'Or am I wrong... is that glow because he has already seduced you?'

Diana felt her cheeks burn under Frances's close scrutiny. The fingers on her arm tightened.

'Oh, my poor child, I am so sorry for you.'

'There is no reason to pity me,' Diana flashed back, but the knowing little smile about Frances's mouth unnerved her. One hand lifted towards the emeralds and she quickly pulled it back, but Frances had seen the movement and her smile grew.

'No? I think it was not only Madame Francot who saw you as a challenge. And who can blame the earl? After all you are here, living in

his house, he would have to be made of stone
to ignore what was so clearly on offer, however
flawed.'

'You go too far, madam!'

Diana rose to her feet, but Lady Frances had
not finished with her.

'Would you deny he gave you those emeralds,
my dear? How very like him to ease his conscience with such a gesture.'

Without another word Diana turned and
walked away. It was not true. It could not be so.
These were stones from the family vault, not
trinkets for some lightskirt. But the doubt remained. She continued to do her duty, a word
here, a smile there, but at length she found a few
moments when she was alone and could stop and
survey the room. Lady Frances was on the far
side, moving towards the harpsichord. She was
almost gliding across the floor, her hips sway-
ing in a provocative fashion that attracted almost
every male eye. Diana glanced at Alex. He was
turned away, talking to Lady Goodge, or else she
had no doubt that he, too, would have been unable
resist watching Lady Frances. Diana fingered the
necklace. How could she have forgotten what Mr
Wollerton had told her, that his friend was always
generous when ending his affairs? She had a sudden urge to laugh. An affair? Their brief coupling
could not even be graced with the term.

The rain had quite gone, but it had cleared the air and there was a deliciously cool breeze coming in through the open windows. Everyone was gathered about the harpsichord, where Lady Frances was entertaining them all with a lively French ditty and Diana took the opportunity to slip outside. The moon was rising, not yet full but sufficient to illuminate the landscape in shades from blue-grey to black. Diana fanned herself gently as she gazed out over the scene and breathed in the heady scents that wafted across from the flower gardens.

A slight movement caught her attention.

'No, do not run away.' Alex stepped out on to the terrace. She could hear the smile in his voice when he spoke. 'I have not been near you all evening and I cannot bear the deprivation a moment longer.'

He was standing so close that her breast was almost touching his waistcoat and she felt her body responding to him, aching to move and bridge the tiny gap between them.

'Alex, I c-cannot, I do not want—'

He put his finger beneath her chin, turning her face up to receive his kiss and she was lost. All reason disappeared as her senses reeled again and his lips demanded her surrender. She melted against him, hands clasping at his coat, her body pressing against him, exulting in the hard, raw masculinity he exuded.

'Will you tell me now that you do not want me?' he murmured, his mouth close to her ear, rousing the slumbering desire deep inside.

'No.' She sighed, resting her cheek against his coat and feeling the thud of his heart through the soft wool. 'I want you too much, I fear.'

A laugh rumbled in his chest and his arms tightened around her.

'You do not know how much that pleases me. But what is this?' His hands slid to her arms and he held her away from him, looking intently into her face. 'What has upset you, Diana?'

She had not thought he would notice her sigh but she knew she must answer him.

'My, my leg, sir. The scar—does it not repel you?'

He looked at her silently for a long moment, then he lifted her hand and pressed her palm against his face.

'Does the scar on my brow repel *you*, my dear, or the one on my chin?'

'No, of course not, they make you what you are.'

He smiled. 'Exactly so.'

He kissed her again, sending the aching desire spiralling through her body. She wished they were alone in the house and they could spend the night sating their lust, but the ripple of applause from the drawing room recalled her to her duty. Reluctantly she broke off the kiss.

'Alex, our guests. We must go in.'

She turned away, but he pulled her close until she could feel his solid chest pressing against her back.

'Must we?'

He nibbled gently at her ear and she almost purred with the pleasure of it. His hands slid over her breasts. They hardened beneath his palms, straining for his touch. How easy it would be to give in, but the soft sound of voices in the drawing room tugged at her conscience. It was an effort to free herself but she forced herself to ignore the urgent call of her body and stepped out of reach.

'We must,' she said. 'We will be missed.'

Alex observed the flushed cheeks, the eyes dark and liquid with desire, and his heart soared. He wanted to carry her off into the gardens and make love to her all over again and devil take the world, but it would not do. She put a hand up to straighten her bodice and gave a little self-conscious laugh.

'I would not give them cause for gossip, sir.'

'Let them gossip all they want,' he said recklessly. 'I would shout it to the world. Diana—'

He reached for her but she evaded him.

'No more, my lord. I must go in. It is growing late and some of our guests might be wishing to retire. It would look odd if neither of us was there to wish them goodnight.'

He watched her turn and walk away, the light setting her hair aflame as she stepped into the drawing room. By heaven, she was beautiful! He had come out to find her with the intention of making her a formal offer of marriage, but all coherent thought had fled when he had seen her standing in the moonlight.

Later. He had promised they would talk when everyone else had gone to bed. There would be no fear of interruption then, he would lay his heart at her feet and ask her if she could love him. Perhaps tomorrow he might send Timothy to London again to bring the rest of the jewels from the vault. There might be a ring there that Diana would like to wear as a token of their betrothal. He sat down on the low stone balustrade that edged the terrace, deciding to give her a few more moments before he followed her indoors. A chance for his body to cool down.

Lady Frances was still at the harpsichord when Diana came in from the terrace, but now she was performing a duet with Mr Hamilton. Diana noted that the gentleman sang in a strong tenor voice without any sign of the stutter that affected his speech. No one had noticed Diana's absence, they were all chattering and laughing and there was a lively air in the room, aided she suspected by the wine that had been flowing all evening.

In one corner Lord Goodge was dozing in a chair while his wife chattered away to Mrs Peters and in another Mr Wollerton and Sir Charles Urmston reclined at their ease, the glasses on the small table between them filled with an amber liquid she suspected was the earl's best brandy. Sir Charles caught Diana's eye and called out to her.

'Miss Grensham, we were just talking of you.'

She smiled politely and moved closer.

'Wollerton and I were discussing tomorrow night's little entertainment. The earl was telling us about it earlier—I believe his wards are to dance for us.'

'Why, yes, in the orangery,' she replied, mildly surprised at his interest. 'They will perform there after dinner tomorrow evening.'

'Excellent news,' declared Sir Charles. 'You know of course, that little Florence is a relative of mine? Yes, her poor mama was my cousin.' He shook his head. 'Bad business, that, killed by her own husband, don't you know.'

'I understood nothing was ever proven,' Diana replied cautiously.

'No, no, of course not, and since nothing has been heard of Florence's father we must suppose he is dead, and we should not speak ill of him, but these Arrandales, you know…' He let the words hang suggestively, but when he saw her frown he laughed suddenly. 'Enough of such sad talk. I wanted to say how glad I am to see the child so happy.'

'Ah, very good. Capital,' murmured Mr Wollerton, smiling blearily. 'They are both dear little souls.'

'I must say I have seen a great change in Davenport, too, these past few months, Miss Grensham,' Sir Charles told her. 'Why, he is becoming positively domestic. Never known him take an interest in children before. In fact, it wasn't so long ago he was wishing his wards in Hades, do you remember, Wollerton?'

'Eh?' Mr Wollerton looked as if he had been nodding off to sleep, but he sat up when Sir Charles addressed him and blinked owlishly. 'Oh, yes, yes. Wanted them out of Chantreys.' He reached for his brandy. 'No mention of it now, though.'

'No, completely changed,' agreed Sir Charles. He laughed. 'Do you remember how it was, Wollerton, that night we were at cards with Davenport? He was completely blue-devilled at not being able to do as he wished at Chantreys.' He gave Diana a conspiratorial wink. 'Back then he was looking for all sorts of ways to persuade you to take the children away.'

'Indeed.' Diana kept her smile in place, but it was a struggle. She did not wish to hear this.

'Why, yes,' put in Mr Wollerton, his eyelids drooping. 'He was all for moving you out at all costs.'

'Yes, he was most put out that you were to be given the last word when it came to the children. He said the late earl considered you a more fit and proper person to look after them,' explained Sir Charles. 'Was that not it, sir?'

'Aye, 'twas,' muttered Mr Wollerton.

Sir Charles rubbed his chin. 'Now what was it Davenport said that night? Something devil-ish amusing—'

His companion gave a laugh that ended with a hiccup. 'I'll tell you what it was, Urmston. He said, "Seduce the wench and send her packing." That was it.'

Sir Charles started and cast a horrified look at Diana.

'No, no, sir. You must have that wrong,' he said quickly. 'I am sure he would never—Miss Gren-sham, take no notice of Wollerton, he is foxed—'

'No, no,' continued that gentleman with the dogged determination of the very drunk, 'I remember distinctly. Those were his words—or somebody's—'

Sir Charles jumped up.

'Nonsense old fellow, you must be dreaming. Do excuse me, Miss Grensham, I think I should take Wollerton off to bed now. Pray ignore his ramblings, it is all nonsense, nonsense.'

'Yes, yes, of course.' Diana stood back as Sir Charles dragged Wollerton from his chair and helped him away.

Diana could never remember how she got through the rest of the evening. The final hour dragged and while she kept her smile in place, inside her rage was building. How could she have been such a fool? Of course she had never meant anything to Alex. With his wealth and position he could choose from amongst the most beautiful women in society, and everyone agreed he was a connoisseur in these matters. He had merely been amusing himself with her. Worse, it had all been an act, a charade to remove her and the children from Chantreys. Even the guests he had invited to this house party were undoubtedly part of his plan. Bachelors to try to win her hand and if that failed and he had to seduce her, the likes of Lord and Lady Goodge were the more respectable of Alex's acquaintances, invited so that the outrage and condemnation at her disgrace would be all the greater. No wonder Alex was not concerned about gossip, he *wanted* her ruin to be known. Diana felt quite sick.

She wanted to retire, to go to her bedchamber and cry her eyes out, but she forced herself to remain until the last of the party had gone. She and Alex were alone, save for the footman who was silently and methodically closing the long windows.

Diana clasped her hands together tightly.

'May we go to your study, my lord? I would like to speak to you privately.'

Silently he followed her across the hall. Candles still burned in the branched stick on the study desk, although one was guttering badly and Alex went across to trim the wick. Diana watched him, remembering those same hands on her body, caressing her. The thought only deepened her agony.

'There, that's better.' Alex turned towards her, that glinting smile in his eyes. 'Now, do you really wish to speak to me or—'

He reached out for her, but she batted his hands away, saying angrily, *'Seduce the wench and send her packing.'*

If any proof were needed that the gentlemen had been telling her the truth she had it now. Alex's hands fell, his brows snapped together.

'Where the devil did you hear that?'

'Mr Wollerton told me.'

'Gervase? What the deuce was he about, to be saying such a thing?'

'Do you deny it? Do you deny that you were planning ways to get me out of Chantreys?'

'You know I cannot deny that, but I said you would go of your own accord.'

'So you tried to marry me off!'

Alex looked perplexed. He pushed a hand through his hair.

'At first that was my intention, yes, but—'

Diana cut him short. 'Oh, despicable, despicable man! And when that failed you—you—' She dashed a hand across her eyes. 'How *dare* you ruin me, just to get your own way?'

'What? Diana, it was not like that—'

'When were you planning to denounce me, on Friday, at the ball perhaps?'

'No!' He caught her shoulders.

'Let go of me!' She shook him off, backing away as she put her hands to the back of her neck and fumbled with the clasp of the emerald necklace. 'No doubt you think I should be grateful for your…your *gift*!'

'No I do not want your gratitude, you little hothead, I want you to listen to me. Those emeralds have nothing to do with what happened between us.' Alex kept his hands at his sides, fists clenched as if to stop himself from reaching out for her again.

'There is no excuse for what happened in the orangery,' he told her. 'I mean to atone for it by marrying you.'

Diana was already in a towering rage and this little speech tempt heightened her indignation. Her eyes flashed.

'La, thank you my lord, I am *vastly* obliged to you for your kind offer but I have no wish to, to sacrifice myself just to ease your conscience!' At last the clasp on the necklace was undone. 'I have money of my own and would infinitely prefer to live with my, my *disgrace* rather than be your wife!'

With jerky, unsteady hands she dragged the necklace from her throat, slipped off the earrings and hurled everything at Alex before running from the room.

The slam of the door resounded around the study before the air settled over Alex in a tense, prickly silence. He stared down at the floor. The earrings winked up at him from the boards and the emerald necklace was draped across one foot like an elegant but old-fashioned shoe buckle.

'You fool,' he muttered bitterly. 'You crass and utter fool.'

Chapter Fourteen

Diana spent a tearful, sleepless night going over the events of the previous day, allowing herself to remember how it had felt to be in Alex's arms, to enjoy the memory of his caresses before the pain of knowing how little it had meant to him was too much to be borne. He had planned it, after he had tried and failed to find a husband for her. Indeed, his attempts in that quarter had been laughable. As if she could ever fall in love with Mr Hamilton just because he liked music or Mr Avery, because they shared a mild interest in gardening. Or any of the other single gentlemen he had brought to Chantreys. None of them had sparked her interest, nor had any of them shown a preference for her.

It was impossible not to think of Alex's kindness to her. The way he had given her the courage to work on that irregular, halting walk, to believe that she could conquer it. But before she could feel too grateful towards him she reminded herself that it had all been in an effort to make her more attractive to the bachelors he paraded before her.

And failing that, he had fallen back on the original plan.

Seduce the wench and send her packing.

The long night wore on. Diana stirred restlessly in her bed. She could not deny she had enjoyed challenging the earl, rebutting his attempts to shock her. It had become a game, but that had all ended yesterday, and not merely because he had seduced her like the practised rake he was.

No, it had ended when she realised how much she loved him.

When at last the grey dawn broke Diana summoned a sleepy Jenny to help her dress. She was determined to get through the day, to see Meggie and Florence perform this evening, but after that she would pack her bags and quit Chantreys. A sigh filled her. She had grown to love Meggie and Florence as if they were her own and leaving them would be agony, but there was no alternative. She was ruined and she could not allow her scandal to touch them. She would admit herself beaten.

A party of pleasure to Upminster had been arranged and everyone was gathered for an early breakfast, which gave Diana the opportunity to make her apologies. There was work to be done in the orangery and Meggie and Florence wished to practise their dance. She made her announcement calmly, not looking at Alex who was at the head of the table. He said nothing, for which she was grateful, even though it showed how little he wanted her company. She thought miserably that it proved his offer to marry her had come from his head, not his heart.

The guests expressed their disappointment that she would not be joining them, Mrs Peters even offering to remain behind and help her with her preparations, but Diana was adamant that they should all go off and enjoy themselves. She slipped away from the breakfast table while Alex was caught up in conversation with Lord Goodge and made her way to the schoolroom, where she remained until the last of the carriages had driven away. Only then did she venture downstairs again. There was much to be done and she hoped fervently that being busy would keep her thoughts away from her own troubles for the rest of the day.

The orangery was looking splendid: Mrs Wallace had worked miracles with the muslin curtains overnight. They had been washed, dried and pressed and were now in place again, softening the lines of the long windows. The pictures Diana had chosen had been carried across and it did not take her long to decide where they should be displayed. Then she turned her attention to the chairs and tables that needed to be arranged so that everyone would have a good view of the dais. A few benches were placed around the walls of the anteroom but everything else was banished to an empty barn, including the old sofa, where she had given herself to Alex. She could not bear to have that reminder of her ruin and disgrace on display.

Mrs Appleton was accompanying the girls' performance that evening and she had been invited to Chantreys for dinner, but Diana had sent a carriage to bring her to Chantreys for an hour at noon to play for the girls' rehearsal. Their dance had been choreographed by Chantal and Suzanne, and as the little girls skipped, jumped and twirled about the stage Diana wished the two dancers could be present to see how well it looked. Indeed, she wished they could have been there to take her place at the side of the stage, from where she would introduce the ballad Meggie and Florence were to sing and narrate the little story they had made up to accompany their dance.

'Too late now,' she told herself as the last notes died away and the girls moved to the front of the dais to make their curtsies to an imaginary audience. 'But tonight I will perform my last duty as hostess here. I shall not stay for the ball.'

As if conjured by her words, a footman came hurrying into the orangery to inform her that Madame Francot had arrived.

'Ah, she has brought your ballgown ready for tomorrow,' cried Florence, clapping her hands. Diana wondered if she should tell the children now that she would be leaving before the ball but she did not have the courage.

'How exciting,' declared Mrs Appleton, mis-reading Diana's hesitation. 'Pray, Miss Gren-sham, go on up to the house and see your modiste. I can easily run through the music again with the young ladies and then escort them to the school-room before I make my way home. You have been so good as to put a carriage at my disposal today, so I am only too happy to do anything I can to help you.'

In the face of such kindness Diana had not the heart to argue. She found Madame Francot and her assistant had already been shown up to her bedchamber, where Jenny was in attendance, her face alight with excitement. A large box lay open on the floor, surrounded by a sea of tissue paper, but that was soon forgotten. Draped over the sofa was a gown of vivid red silk embroidered with gold thread at the neck and hem.

It was so lovely that Diana had to steel herself

to utter the words she had been rehearsing all the way from the orangery. She dismissed her maid and then turned to face the modiste.

'Madame Francot, so good of you to come but I am afraid it is a wasted journey. I shall not now be requiring the ballgown.' When the lady's pencilled eyebrows rose alarmingly she felt compelled to explain. 'I am not going to the ball tomorrow after all. You will be paid in full, of course…'

'Tsk, that is unfortunate, *mademoiselle*,' replied the modiste. 'I shall not ask you why. I can see from your sad face that something most *catastrophique* has occurred. But tell me, if you please, if you are withdrawing for ever from the eye of the public? Are you, per'aps, to become a nun?'

Even through her misery Diana was obliged to smile.

'No, nothing like that.'

'*Bon.* Then the journey he is not wasted. *S'il vous plaît, mademoiselle*, to try on the gown and we will make the final adjustments.'

In vain did Diana argue, Madame Francot stood as one not to be moved and in the end it was simpler to acquiesce.

'*Voilà,*' declared Madame Francot. '*C'est fini.*' Diana regarded herself in the long glass. A stranger looked back at her. The face was pale, but despite her unhappiness the vivid red of the gown made her eyes sparkle like jewels and it enhanced the rich fiery glow of her hair. She had been very uncertain when *madame* had suggested the colour to her, but now she saw that the modiste had been perfectly correct, the scarlet silk became her very well. Diana felt a sigh building up inside her.

'If you cannot wear the gown tomorrow night then I am sorry for it,' declared Madame Francot, regarding her with a professional eye. 'But this gown, it is a triumph. You must keep it to wear on another occasion.'

Without waiting for a reply she turned to her assistant, rapping out her orders to pack away the needles and thread. Diana took one last look in the mirror, thinking of what might have been. Then she sent for Jenny to help her back into her day gown before she slipped away, leaving her maid to reverently pack away the gown and see Madame Francot off the premises.

Diana was descending the stairs when Alex came in, dusty from riding. She quickly turned back but his voice stopped her.

'I would appreciate a few moments of your time, Miss Grensham.'

With Christopher the footman standing

wooden-faced by the front door Diana felt she could not refuse. She descended the last few steps to the hall.

'I did not expect to see you until dinner, my lord.'

'No, I left the party in Upminster and rode back ahead of them.' He strode to his study and held open the door. 'I am expecting my great-aunt and her protégée later today.'

'I am well aware of that. The arrangements for their reception are in hand.'

'I beg your pardon, I did not mean to question your ability to welcome them.'

We are talking like mere acquaintances, thought Diana as she went into the study. Polite, civil. Distant.

Excruciating.

Alex shut the door. 'Diana, about yesterday—'

'No!' That wound was too raw. 'We will not discuss it further, if you please.'

'But we must. I would not have you think that what happened in the orangery was part of any plan to remove you from Chantreys.'

'Nevertheless you have succeeded in your original design,' she replied coldly. 'I cannot remain here. And I can no longer act as governess to Meggie and Florence.'

'*What?*'

His shock only increased her anger. She said

bitterly, 'What did you expect to happen? I acted foolishly. I no longer consider myself a, a *fit and proper person* to look after the children. I will leave in the morning.'

His brow darkened. 'You cannot quit so abruptly. You are my hostess.'

'Better I go now than wait to be denounced. Lady Frances has already guessed what happened yesterday. I will not remain to be publicly humiliated.'

'No one is going to humiliate you,' he ground out. 'I will speak to Frances.'

Diana's hand fluttered.

'There is no point. What's done is done.'

He caught her fingers.

'There is a solution, Diana. Marry me. We will announce our betrothal at the ball. That would place you firmly under my protection.'

She snatched her hand away. 'To save my name? No, I thank you.'

Somehow she kept her head up. He must never know how much he had hurt her. All she had left now was her pride and she must hold on to that at all costs. She took a deep breath and pronounced with slow deliberation, 'If I loved you, my lord, then perhaps I might accept your offer. As it is I prefer to make my own way in the world.'

Diana forced herself to look steadily into the slate-grey eyes that stared at her beneath the dark and frowning brows. She tried to forget when she had seen those same eyes smouldering with passion, she thrust from her mind the memory of being held in his arms, surrendering to his kiss. Even now, if he had dragged her into his arms she knew she would crumble.

The silence stretched on. A tiny, almost unacknowledged hope flickered that he might beg her to stay, tell her that he could not live without her.

He turned away. Hope died.

'Very well.' Alex stared down at the desk, idly moving the inkwell and straightening the pens. He had spent the night preparing for the meeting, vowed he would not hurt her any more than had already done. She did not want him, did not love him. He must respect that. At least she was honest enough to admit it. She was not like all the others, who pretended to care when all they wanted was his money and his title. Even his first, disastrous love affair had been a lie. The older woman had used him because her ailing husband could not satisfy her. She had never loved him and he had soon been replaced by another, more experienced youth. No woman had ever loved him for himself, but he had thought it did not matter. After that initial schoolboy infatuation he had never allowed it to matter.

'Very well,' he said again. 'I cannot force you

to remain, but I would beg you to consider the children. To leave so precipitately would cause them great distress.'

'If I leave tomorrow you will still be here for them.'

'But I am not you, Diana.' The words were wrenched from him. 'You have been everything to them since their parents died. You were their sole comfort in those first months while I—' He broke off, swallowing hard. 'I was too caught up in my own grief to spare a thought for their loss. If you go, without a word, it will break their hearts.'

And mine.

He looked up. 'At least stay until I can find another governess to take your place. I need your help for that. You know what will suit the girls. John Timothy will draw up a list of suitable candidates and I will send them down to you for approval.' He saw the flicker of indecision in her eyes and pressed home the advantage. 'In a day or two the guests will be gone and I shall return to London. You and the girls will have Chantreys to yourself again.'

'That would give Meggie and Florence time to grow accustomed to my leaving,' she acknowledged.

Alex felt the weight lifting from his chest. He had some irrational feeling that if he could keep her at Chantreys there was a chance she might change her mind.

'And you will continue as my hostess?'

'I will stay for the girls' performance tonight, but that is all.'

'But the ball—'

'Nothing would persuade me to attend!'

Her vehemence cut him. He realised how much he had been looking forward to seeing her in all her finery, dancing with her, showing her off as his future bride. How on earth had he handled things so badly? She was close to tears and he knew he must tread carefully.

'As you wish. But tomorrow I would like Meggie and Florence to spend some time with my great-aunt and I am aware she can be quite formidable, they would be much more comfortable if you were with them. And it would be a pity for you to miss the dinner, when you went to such pains to plan it with Cook.' He went on quickly. 'You need not think that I shall impose my company upon you, or importune you any further. You may slip away directly after dinner, when everyone goes off to change. I will tell the marchioness then that you have been taken ill and ask her to stand in as hostess.'

'Yes, yes, that will do.'

Diana felt the tears pressing. If she did not get

away soon they would spill over and she was determined not to show such weakness before him.

'You agree to my plan?'

Another steadying breath was required before she could speak.

'Yes, I agree. Now if you will excuse me I must get on—'

She almost ran to the door.

'Diana.' His voice halted her. She stood with her back to him, her hand grasping the door handle. 'I never meant to hurt you.'

She closed her eyes, squeezing back the hot tears. He sounded so humble that she almost believed him.

Almost.

Diana fled to the schoolroom, where she found that Jenny had taken Meggie and Florence for a walk, the girls being far too excited about their forthcoming performance to settle to any work. That gave Diana an opportunity for a little quiet reflection in her room, which did much to restore her equilibrium and make her see the sense in remaining at Chantreys, at least for the moment. Much as she would prefer a quick, clean break, it would be better for Meggie and Florence if they were prepared for her going. It would be painful for her to continue as hostess and act as if nothing had occurred, but she would do it, for their sake.

*　*　*

It had been agreed that Diana would take the girls to the drawing room before dinner to be introduced to the Marchioness of Hune and her protégée, Miss Ellen Tatham, but even on the top floor of the house it was impossible to avoid news of their arrival. Nurse came puffing up the stairs to announce that the marchioness was come and with such a quantity of luggage that Mrs Wallace was in despair as to where it would all go, and when Jenny arrived to help Diana and the girls to change their gowns she was clearly impressed by her ladyship's dresser.

'Miss Duffy, she is, and she has 'em all in a spin below stairs,' Jenny declared as she took a brush to Meggie's tangled curls. 'When I saw her in the hall she looked down her nose at me in *such* a way that I mistook her for the marchioness herself!'

'I believe it is often so with retainers of long standing,' Diana replied calmly, not wishing to make the girls nervous of meeting Lady Hune.

'Perhaps it is, miss,' said Jenny cheerfully. 'Now, then, Miss Grensham, what are *you* going to wear tonight? The rose-green looks very well.'

But if she wore that Diana thought someone might comment upon the fact that she was not wearing the emeralds.

'The teal,' she decided. 'I shall wear the teal and my pearls.'

* * *

The summons came soon afterwards and Diana escorted her charges to the drawing room. Alex was waiting for them and as they came in he fixed Diana with a dark, enigmatic stare.

'Davenport is worried I might frighten you all away if he is not here to protect you.'

The voice, rich with amusement, brought Diana's attention to the old lady sitting in regal state in one of the arm chairs. So this was the Dowager Marchioness of Hune. She was dressed all in black with quantities of silver lace at her wrists and neck and held an ebony cane in one gnarled and beringed hand. Her silver hair was neatly piled about her head and the faded blue eyes were sharp, but not unkind as they surveyed Diana and her charges. Alex performed the introduction and the girls made their curtsies before moving to sit on the sofa near the dowager's chair.

Lady Hune turned to Diana. 'I believe you are the girls' governess, as well as sharing guardianship with my nephew?'

'Yes, ma'am, for the moment.'

'Why do you say that? Is there some doubt of your continuing here?'

Diana was trying to frame an answer when there was a welcome distraction. The door opened and a young lady appeared, a golden-haired vision in cream muslin sprigged with tiny blue flowers that matched the cerulean blue of her large eyes. She was, thought Diana, startled, the loveliest creature she had ever seen.

'I beg your pardon, Duffy could not remember where she had packed my Norwich shawl and in the end I have come down without it, for I did not wish to put off meeting Lord Davenport's wards.' Her pleasant voice was laced with laughter as she crossed the room. 'My goodness, but you are both so pretty, no—do not tell me, let me guess. You must be Lady Margaret, yes? And if that is so then you are Miss Florence.' Having delighted the children with her friendly manners the vision addressed Diana, who was standing a little to one side. 'And you must be the famous Miss Grensham,' she said, dipping a little curtsy. 'Lord Davenport has told me so much about you.'

'And this baggage,' declared Lady Hune with mock severity, 'this is my protégée, Miss Ellen Tatham, putting me to the blush with her lack of manners.'

'Oh, fie, ma'am, you know we stand on no ceremony with Lord Davenport,' Miss Tatham responded, casting a mischievous look at Diana. 'He is Lady Hune's great-nephew, you see, Miss Grensham, and obliged to be courteous to me and to stand up with me whenever we meet at the balls and assemblies, so we have become great friends.'

'This is your first Season, I believe?' murmured Diana, sinking down into a chair even as the vision disposed herself gracefully on the sofa next to Florence.

'Yes, and Lady Hune has been good enough to sponsor me,' replied Miss Tatham. 'It was intended that Phyllida, my stepmama, would present me, but not only was she disobliging enough to fall in love last autumn, she felt it necessary to marry *and* to set up a nursery immediately, so she has not been in any fit state to be jauntering around London. It was proposed that my Aunt Hapton would step in, but *fortunately*, Phyllida's husband is another of Lady Hune's greatnephews, so I am part of the family now, which makes it perfectly proper for her ladyship to bring me out.'

'And your stepmama?' enquired Diana, smiling at this breathless recital.

'She has presented her husband with a lusty heir,' Miss Tatham said. 'But Lady Hune thought it best to leave the doting parents to coo over their baby while we continue to enjoy ourselves.'

'Enjoy?' declared the dowager. 'If I had realised how fatiguing it would be, I should have remained in Bath and left you to your aunt's ministrations.'

Miss Tatham was not a whit cast down by the words, nor the scowl that accompanied them. She merely laughed.

'You know you love every minute of it, ma'am, and looking after me stops you from worrying yourself into a fever over Lady Cassandra.'

'Lady Hune's granddaughter,' Alex explained to Diana. 'She and her husband were in Paris when war was declared.' He turned back to the dowager. 'Is there any news of Cassie, ma'am?'

Lady Hune shook her head.

'I had one letter soon after hostilities resumed, to say they had been detained. Since then it has been difficult to discover just what has happened to them. I hope, if her cousin had indeed escaped to France…'

'Ah, the infamous Wolfgang Arrandale,' said Alex. He glanced at Diana and said, by way of explanation, 'Florence's father.'

She nodded. She knew the story, how Florence had been born as her mother lay dying and the wild young man who was her father had fled abroad, accused of murdering his wife.

Alex turned to Lady Hune and said gently, 'You are aware, ma'am, that nothing has been heard of him for years.'

'But there was a rumour he was living in France under an assumed name,' the dowager replied. 'If that is so, he might be able to help Cassandra.'

Alex gave the slightest shake of his head. 'I fear you are clutching at straws, Aunt.'

'I fear so, but I have to *try*. The boy certainly had friends in France. I have tried to contact them, but it is impossible to know if my letters ever arrived. And even if they did, there is only a small chance they would be of help to Cassandra.'

For a moment the mask slipped. The thin hand holding the cane clenched until the knuckles gleamed white and Diana saw the haunting sadness in the old lady's face, but only for a moment, then Lady Hune seemed to straighten her shoulders. 'However, there are reports that many of the English have gathered in Verdun and are enjoying themselves vastly. They have made themselves at home there with entertainments and gambling and horse-racing.'

'Yes, I have heard that.' Alex nodded. 'I believe they call it Little England. Let us hope that Cassie and her husband have found their way there.'

'Yes, let us hope that.'

The sorrowful note in the dowager's voice was not lost on Miss Tatham, who immediately jumped up.

'You must be tired from the journey, my lady. Let me take you upstairs where you may rest until it is time for dinner. I am sure Miss Grensham will excuse us.'

Miss Tatham suited actions to her words and gently led the dowager away, leaving Alex and

Diana alone with the girls. The room seemed suddenly very quiet and Diana sought for something to say to break the silence.

'Miss Tatham is a lively companion for the dowager.'

''She is, but she is also very conscious of my great-aunt's age and takes great care of her,' Alex replied. 'The arrangement works exceedingly well.'

Another silence stretched. Alex felt the awkwardness and wished he could say something to ease it.

'Diana—'

'We must be getting upstairs, too.' She rose and held out her hands to the girls. 'Meggie and Florence have to prepare for their performance tonight.'

Meggie looked up at Alex anxiously. 'Will everyone be coming to watch us?'

He smiled and ruffled her hair.

'Why, yes, I will not allow anyone to miss it. I am sure you will sing and dance delightfully.' He glanced up. 'Can the girls not make their own way to the schoolroom? We might take a walk in the garden—'

The suggestion made her shy like a nervous colt. She murmured, not looking at him, 'You promised, my lord.'

Yes, he had promised and he must keep to it. Alex went to open the door.

'Of course. Off you go then. Until dinner, Miss Grensham.'

Chapter Fifteen

There was no doubt that Lady Hune and Miss Tatham made a welcome addition to the company gathered in the drawing room before dinner. The dowager was happy to converse upon any subject, while Miss Tatham's liveliness lifted the spirits and charmed everyone, not just the gentlemen who gravitated towards her.

'Like bees around a honeypot,' observed Lady Frances, stopping beside Diana. 'Ellen Tatham has everything, she is young, handsome and endowed with a considerable fortune.'

'Indeed, she is a very fortunate young woman,' agreed Diana, looking across the room to where Alex was laughing at something Miss Tatham was saying.

The leaden weight around her heart grew heavier and she turned away, but Lady Frances followed her.

'The earl has been seeing a great deal of her in town the past few months.'

If Frances was trying to make her jealous she was missing her mark, thought Diana, and in any case it no longer mattered, since she would soon be leaving Chantreys and Alex for ever. The lady continued in a low voice.

'There is much talk in town that they will make a match of it.'

'I wish them well then,' muttered Diana.

'Yes, it is best to accept the inevitable,' murmured Frances with spurious sympathy. 'Even though you have worked so hard to minimise that ugly walk of yours, Miss Grensham, you could not compete against such a beauty.' Her contemptuous look raked Diana from head to toe. Suddenly the teal gown with the gold-silk tambouring felt no more special than a rag upon her back. 'Your transformation came too late.'

Diana remained rooted to the spot as Frances walked away. How was she to bear another full day of this?

You must. It is for the children's sake. Hide your grief and keep your head up, Diana.

Dinner was easier. Diana kept her attention fixed upon her food and entertaining those guests seated immediately around her. On her left she had Sir Charles Urmston, and although she could not like his rather unctuous courtesy, it was some comfort that he did not spend the whole time staring stupidly at Miss Tatham, which she noticed Mr Avery and Mr Hamilton were doing.

As soon as the ladies withdrew Diana excused herself and went off with Mrs Appleton to collect Meggie and Florence and take them to the orangery. She knew Alex would not allow the gentlemen to linger over the brandy tonight, so they had less than an hour to prepare.

The candles were burning brightly in the orangery by the time the earl and his guests came in. Mrs Appleton played a selection of music that blended with the chatter of the audience as everyone took their seats. Diana kept Meggie and Florence beside her, sitting quietly on a bench behind the pianoforte. From there Diana watched Alex walk in with the dowager on his arm, Mr Wollerton following with Miss Tatham and they settled themselves on the front row of seats with Alex sitting between Lady Hune and Ellen Tatham.

Once everyone was settled Diana rose to introduce the ballad Lady Margaret and Miss Florence Arrandale were to sing. She was nervous, but not overly so. It was as if she was looking down upon the scene, watching herself walk slowly to the front of the dais. The skirts of her gown caught the light, shifting from green to blue and whispering about her as she moved gracefully across the raised platform, her steps even and steady. Alex was regarding her intently, a look of approval on his face. Of pride. And why should he not? Whatever wrong he had done her, she could not deny that he had given her the courage to stand tall and face the world. A small victory and a bittersweet memory to take with her when she left Chantreys.

She stood to one side, her back to the audience as the girls sang. She smiled encouragement, mouthed the words and led the applause that followed their rendition. Then she stepped forward again. There was silence in the room, every eye was upon her, expectant, waiting. She cleared her throat and began her next little speech, inviting them to imagine a leafy glade and two fairy sprites dancing therein…

Diana took her place at the side of the dais while the music flowed and soared, filling the room. Meggie and Florence danced the routine Suzanne and Chantal had created for them, their flowing white dresses sashed with dark green and wreaths of evergreens upon their heads. They jumped and twirled and skipped about the stage quite beautifully and when it was over the audience showed its appreciation, the gentlemen clapped, the young ladies exclaimed in delight and the matrons in the audience sighed and wiped away a tear. It was done and it was a success.

'Well, that went very well, I think,' declared Mrs Appleton when Diana went over to thank her.

'Very well indeed.' Diana smiled and looked across to where Meggie and Florence were being praised and fêted by a group that included Alex and Miss Tatham. 'You will stay for refreshments, Mrs Appleton? I have asked Fingle to bring wine and cakes and lemonade for everyone.'

The room was already being rearranged into a more informal setting. Tables were brought in and servants began to circulate with their heavily laden trays.

'I must say, Miss Grensham, you have worked wonders with the little ones,' observed Mrs Appleton, packing away her music. 'When one thinks that it is not yet a year since Lady Margaret lost her parents. I am sure it has been a great comfort to the little girls that you have been here to look after them.'

'Thank you, ma'am.' Diana's restless gaze wandered over the room, quickly moving on from the sight of Alex laughing at something Ellen Tatham was saying. Had Fingle sent in enough wine? Should she ask him to bring in more lemonade, or ratafia, perhaps, for the ladies…?

'And what changes will the future bring, hmm?' continued Mrs Appleton, turning a beaming smile upon Diana. 'Are we to expect an announcement tomorrow night, my dear?'

Diana's wandering thoughts snapped back. 'An announcement, Mrs Appleton?'

'Why, yes, one cannot live in a small place like this without everyone knowing what is in the wind, my dear. The new earl paying you such distinguished attention, bringing a house party to Chantreys with you as his hostess and tomorrow, when the whole neighbourhood is gathered here, you will be standing beside him—*such* an exciting time, Miss Grensham!'

'M-Mrs Appleton, I assure you, you must not expect anything tomorrow other than the ball.'

'Now, now, there is no need to colour up.' Mrs Appleton patted her hand. 'I do not wish to spoil the moment, but just to let you know that we are all delighted at the prospect. Delighted.'

Cheeks flushed, Diana murmured her excuses and moved away. If ever anything was needed to convince her she must not appear at the ball, that was it.

'What an excellent display, Miss Grensham.' Lady Frances came up, her smile honey-sweet. 'I vow I have never seen children dance better. You were clearly born to be a governess.' Diana met her comment with a stony silence and the lady's smile widened before she turned to address the company. 'Since we are all here then should we not make the most of this beautiful instrument? Mr Hamilton, will you not join me to sing for the company?'

The idea of a musical evening was greeted enthusiastically. Mrs Appleton declared herself only too delighted to play for anyone who needed her and everyone refilled their glasses and milled about the room while those who wished to perform took their turn on the dais.

Diana could not be persuaded to join in, saying she must look after the children, although in truth Meggie and Florence were sitting at a table with Miss Tatham enjoying a treat of cake and lemonade. She wandered about the room, accepting compliments on behalf of her charges, but keeping well away from the dais. And from Alex.

When Jenny arrived at the appointed time to collect Meggie and Florence Diana had to prise them away from Miss Tatham. They parted reluctantly and only after that young lady had promised to join them for their walk the following morning.

'No, pray do not you rush off, Miss Grensham,' said Ellen, when the children were finally consigned to the maid's care. 'I would very much you to sit with me for a little while.'

She signalled a passing footman and procured two full glasses of wine.

'I would have thought you would like a little peace and quiet after sitting with the girls for so long.'

Ellen laughed. 'They are charming, Miss Grensham—no, I shall call you Diana, and you shall call me Ellen, if you please—Meggie and Florence are delightful children and a credit to you. Lord Davenport has told me how you have been like a second mother to them. But as their governess I hope you will forgive me for spoiling them a little tonight. I promise you I did not allow them too much cake, but they are so excited I am afraid they will not wish to go to bed.'

Diana chuckled. 'I think you are right. I am sure they will not go to sleep until they have described to Nurse and Jenny their triumph this evening.'

'They performed beautifully.' Mischief danced in Miss Tatham's eyes. 'Oh, dear. I do hope it has not given them a taste for the stage. Lord Davenport was telling me he sent down a couple of opera dancers to tutor them in the steps.'

'*Ballet* dancers,' Diana corrected her, a twinkle in her own eyes. 'I was assured they were young ladies of the highest respectability.'

'And *I* am sure you would have sent them packing if they had been anything else.'

'I should, but I knew I could rely upon the earl not to do anything that might harm the children.'

Diana sipped her wine. How long ago that seemed now. She and Alex had understood one another then and she had enjoyed the game. Now it was over and very soon she would pack up and remove herself from Chantreys and the girls for ever. She shrugged off the melancholy thoughts as the atmosphere around them changed again. Lady Goodge had finished playing a fiendishly difficult piece by Mr Mozart and the room was filled with applause and excited chatter. She heard calls for the earl and Lady Frances to sing another duet and she was surprised when the lady demurred.

'I think we should invite Miss Tatham to sing with Lord Davenport,' said Lady Frances, at her most gracious.

There was no doubting Ellen's surprise. Across the small table Diana forced herself to smile and nod encouragingly and while Ellen went off to join Alex by the pianoforte, Diana moved to one side of the room where she could watch the performance. Lady Frances wandered by and paused when she reached Diana.

'Do they not make a perfect couple, Miss Grensham?' she purred. 'They are constantly to-
ether in town.' She gave a sigh and said sadly
he moved on, 'I have quite resigned myself

to the match. Even *I* cannot compete with the heiress's charms.'

Not by the flicker of an eyelid did Diana respond. She kept her eyes on the duo, listening to the melodious sound their voices made together, but inside the splinter of unhappiness was working its way deeper into her heart. Ellen Tatham was indeed perfect. An ideal consort for an earl who was renowned for his love of beautiful objects. Meggie and Florence liked her, too, which augured well for their future. Diana felt the hot tears pressing. The girls would not miss her for very long, if they had Ellen Tatham to comfort them.

Gervase Wollerton was waiting when Alex led his partner from the dais.

'An excellent rendition, Miss Tatham,' he declared. 'And you, Davenport. Never heard you in better voice.'

Alex said nothing, merely standing, frowning, while Ellen Tatham accepted Gervase's compliments with a pretty grace. When she was called away Alex and Gervase were left staring at one another in silence.

'Alex, old friend—'

'Enough, Gervase. Let us forget the matter.'

'But I can't, Alex.' Gervase glanced around. Everyone else was engaged in chatter, no one was taking any notice of them. 'I cannot,' he said again. 'I have racked my brains to think how I could have been such a fool last night, to say what I did to Miss Grensham. I didn't even remember it until you tackled me about it this morning.' He shook his head. 'I cannot even blame it on the brandy, you would never allow a bad barrel in your cellars.'

Alex felt his scowl deepening. 'Urmston got you drunk and primed you with what to say. I have seen him do as much before, with other fools.'

Gervase took the insult without a flinch. He said, 'I remember sitting down with him, but I did not think I had had that much to drink.' His usually cheerful face was full of grief. 'I am more sorry that I can say. If you want satisfaction—'

'And make a bad situation even worse? No. What's done is done, Gervase. I was a fool to allow Urmston anywhere near Chantreys. Where *is* he, by the bye?'

Wollerton looked around him.

'No idea. Lady Frances is still here, so—' He broke off and cast an anguished look at Alex.

'Don't worry about offending my sensibilities in *that* quarter,' he said grimly. 'I have long suspected they are more than friends. I think they have been working together to poison Diana's mind against me—did you see the way Frances encouraged me to sing with Ellen Tatham?' He shrugged and gripped Wollerton's arm. 'Cheer up, Gervase. I do not hold you wholly responsible for what occurred. I have been a blundering fool where Miss Grensham is concerned. In fact, the blame for this whole fiasco rests squarely at my door and I must take the consequences.'

With all the confusion of chatter and singing and the servants moving between the guests to supply them with refreshments, Diana thought no one would miss her if she slipped outside. She needed a few moments to compose herself and to force back the silly tears that were never far away.

It was blessedly cool on the terrace and there were deep shadows between the blocks of light that spilled out from the long windows. She stepped into one of the shadows and wiped her eyes.

'Miss Grensham, are you quite well?'

Diana jumped as Sir Charles Urmston approached her.

'Oh, th-thank you, sir. I am very well. Suffering a little from the heat and the noise, that is all.'

'Ah.' He came closer and Diana found herself stepping back further into the shadows. 'It is very hard, is it not, when one's dreams are shattered.'

'I'm afraid I do not understand you…'

'Davenport and the heiress. An ideal match. I saw Miss Tatham in Bath last year. She was even then a piece of perfection, but so well *guarded*. At the time I thought it a little excessive, but I see now that the marchioness was keeping her for Davenport. He is her great-nephew, you know, and the Tatham fortune will enhance the Arrandale coffers.'

When Diana did not speak he continued in a reflective tone.

'Yes, one can quite see that she will suit him perfectly. Another beautiful object to add to his collection. You know, of course, that Lady Frances had hopes of being his countess. She has been so, in all but name for some time.'

'Really, Sir Charles, I do not think you should be telling me this.'

'Oh, but it is a relief to be able to speak without restraint about these matters, to talk to someone who *understands*. I have known Lady Frances for many years and I had thought, with Davenport out of the way...' He sighed. 'But she is heartbroken and she will not let me comfort her.'

Diana began to feel uneasy.

'I really think I would like to go in now—'

He caught her hand.

'Not yet. We should ease each other's pain.'

'No, I do not want—'

He dragged her into his arms. Diana struggled, but Sir Charles was too strong, he was holding her so tightly against his body that it was difficult to breath. Panic was rising, but she had to contain it.

'Let me go!'

Her hands were against his chest but she could not push him away. She kept turning her head to avoid his lips until he grabbed her hair, forcing her head back. He was squeezing her so hard that she could not find the breath to scream.

'A kiss,' he muttered, his breath, thick with wine and spirits, was hot on her face. 'Let me show you that in the dark one man is very much like another—'

The kiss never came. Suddenly Diana was free and she staggered back, unbalanced. She heard a growl, a tussle in the darkness and the sickening thud of a punch. By the time she had recovered her balance and looked up Sir Charles was lying on the floor with Alex standing over him, fists clenched. Even in the shadows Diana could see the naked fury in his face. She gave a little gasp and, as if recalling her presence, Alex stepped back.

'Get up, Urmston,' he barked. 'Pack your things and leave my house. There is a good moon, I want you gone within the hour.'

Sir Charles scrambled to his feet and stood for a moment, rubbing his jaw.

'Very much dog in the manger, ain't you, Davenport? You don't want the lady but no one else shall have her either.' He gave a savage little laugh. 'And I thought you might appreciate my helping you out of a predicament by taking the wench off your hands.'

With a muted roar Alex advanced, but Diana grabbed his arm.

'No, please!'

Sir Charles watched them, his lip curling.

'She is right, Davenport. You would not want your guests to witness an unseemly brawl, especially the lovely Miss Tatham.'

'Get out of my sight, now, or I will mill you down again and to hell with who sees it!'

With a final, malevolent glare Sir Charles dusted himself down and lounged away. Alex turned back to Diana.

'Did he hurt you?'

'N-no. I was merely shocked, that is all.' She sank on to the balustrade restlessly clasping and unclasping her hands. Alex sat down beside her.

'Another wrong to lay at my door.'

'I will not blame you for Sir Charles's actions, my lord.'

He reached out and caught her hand, holding it in a warm, sustaining clasp.

'I blame myself for putting you in his way. Diana, I want to protect you from men such as Urmston. I want to make sure such a thing never happens again. I have wronged you and I want to put everything right. Marry me!'

Diana knew it would be so easy to lean against that strong shoulder, to give in to her heart and say yes, but she must not. She loved him, but it was not reciprocated. A vision of her life stretched ahead of her, bound to a man who had married her out of duty. Out of guilt. Such a marriage would make neither of them happy. Gently she pulled her hand free. She must end this, now and for ever.

'In my world, Lord Davenport, if a marriage cannot be a love-match at the very least it must be based upon mutual respect, affection and trust. There would be none of these things in our union and therefore it cannot go ahead.'

So that was it. His brave Diana, even after the indignity of Urmston's attentions—and he had seen how she fought against the brute—even after such a shock she was still determined to refuse him. What had she said? *If it cannot be a love-match.* Nothing could be clearer. He pushed himself to his feet.

'Very well, madam, I shall say no more on this matter.' He rose. 'But Chantreys has been your home. There is no reason why you should give up your place here.'

'There is every reason, my lord. The children

need a governess who is above reproach. In all conscience I cannot claim that for myself.' She rose. 'You will instruct Mr Timothy to find another governess, if you please. As we agreed.'

'But you will remain their guardian?'

'Of course. Any communication can be dealt with by our lawyers.'

'If that is what you wish.'

'Then it is all settled.' Her voice was firm, matter of fact. 'I will fulfil my duties here tomorrow and then I shall prepare the children for my departure.'

Alex nodded. His right hand was throbbing where it had come into contact with Urmston's jaw but it was nothing to the pain of the iron band that was squeezing his chest.

'Now if you will excuse me, I will return to our guests.'

She swept past him and in through the open window, head held high and with never a backward look.

Chapter Sixteen

⟡

There was no chill to the bright September day when Diana stepped out of the house with Meggie and Florence the following morning. She had not expected Ellen Tatham to remember her promise to join them, but a message had come upstairs while the schoolroom party were breaking their fast to say Miss Tatham would be waiting for them in the rose garden.

As soon as they saw Ellen strolling amongst the roses, Meggie and Florence ran up to her and Diana tried hard not feel resentment. Miss Tatham greeted the girls with genuine pleasure and waited for Diana to join them.

'Is it not a glorious day, Miss Grensham? Shall we walk in the park?'

They set off at a brisk pace, the little girls skipping along beside them and chattering happily to their new friend. Soon they were telling her all about the secret lake and suggesting they should go exploring in the woods. Diana's heart sank. She had not been to the lake since Alex had surprised her there and she was very much afraid that the memories it evoked would prove too much for her. She feared her reluctance was apparent, for after a quick glance in her direction Ellen said she thought they should save such a treat for another day, when there was more time.

'I really think I must save my energy for the ball tonight,' she told them, smiling. 'We are to dine early, I believe, so we may all have time to change into our finery before the festivities begin.'

'Diana has promised that we may watch for a little while, so we shall be able to see you dancing,' Florence confided.

'Will you indeed?' exclaimed Ellen. 'How exciting.'

Meggie nodded solemnly. 'Jenny will take us to the orangery to watch the first dance, and then when we come back I hope we can have macaroons, and orange flummery and lemonade for our supper!'

'I am sure Mrs Wallace will be able to send up a selection of treats for you, if you are very good today,' said Diana solemnly.

'We are always good,' replied Meggie, affronted.

Ellen laughed and linked her arm with Diana's.

'What a wonderful place this is,' she declared. 'I love it here and I am sure we are going to be very good friends.'

Diana smiled and realised how much she would like to have Ellen for a friend, but it was not to be. As soon as another governess could be found to look after the children she must cut all ties with Chantreys and the Arrandale family.

They made their way back through the formal gardens, the girls running on ahead to ask the aged gardener if they might pick some flowers for the schoolroom.

'Now we are alone there is something I wanted to ask you.' Ellen lowered her voice. 'Did Sir Charles Urmston try to molest you on the terrace last night?'

Diana flushed at the forthright question, but she found it impossible to be offended with Ellen Tatham. She decided to answer frankly.

'Yes, he did.'

'I thought as much. And Lord Davenport came to your rescue. How romantic.'

'Not at all. It, it was quite horrid.'

'I saw Urmston step out of the orangery last night and he never reappeared. Then this morning we learned that he had left Chantreys. It was put about that urgent business called him back to town, but I am not deceived. Davenport threw him out and I am very glad of it.' Ellen lowered her voice, saying confidentially, 'Sir Charles is not at all to be trusted, Diana. He tried to do me a great disservice in Bath last summer. He was part of a wicked wager to dishonour me.'

Diana stopped and stared at her in shocked dismay.

'Is that all Lord Davenport and his, his *cronies* can find to do with their time?' she exclaimed.

'Oh, Sir Charles is no friend of Davenport's,' said Ellen cheerfully. 'It was Lady Frances who invited him to Chantreys. The earl was most put out about it, he told Lady Hune as much when we arrived. Of course the dowager has said nothing to Alex about the wager, but nevertheless I know Lord Davenport dislikes Sir Charles, and I suppose seeing him trying to kiss you last night was the last straw. Did he mill him down? I do hope so, for Urmston is an odious toad and if there is any mischief to be made he will do it, you may be sure.'

'Lord Davenport was certainly very angry,' Diana admitted.

'Of course he was, to see that beast manhandling the woman he loves. I am sure he was incandescent.'

Diana stopped.

'No, no, you are quite mistaken. Lord Davenport does not care for me.' She added earnestly,

'Indeed, Miss Tatham, you must put that silly idea quite out of your head. He feels an obligation to me, but nothing more than that, I assure you.'

Ellen did not look convinced, but as the children came up at that moment with an armful of flowers she turned to them.

'Well, you have collected so many, there is nothing left for me to do,' cried Ellen. 'Shall we go indoors and find a pretty vase to display them?'

'You go on ahead,' Diana urged them. 'I think I will remain in the gardens a little longer.'

She watched them walk off and as soon as they were out of sight she slipped into the shrubbery to think about what Ellen had said.

Alex could not love her. It was not possible. It was merely Ellen's romantic nature that had made her imagine such a thing. Ellen Tatham was very young and had most likely lived a very sheltered life. She would not yet understand that a man might desire a woman physically and yet feel nothing more than a passing fancy for her.

'Miss Grensham, do I disturb you?'

Diana jumped. She had been so wrapped up in her thoughts she had not heard Mr Wollerton approach but now he was before her. She summoned up a smile.

'No, sir, not at all.'

'Good.' He turned and fell into step beside her.

'And I am glad that I have found you alone. I want to apologise for what I said the other night. It has been on my conscience ever since.'

'About the earl wanting to ruin me?'

The gentleman winced at her frankness.

'There is no excuse for it, I was foxed in your drawing room, Miss Grensham, and I humbly beg your pardon. But here's the thing, I may have given the impression that it was Alex who said those words, but do you know, I am not sure that it wasn't Urmston's idea.'

Diana gave a bitter little laugh.

'That I can believe! But it makes little difference, Mr Wollerton. The earl did not dismiss the idea out of hand, did he? You need not hesitate to be frank with me, sir. Lord Davenport told me as much himself.'

'Well, no, he did not. But I think—I *believe*, Miss Grensham—that once Alex became acquainted with you he quickly changed his mind about moving you out. Quite the contrary, in fact.'

'Oh?'

'Yes, yes,' declared Mr Wollerton eagerly. 'I heard him only yesterday, telling Lady Hune that there was no one better suited to looking after his wards.'

'Yes, I was born to be a governess,' she muttered, recalling Lady Frances's words.

'And now Alex tells me you are determined to leave. He is quite cut up about it and I know he blames me in part, for repeating something that you should never have heard.'

'But it was not totally false, was it, sir?'

'No, but I do not think it was ever Alex's intention to resort to such measures.'

'Whatever the earl's *intentions*, Mr Wollerton, things have come to such a pass that I cannot remain at Chantreys. As soon a suitable governess can be found I shall leave.'

The gentleman's cheerful countenance took on a mulish look.

'I do not think you should, Miss Grensham. I have never seen Alex in such a mood before. I think he is in lo—'

She stopped him, feeling an angry flush building inside her.

'If the earl is in a bad mood it is because for once he cannot have his own way. He, he has made it impossible for me to remain as instructress to Meggie and Florence and I can never forgive him for that!'

With a twitch of her skirts she left him and hurried back to the house.

Diana put on her teal gown to go down to the early dinner. She had considered wearing her lavender silk, which would have been more in keeping with her mood but compared to her new gowns it was very sober and old-fashioned, and with a sudden flash of spirit she knew she did not wish Alex to remember her as dowdy.

She gazed with a quiet defiance around the crowded drawing room. Alex was standing by Lady Hune's chair. Had he told her yet that she would be required to act as his hostess later this evening? Perhaps it was too much to ask of such an old lady. Lady Frances drifted into view, looking beautiful and untroubled. Perhaps Alex would ask her to stand at the door to greet his guests.

The idea woke the insidious worm of jealousy in Diana but she would not allow it to subsume her. After all, what did it matter? Soon nothing at Chantreys would be her concern, and even her involvement in the children's welfare would be reduced to correspondence between lawyers.

Across the room Alex watched Diana, so absorbed in his thoughts that he did not realise Lady Hune was addressing him until he felt her stick bang against his leg.

'I beg your pardon, ma'am, I was not attending.'

'That is quite evident,' came the sharp reply. 'I was saying that Miss Grensham looks a little distracted.'

'Perhaps she is pining,' murmured Ellen

Tatham, coming to sit down beside the dowager. 'I think she is suffering from unrequited love.'

'Then more fool her,' uttered the dowager.

'Indeed, ma'am, I think perhaps it is the *object* of her affections who is the fool.' Miss Tatham carefully arranged her skirts. 'I suspect he is quite as besotted as Miss Grensham, only he has not had the wit to tell her so. I fear they will go their separate ways and both be equally miserable, all for the want of a little resolution. Do you not agree, my lord?'

Alex dragged his eyes from Diana's graceful figure and looked down to find Miss Tatham's wide, enquiring gaze fixed upon him.

'What a cork-brained idea!' he declared savagely.

There was an air of excited anticipation in the drawing room. Diana felt it but was unmoved, after all she would not be at the forthcoming ball. When anyone commented that she was quiet, or pale, or abstracted, she explained she had a headache. It was not completely untrue and would be remembered when she sent her apologies later in the evening. She spent the short time before dinner mingling with her guests but carefully avoiding the earl. The few times they had found themselves in the same group they had been studiously polite to one another. There were no shared jokes, no laughing looks. Diana found that even more painful than if he had not been there at all. She glanced at the clock. A little more than half an hour until dinner was announced. She would engage Mrs Peters and Miss Prentiss in conversation until then.

'Miss Grensham, I would like a word with you, if you please.'

Alex was at her shoulder, his face a polite mask. What could she say, in front of everyone?

'Of course.'

A smile, cool and distant as his own, and she went with him to his study. He shut the door upon them but did not speak immediately. Instead he walked to the window, then to the mantelshelf to straighten an ornament. At last he turned to face her.

'I needed to make sure you had not changed your mind. You are determined to stay away from the ball.'

'I am.'

'Then after dinner I shall ask the dowager marchioness to stand in for you.'

His words were harsh, his face unsmiling and for a moment she allowed the hurt inside her to creep to the surface.

'Mayhap you would prefer Lady Frances to take my place!'

As soon as the words were out Diana regretted them.

'I beg your pardon, I should not have said that.' She turned away, blinking rapidly. 'Of course Lady Hune is the most proper person to be your hostess. Now if you will excuse me—'

'No. Not yet.' He caught her arm. 'Why should you think I would do that? Why should I put Frances in your place?'

'Sir Charles told me—'

'Hah! I should have known Urmston would stir it up if he could. Go on, what poison did he drip in your ear?'

She shook off his hand, disturbed by the reaction his touch caused in her, the way her stomach swooped and the sudden compulsion to throw herself into his arms. She clenched her fists, digging the nails into the palms to help her keep calm.

She said, 'He told me you and Lady Frances were very close. That she had hopes of becoming your countess.'

His dismissive laugh shocked her.

'He said she loves you, my lord.'

'Frances? The only person she loves is herself.'

'How can you say that?

'Because I know the woman.'

'I thought you and she were friends.' Diana

frowned a little. 'I thought, perhaps, you were even more than that.'

'Lovers?'

Diana nodded, her eyes sliding away from his piercing gaze. They stood in silence for a long moment until at last he spoke.

'I did have a brief liaison with the lady. It was when I first came to town. Frances likes novelty, but it came to nothing and we parted on good terms and we remain—remained friends. We have many acquaintances in common, you see. I admit I enjoy her parties, the company she gathers about her is interesting, there are few women, in general the men are sportsmen and gamblers and one is not constantly on the alert for the parson's mousetrap.'

He walked back to the window and stared out, his hands clasped lightly behind him.

'My reputation is bad, Diana, but that is mostly because when I came to town I would not conform to society's rules. I am not a recluse, but I have avoided those parties and assemblies where one is expected to do the pretty with a host of young ladies all on the catch for a husband. My fortune has allowed me to indulge my passion for sport and collecting those works of art that appeal to me.

'Lady Frances has been very useful, I do not deny it. She has been on hand to act as my hostess upon occasion when I have held my own parties in town and because I have had no one to please but myself those attending such parties were not the most respectable. And occasionally Frances and I appear in public together. It is convenient. She is generous with her time and I ensure she is well rewarded. I have no illusions about the lady's interest in me, it was non-existent until I became earl, but in the past months she has been trying to beguile her way back into my bed.' He swung round. 'She has not succeeded, Diana. I realised at the outset that Lady Frances is one who likes to share her favours and that is not my way. I have also come to realise that there are far too many men like Urmston in her circle. In fact, I think I have outgrown such company now.'

He came to stand before her again and Diana fought down the urge to flee. This might be the last time they would be alone together. Even when he reached out to take her hands she did not resist.

'I have been a fool, Diana. I could not see what I wanted when it was here all the time.'

'Please,' she whispered, forcing the words from her drying throat. 'You gave me your word you would not speak of it again.'

'I know, but let me beg you one more time to accept my hand in marriage, Diana. I do love you, you know.'

'No.' Tears misted her eyes, she wanted to run away from the temptation Alex was offering her, but he was holding her hands, his thumbs gently caressing the soft skin of her wrists and she could not move. She tried her best to argue, to fight him with reason. 'It is not love, my lord. It is merely lust, and having given in to it you think you need to make reparation. You do not. I would not tie you to such a bleak existence.'

'I do not see it that way. Do you not think you could love me, if you tried?'

His voice was low and coaxing. Those circling thumbs were drawing up the aching longing from deep within. Diana felt it spreading through her limbs, taking away her ability to move, to think clearly. He was so close now, towering over her. If she looked up into his face she would be lost. He released one hand and put his fingers under her chin, gently lifting it.

'Diana, my beautiful woodland goddess.'

He was lowering his head. Her eyes fixed on his lips and her own were already parting in anticipation. She remembered how his kiss had ravaged her before, how his tongue had plundered her mouth, demanding a response and she longed to respond to him again. To give herself to him again.

'I say, Alex, have you seen my—oh. I beg your pardon.'

Mr Wollerton's entrance and clumsy apology brought Diana back to reality. It was as if a pail of icy water had been thrown over her.

Even as Alex looked up she stepped away from him. How could he love her, how could he in all honesty call her beautiful? She was small and thin and insignificant and he was an expert on beauty. It was true she no longer walked with that ugly, halting gait but the scars were still there. That long ridge on her thigh would never disappear.

His intentions were honourable but he was lying to her. It was all a trick. He had decided she should marry him to save her reputation and he knew she would not enter into a loveless marriage so he was trying to make her believe he had fallen in love with her.

All those years of discipline now came to her aid, those years when she had had to summon every ounce of pride and spirit to get her through the door, to smile as if she could not hear the whispers or see the pitying looks as she limped into a room.

'Do come in, Mr Wollerton,' she said now with admirable calm. 'Lord Davenport and I have finished our conversation and I must return to my guests.' She raised her head and fixed the earl with a clear, steady look. 'Thank you, my lord, for your kindness, but my decision has not changed.'

Chapter Seventeen

Alex watched Diana walk out of the room and close the door. Such calm, such poise did not belong to a woman labouring under strong emotions.

'Have I interrupted something? Alex?'

He realised Gervase was still in the room and staring at him.

'What? Oh, no, no. What is it you want?'

'I thought I might have left my snuffbox in here. Can't find it anywhere.'

Alex waved a hand. 'Feel free to search the room, then.'

He went back to the drawing room, pausing for a moment before going in. If Diana could refuse his proposal with such sangfroid then he must accept it with the same cool composure. It was over.

Diana sat at the foot of the dining table and ate a little from every dish with an outward appearance of enjoyment, but despite Cook's exceptional efforts, every mouthful tasted like ashes. She wanted to weep and cry and rip and tear, instead she had to smile and make polite, meaningless conversation. By the time she led the ladies out of the dining room there was no doubting that she was unwell. Several of the ladies remarked upon her pallor as they drifted into the hall, so she had the dubious comfort of knowing that when Alex announced she was too ill to attend the ball no one would doubt him.

She dawdled in the hall, pretending to straighten a stray bloom in the arrangement at the bottom of the stairs while the ladies began to make their way upstairs, but at last she knew she must go, too. As she put her foot on the first step she found Lady Frances at her side.

'My dear, you look positively *grey*. Pray, let me help you up the stairs.'

She supported Diana in what must appear to any onlooker as a friendly grasp. To Diana it felt more like the jaws of a mastiff clamped around her arm, but to throw her off would have taken effort, and Diana was too exhausted to care. There were other ladies on the stairs but no one close enough to overhear Lady Frances's soft murmur.

'Very convincing, my dear, I take it you will not be appearing again this evening.'

'No, I do not think I will.'

'So you have seen the folly of your ways? You see now what a fool you would be to stand beside Davenport and meet his guests, his neighbours. How small and insignificant you would be beside him, my dear, with all your...imperfections. Better not to put yourself through that humiliation, would you not agree?'

Diana lifted her head.

'I have nothing to be ashamed of—'

'Have you not?' Lady Frances purred out the words. 'Would you deny that you have given your silly little heart to Davenport?' Her knowing smile was a mixture of pity and contempt. 'And you have as good as told me the earl has taken more than your heart, has he not? Just as he intended.'

Diana stopped, wrenching her arm free. 'How dare you insult me.'

'Oh, I dare.' Lady Frances halted on the next step up, as if to increase Diana's humiliation by the extra height. 'What will you do about it, go crying to Davenport? He has given you little support thus far. Do you remember, my dear, when I mentioned that ugly limping gait of yours? I must say you have done very well to disguise it.'

Diana was too angry to be intimidated. She marched up the next two steps until she was eye to eye with Frances.

'I am not your dear and I remember it very

well. But then, as now, there is no need for anyone to support me against...' she breathed in, allowing her rage full rein '...against the railings
of a toadying mushroom with the manners of an
alley cat!'

The stunned look on Frances's face was very
satisfying, if Diana had been in the mood to appreciate it, but she was too shocked at her own
outburst. She ran quickly up to the top floor, anxious that her fury should not betray her into any
more unladylike behaviour.

Alex did not encourage the gentlemen to tarry
once the ladies had departed. They drifted out of
the dining room and at last Alex was alone with
his thoughts. He poured himself another brandy,
carried it to the window and gazed out without
seeing the landscaped grounds looking their best
in the late afternoon sunshine.

'Not feeling quite the thing, old boy?' Gervase
appeared at his shoulder.

'I did not hear you come back in.'

'No, you was lost in your own thoughts, what?
I hope your neighbours are impressed by you putting on a ball for them.'

'I wish I had never started this whole thing,'
Alex muttered. 'I should have bought another
house for my treasures and my amusements and
left Chantreys well alone.'

'Yes, well, it's a little late to think that now.'
He coughed delicately. 'I tried to put it right with
Miss Grensham. Told her it was never your plan
to ruin her.'

'And did she believe you?'

'Well, no…'

Alex gave a tight little smile.

'No, she wouldn't. Not after we had—' He
broke off and rubbed one hand across his eyes.
'I have ruined her life, Gervase, and she will not
let me put it right. She says she won't enter into
a loveless marriage.'

'Aye, but would it be?' murmured Gervase,
rubbing his nose.

'Not on my part,' said Alex quickly.

'That's what we thought.'

'We?'

Gervase waved his hand. 'Figure of speech,
old boy. Well, I had best go. I told my man to
bring up the hot water early, before it is all taken
by the ladies.' He laid a hand on Alex's shoulder.
'Cheer up, my friend. It may all yet turn out well.'

The earl's only answer to his friend was a
grunt.

Upon reaching the schoolroom floor Diana
went directly to her bedchamber, but the first
thing that met her eye was her new evening

gown, thrown over a chair with its voluminous skirts flowing out like a scarlet waterfall.

'What is that doing here?' she demanded of her maid. 'I told you it would not be required tonight.'

Jenny bobbed a nervous curtsy.

'If you please, miss, I *had* packed it away, like you said to do, but when I was downstairs Mistress Duffy came up to me and told me that I must shake it out and leave it over a chair, to prevent any creases.'

'My gowns are not the business of Lady Hune's dresser,' exclaimed Diana angrily.

'I know that, miss, but she was so insistent, and I thought she would come and see that I had done as she bade me...'

With a huff of exasperation Diana turned on her heel and walked out. She went into the schoolroom, where Meggie and Florence were working on their samplers under Nurse's indulgent eye. When they saw Diana they demanded that she come and inspect their progress. Diana's anger faded and was replaced by the aching realisation that they would not be in her care for very much longer. She sat with them for a while, wondering how best to explain that she was leaving them, but just the thought of it made her head pound even more. She decided she would broach the subject in a day or two, when all the guests had departed and they could be quiet again.

At last Nurse took the girls away but long after they had gone Diana remained alone in the schoolroom, sitting at the big table with her head in her hands.

'May I come in?'

Diana sat up.

'Oh, Miss Tatham. Yes, please do come in. Did you wish to see Meggie and Florence? They have gone to lie down on their beds for a while.'

'Well, then, I shall not disturb them.' She looked around her with lively interest. 'It is so lovely and peaceful in here, may I stay for a while, Miss Grensham? I think we are very alike and do not wish to be hours at our dressing table, preparing for a ball.'

'I, um, I am not going,' said Diana. 'I am not well.'

'Oh, dear, and here am I, chattering on, when no doubt you wish to lie down upon your bed.'

'No, no, there will be plenty of time for me to do that later,' Diana replied politely. 'Please, stay as long as you wish.'

'Thank you.'

Ellen wandered around the room, inspecting the paintings on the walls, running a finger along the spines of the books on the shelves.

'You have made this very comfortable, Miss Grensham. I never had a schoolroom, only the nursery and my lovely Matlock to look after me.

I was sent away to school at an early age, you see. Papa thought it best that I should learn something of the world before my come-out. It was an excellent establishment and I learned a great deal.' She bent a mischievous smile upon Diana. 'Probably much more than Papa ever intended.'

'And now you are enjoying your first Season,' offered Diana.

'Yes, I am, very much.'

'And...' Diana traced a crack in the table top with one finger '...I expect you have any number of suitors.'

'Yes, dozens.' Ellen gave a trill of laughter. 'Does that sound very conceited? It is the truth, but it is not really anything to boast of. Most of them are attracted by my fortune.'

'And, do you have any particular favourite amongst all these suitors?'

'Oh, I find them all most diverting, in their way.'

'And, and Lord Davenport?' Diana tried to sound unconcerned. 'He clearly has the advantage of being related to Lady Hune, who is your sponsor.'

'Yes, I suppose that is true,' said Ellen, sitting down at the table. 'We have met frequently in town this Season and he was good enough to escort us to several parties. But he is an Arrandale and the family has the most shocking reputation.'

'I think Lord Davenport could be a very good husband,' Diana observed, a little wistfully.

'I believe you are right, Miss Grensham. But I have no intention of marrying for years yet and certainly not the earl.' She smiled at Diana's surprise. 'Oh, he is very charming, but he can be a little tiresome. When we met in London all he talked of was his wards and their governess.' There was a mischievous look in Ellen's eye. 'Mr Wollerton and I think he is quite enamoured of her, you know.'

Diana quickly returned her attention to the crack in the table, not knowing what to say. The schoolroom clock began to chime the hour.

'Goodness, is that the time?' Ellen jumped up. 'I must go and change. Thank you for your company, Miss Grensham.' She ran to the door and stopped to look back at Diana, who had not moved. 'Oh, and talking of Lord Davenport and the governess—I believe he is hers for the taking, if only she would put herself to the trouble of catching him.'

She was gone before the clock had chimed its final note, leaving Diana to stare at the closed door.

The sky was glorious, the final blaze of the evening sun sending streaks of red and gold through the darkening azure. Torchères had been placed around the drive and along the covered walk to the orangery, where the musicians were tuning up in readiness for the evening's festivities. The air was so calm and clear their discordant notes could even be heard floating in through the open windows of the drawing room. Alex was there alone. Most of his guests were already making their way to the orangery but he had sent a message to Lady Hune to join him here. He did not want an audience when he asked her to act as his hostess for the evening. He turned as the door opened.

'Frances.' With an effort Alex prevented himself from frowning. 'Everyone has gone to the orangery.'

'Not quite everyone, Alexander.' She came towards him, resplendent in white silk trimmed with blue and silver, the diamonds and sapphires he had given her sparkling at her throat. 'Your little *ingénue* will not come up to scratch. I believe she will cry off.'

'She is unwell,' Alex replied shortly.

'Really? I rather thought she was suffering from a guilty conscience.' When he did not reply she gave a soft laugh. 'Poor Alexander, you spend all your time in town avoiding those matchmaking mamas only to become entangled with a governess.'

'Miss Grensham is joint guardian of Meggie and Florence,' he corrected her.

'And that makes it all so much more complicated, doesn't it?' She came closer and brushed a speck from his evening coat. 'She is not of our world, my lord. She does not understand the games we play.'

He said heavily, 'I do not play games, Frances.'

'No? Then why did you invite the tedious Mr Hamilton and Mr Avery to Chantreys? Not for your own pleasure, surely. And then there was Madam Francot and the two dancers you sent here. Were you not trying to shock Miss Grensham?'

'Yes, yes, very well. I wanted her out of Chantreys,' he admitted, turning again to the window, but not taking in the pleasing view. 'But all that has changed.'

'I know it, but there is no going back, my lord. The damage is done and the question is, what happens next? Have you asked Miss Grensham to marry you?'

His shoulders lifted a fraction. 'She will not have me.'

'Well, I am glad one of you is showing some sense.' His keen ears caught the rustle of silk as she moved closer. 'You and I both know that an innocent like Diana Grensham would bore you within a month. You need a woman, my lord, someone who can amuse you without desiring your constant attendance, or throwing a tantrum every time your eye is taken by a pretty face.'

Bore him? Alex could not agree. Diana would infuriate, challenge, argue, even surprise him, but life with her would not be boring.

But she has refused you.

Frances was at his shoulder, her voice soft and seductive. 'We are not in love, Alexander, but we understand one another. You need a wife and I would like to be a countess. You know I am perfect for that role. I could run your houses, see to your…comforts and provide you with an heir. I was brought up to do that, bred for it. Your life need change very little, we would be obliged to entertain your neighbours occasionally, very much like this evening, but otherwise we might continue to enjoy ourselves as we do now. I would not complain if you wished to take your pleasures elsewhere. It would be a very civilised arrangement and no one would suffer.'

A civilised arrangement. No raging passion that would overwhelm him, none of the pain that was now tormenting him.

'Think it over, Alexander,' the soft siren voice murmured in his ear. 'Think how pleasant it would be to have a wife who wants nothing but your comfort, who will not disturb your peace with tears and arguments and will let you go your own way, whatever that may be.'

Her fingers squeezed his arm and then she was gone, he heard the soft click of the door as she went out. There was no doubt it was a tempting prospect, thought Alex. He would have to marry at some point, and this way he could go back to his old hedonistic lifestyle, knowing he had done his duty.

And in time the memory of Diana would fade.

He heard the door open again and turned to see the Dowager Marchioness of Hune coming into the room.

'Well, Nephew, you wanted to see me?'

Chapter Eighteen

It seemed to Alex that there was an endless procession of guests filing in from the anteroom. The orangery was already crowded and noisy with loud, chattering voices, but still they came. Some were acquaintances from town but many were strangers, neighbours invited here to meet the new earl.

He told himself it did not matter that Diana was not beside him to make him known to the local families, Fingle took each guest's name and announced it in a majestically sonorous tone. Most of those coming in were too awed at being met with not only an earl but a dowager marchioness to do more than make their obeisance and move on, but one or two, like Squire Huddlestone and Mrs Frederick, were emboldened to ask after Diana.

Their disappointment and concern when they heard that Miss Grensham was indisposed was clearly genuine and from their comments Alex realised that although Diana might not go into society a great deal, she had made some good friends at Chantreys. His eyes wandered around the room. With the exception of Gervase, how many of those who called themselves his friends would care if he were ill?

'Well, Nephew, have you decided whom you will honour with the first dance?'

Lady Hune's voice recalled his attention. The doors to the anteroom had been closed, his guests were all assembled and the orchestra was tuning up. He must find a partner, but he was well aware of the speculation that would arise when he made his choice.

'Perhaps it is fortunate Diana is not here to stand up with you, since you tell me you have no intention of offering for her,' said the dowager, as if reading his mind. 'Pity, though. I thought she would suit you very well.'

'Unfortunately the lady does not agree with you,' he muttered. 'I wish to goodness I did not have to do this.'

'With rank and privilege comes responsibility, Davenport.'

'You need not tell me that, ma'am.'

'So who will it be? Not Ellen. We both know my protégée is not for you so let us not raise any

more conjecture there. You must find a partner,
Davenport.'

Alex looked about him. Frances had moved
closer and was standing with Miss Prentiss and
Mrs Peters, smiling graciously at something the
older lady was saying. A few steps would take
him to her side. She was clearly ready and waiting for him to invite her to dance. Ready to become his countess. And why not? As she had
said, they understood one another. It would be a
very elegant solution. She looked across at him
and her smile widened. He could see the triumph
in her eyes.

An expectant hush had fallen over the room.
The musicians were waiting for his signal to
begin, the guests were all turned towards him.

He raised his hand.

'Davenport.'

Lady Hune's urgent tone and tap on his arm
made him swing around to see that the doors
of the anteroom had been thrown wide again.
Framed in the opening was Diana, dressed as
he had never seen her before in a scarlet ballgown that glowed in the candlelight. It was cut
low across her breast and fell in soft, shimmering
folds from the high waist. Her red hair was piled
on her head and only one glossy ringlet had been
allowed to escape, falling like a narrow tongue of
flame against the cool ivory skin of her shoulder.

She wore no jewels, just a simple length of red ribbon around her throat, but as she came slowly into the room the flickering candlelight was reflected in her eyes, making them glow with sparks of emerald and amber. Those same eyes were fixed anxiously upon Alex and in the near silence that now filled the room he heard her soft, musical voice addressing him.

'Am I too late?'

It had taken all Diana's courage to come to the orangery. When she reached the anteroom and saw the doors were closed she would have run away again, but Fingle was blocking her retreat.

'Forgive my impertinence, miss, but it would be a shame to come thus far and not go in.'

There was understanding in his voice and in the smile he bestowed upon her. He was right, she had to do this. Diana turned towards the ballroom, put back her shoulders and lifted her head another inch.

The butler moved ahead of her. 'Shall I announce you?'

Diana gave a little shake of her head. Silently he threw wide the doors and, gathering up all her courage, she stepped forward in a whisper of scarlet silk. She had a sudden, vivid image of Mrs Siddons, making an entrance at Drury Lane.

The room was hushed and every eye was turned towards her—or perhaps not.

Perhaps they were watching the earl putting out his hand to Lady Frances.

As Alex turned to look at Diana she took another few steps into the room.

'Am I too late?'

She prayed Fingle had not closed the doors behind her. One look, one word from Alex and she would turn and flee. Her heart was hammering against her ribs and the blood was pounding so loudly in her ears that she feared she would not hear Alex's response, but it did not need words. There was no mistaking the explosion of joy that lit his face. He came towards her, both hands reaching out, and any lingering doubts fled when she read the message in his eyes. They glowed with love and pride.

'No, you are not too late,' he murmured, smiling down at her in a way that made her spirits soar. 'Never too late, my love. My goddess.'

He pulled her closer and as he lowered his head she forgot about the crowded room and raised her face to accept his kiss. Gasps of shock and outrage rippled around the room but they were quickly replaced by laughter and a smattering of applause. Diana heard Gervase's voice calling out cheerfully, 'And about time, too!'

As Alex raised his head Diana felt her cheeks

burning and turned an apologetic look towards
Lady Hune, but the dowager was smiling broadly,
while beside her Ellen Tatham was laughing and
clapping. In fact, as Diana looked about the room
everyone was beaming at her. Even Lady Frances had managed a forced smile.

Alex led Diana to the centre of the floor and
signalled to the musicians to strike up.

'Do you realise that we have never yet danced
together?' he remarked as guests flocked to take
their places in the set. 'If you recall, I have been
assured that you dance beautifully.'

He was grinning at something over her shoulder and she glanced around to see Meggie and
Florence peeping in from the anteroom. Heavens,
they must have followed her down the path! She
turned back to find Alex regarding her seriously.

'Do you mind if we stand up for just one
dance?' he asked her. 'I want the children to hear
our announcement before they go off to bed.'

'Our...our announcement, my lord?'

'Why, yes.' The first notes of the dance filled
the air and they saluted one another. Alex stepped
up and held out his hand to her, ready to execute
the first move. 'I think they should be here when
I ask you to marry me, don't you?'

'Alex, you c-can't ask such a thing here, in
front of all these people!'

He stopped abruptly. Immediately everyone else stopped dancing and the music died away.

'Why not?' Alex's deep voice filled the awkward silence. 'After all, you *kissed* me in front of all these people.'

A laugh caught in her throat.

'I—that is—'

He interrupted her disjointed protest. 'Are you going to refuse me?'

Another startled murmur fluttered around the room as Alex went down on one knee in the middle of the floor. He was still holding Diana's hand and he spoke with ringing clarity.

'Miss Grensham, will you do me the very great honour of becoming my wife? Will you allow me to bestow upon you my hand and my heart?' His grip on her fingers tightened. He said more quietly, 'It is a long time since I wanted you to leave Chantreys, Diana. Now I want you to be its mistress. For ever. Pray, answer truthfully, refuse me if you must, you have my word that whatever you decide, Chantreys shall remain your home, Meggie and Florence shall remain in your care, our care, for as long as you wish it.' He glanced about him. 'There are enough witnesses to my declaration that you can be sure I shall not go back on my word. On my honour.'

Once again she was the centre of attention. A few months ago she would have cringed to be in such a position. Now, she barely noticed the crowd. Only Alex, kneeling at her feet. She said slowly, 'I have never doubted your honour, my lord, but...can you really *love* me?'

She read the answer in his eyes.

'With all my heart and soul,' he said ardently. 'If you return my regard, if you love me and can agree to become my wife, you will make me the happiest man on earth.'

His image became blurred and she blinked rapidly.

'Oh, Alex, I do,' she whispered. 'I do love you, and—'

Her words were cut off as Alex jumped to his feet and dragged her into another fierce embrace. His kiss was brief but ruthless and when it was over Diana hid her face in his shoulder. It was shameful, totally outrageous to behave this way in public. What would everyone think? She felt a laugh bubbling up inside. She did not *care* what anyone thought!

'We will be married by special licence,' he murmured. 'But even that is too long to wait. As soon as everyone is gone I shall take you to bed and worship you, my goddess. But only if you wish it, Diana.'

A glow suffused her body at the thought and she could not suppress a beaming smile of happiness.

'I would like nothing more,' she whispered to him.

With a laugh Alex released her, but only to pull her hand on to his arm.

'Head up, Diana,' he murmured, smiling down at her. 'We have an announcement to make!'

* * * * *

This is the second story in Sarah Mallory's exciting Regency quartet,
THE INFAMOUS ARRANDALES.
The first book,
THE CHAPERON'S SEDUCTION,
is already available.
And look for further books in the series,
coming soon!

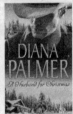